Barbarians at the PTA

Barbarians
at the
PTA

STEPHANIE NEWMAN

Skyhorse Publishing

Skyhorse Publishing books may be purchased in bulk at special discounts for sales promotion, corporate gifts, fund-raising, or educational purposes. Special editions can also be created to specifications. For details, contact the Special Sales Department, Skyhorse Publishing, 307 West 36th Street, 11th Floor, New York, NY 10018 or info@skyhorsepublishing.com.

Skyhorse® and Skyhorse Publishing® are registered trademarks of Skyhorse Publishing, Inc.®, a Delaware corporation.

Visit our website at www.skyhorsepublishing.com.

10 9 8 7 6 5 4 3 2 1

Library of Congress Cataloging-in-Publication Data is available on file.

Cover design by Daniel Brount

Print ISBN: 978-1-5107-5824-7
Ebook ISBN: 978-1-5107-5985-5

Printed in the United States of America

To Michael, Arianne, and Peyton,
with all my love

Contents

Chapter 1:   Best Day   1
Chapter 2:   Mayfair Memes   16
Chapter 3:   This Old House   27
Chapter 4:   A Visit   37
Chapter 5:   Carpool   48
Chapter 6:   MIA   57
Chapter 7:   I'll Never Do Lunch in This Town Again   69
Chapter 8:   Lunch Ladies   80
Chapter 9:   Mayfair Memes 2   89
Chapter 10: Benched   98
Chapter 11: Hooky   105
Chapter 12: Pilgrim's Progress   116
Chapter 13: Back at the Cafeteria   129
Chapter 14: Buckets   141
Chapter 15: Dead Ends   153
Chapter 16: Thin Ice   160
Chapter 17: Into the Dark   174
Chapter 18: The Arms Race   183
Chapter 19: One For the Team   190
Chapter 20: The Social Networks   198
Chapter 21: Cyber Nothings   215
Chapter 22: Beasts of Burden   227
Chapter 23: Him   240
Chapter 24: Working It   249
Chapter 25: Front Row Action   261

Acknowledgments   265
Book Club Questions   267

One

Best Day

I've always told my therapy patients that endings are inevitable; it's best to understand feelings and move on without looking back. Having survived my share of losses and goodbyes, I knew that as soon as one door closed, another opened.

These were heavy thoughts for a Tuesday at 8 a.m., but Rachel was starting a new elementary school. Transitions were on my mind.

I headed down the hallway, wood floors creaking, causing my heart to do a little butterfly flip. It had only been a couple of weeks, and I still hadn't adjusted to all the sounds and scents. Our new house was full of them—and who knew what else. Well, what did I expect; the place was built before women had the right to vote.

Rachel's room looked like a disaster relief site, with cartons and cast-off clothing at every turn. She sat on the bed, staring into her laptop: a photo of several girls at a back-to-school picnic. I glanced at her leggings and T-shirt; they were identical to those in the picture. My little Margaret Mead, conducting field research on the first day of her new school.

"Come on, Rach. Let's get moving."

We got into the car and made our way over, taking the short-cut. It was muddy, littered with leaves and twigs. Driving to a nearby cul-de-sac and cutting through the back meant we didn't have to deal with the scene in the parking lot. I'd heard it took forever to get out of there, and I had to get to work.

We were almost at the path to the entrance. Several girls who looked to be about Rachel's age pushed past—why were fifth graders wearing makeup and pointy boots? And why was every car in the traffic line a gigantic SUV? My daughter was poker-faced, staring straight ahead and gripping her phone. I felt a stab of guilt; she'd been through a lot already without having to switch schools.

Thinking about all of the recent changes brought me back to a dark time only six months earlier. Once-buried details resurfaced in my mind: clear blue skies, the rectangular building at the edge of the floral district, a labyrinth of hallways leading to the Justice's chambers. The three of us had stood, bodies knitted into a tight semi-circle.

Now I closed my eyes, hoping to will the sadness and anger away. But it was too late; memories of that terrible scene at the altar flooded in.

Despite the presence of scores of friends and relatives, their folding chairs running the length of the room, it was my late Great Aunt Pearl's voice I'd heard over and over that morning, her well wishes uttered over the phone, from her bedside at the retirement community in Boca: "I hope you have the best day, my dear girl." She was almost 94—too old to make the trip.

Aunt Pearl's words and the image of doors closing had been etched in my brain, forming an unexpected pairing, sort of like Colin and me. I glanced across at him, thrilled by his smile.

Colin and I were getting married! My chest prickled with excitement at the thought that my daughter and I wouldn't be alone anymore. Instinctively I reached over to squeeze her shoulder. At ten years old, she was proud of her first salon blowout. Her brown hair and silky white dress was an identical match to my dark chignon and plain sheath. The basket of petals captivated

Rachel; with every toss, each bloodred flutter, her face split into a wide grin.

Colin grabbed my hand. His chocolate-colored eyes stared straight into my soul. He was smart, handsome, *and* successful, a partner at his law firm. A bookish psychologist and single mom, I could hardly believe I'd met someone who cared for me and was good to my daughter.

The Justice was speaking about blending—how Colin, Rachel, and I were now one—I bathed in the warmth of her words, part of a family for the first time since my parents' fatal car accident my senior year of high school. I'd been mostly alone after that, until Rachel came along.

Glancing over the sea of dark suits and deep green, navy, and red dresses, I took it all in: The beautiful ceremony, my daughter and I surrounded by love. Everything had happened quickly: Colin and I meeting eighteen months ago and moving in together last spring as we finalized the details of the wedding. It was almost too good to be true. I fought off shivers of doubt. How well can you ever really know another person? If things didn't work out, would Rachel be scarred for life? Would I? I glanced back at Colin's parents, seated in the front row and radiating approval. Behind them were friends and colleagues, along with families from Rachel's school; nods and smiles in every direction.

The Justice continued: "If there is anyone who knows of any reason why these two should not be joined in holy matrimony, let him or her speak now."

There was no sound, except for a communal swish of air, heads turning until everyone was satisfied that there were no objections.

"Victoria," the Justice was beaming in my direction. "Would you like to read the vows you have written?" I nodded and gripped Colin's hand as I recited the words I'd composed and memorized: "You came into our lives after we'd been alone for so long. You made everything fun and helped me to believe in happy endings."

Rachel was giggling, pleased that the service we'd rehearsed over the past few days was finally happening. I cupped her under the chin and shifted back to Colin: "You treated my beautiful daughter as if she were your own child."

There were sniffles and cooings from behind me. "I love you . . . ." The room was still. Then, an explosion of activity erupted as everyone was suddenly on their cell phones, grasping and hissing, metal chair legs pushed backward by the jerking of bodies and shifting of feet. It was the unexpected screeching of the furniture that caused me to turn toward the crowd.

Julie, my closest friend since grad school, caught my eye and waved frantically from the first row. Though technically a bridesmaid, we agreed she should sit it out with her young daughter and newborn, who'd been sleeping in a portable car seat atop one of the folding chairs. The seat backs were joined by winding strands of leaves that had been woven especially for the occasion to symbolize the bonds of eternity.

My body tensed. Usually the bride didn't have to compete with swooshes and pings. I was about to telegraph a withering glance, shush the audience. Whatever it was could wait. But Julie's look stopped me. In the seconds that followed, she placed her husband's hand on the baby carrier and stood up, walking toward me. All I could think was that I finally understood what was meant by the phrase "ashen complexion." Hal, her husband, was trying hard not to look my way.

My aunt's "best day" comment ran through my mind as Julie stepped quickly. I shrugged at Colin and squeezed Rachel's hand, wondering what to do.

But it wasn't up to me. There was another explosion of whispering, gasping, and shifting, along with a chorus of pinging. My panic rose. Something really bad must be going on, like a terrorist attack or other international crisis.

"Excuse us," Julie said as she began dragging me toward the

private room at the side of the chambers. I couldn't help noticing how pretty the contrast was between her auburn hair and teal blue shift.

I hissed, "What on earth?"

She shut the door, encasing us in a small, paneled room that held only two winged chairs upholstered in a faded red. There was no air. But I hardly noticed because so much was going on at once: Colin began pounding on the door, Rachel was calling from the hallway, and Julie was shoving her iPhone at me.

There was pity all over her face.

"Vic, I'm so sorry." Her voice was shaking.

"What's going on?" Whatever made her drag me out of my own nuptials had to be bad. I wanted to feel the reassuring grip of my daughter's hand and steel myself against my fiancé's shoulders. "Let's get Colin and we'll figure it out together," I said, moving toward the locked door. But Julie grabbed my arm: "NO!"

I heard his voice: "Vic, open the door." His tone was high-pitched, almost a whine.

"Mom?"

Rachel sounded upset. I tried to wrench myself away from Julie, but she pulled me back and pushed her phone at me. "You need to look at this."

The video was grainy and poorly filmed. A beautiful and naked blond woman was on all fours, grunting with pleasure. Her long, yellow hair swayed as she moved back and forth, groaning.

Her moan became insistent as she threw back her head: "Yes. Yes, baby. Yes."

What did this X-rated display have to do with me? Tasteless though it was, I couldn't avert my eyes. Time slowed as Colin pounded on the door and Rachel begged me to let her in. My mind fought to make sense of why a blond with exposed butt cheeks had interrupted my wedding.

"Baby, more. More." She turned to the camera briefly, lifting a brow and flicking her hair, then moved slightly to reveal the chest and arms of the man below. His back arched in pleasure as he groaned.

"Smile for the camera baby," she urged him.

"Huh?" The man's voice was sleepy, confused. He slowly propped himself up on one elbow, revealing first his jawline, then cheekbones, until finally the chocolaty-brown eyes came into view.

I fell against one of the red chairs as the small screen went dark. There was no mistaking what I'd seen.

"Victoria!" Colin's pounding was like a jackhammer.

Julie was crying and telling me how sorry she was. For the next several moments as my heart raced and chest closed, I didn't know what to believe. "Maybe it's an old video?" I whispered.

Julie shook her head. "There's been a barrage of stuff throughout the ceremony: this video, Facebook posts, tweets." As Colin pounded for me to let him in, Julie showed me her phone. It was open to Instachat, a popular social media app, to an account named Nymphette, which appeared to belong to the same willowy blond in the video. I grabbed one of the chairs to steady myself. In a post that was dated yesterday, the two of them stood arm-in-arm, my fiancé dressed in a shirt we'd picked out only a couple of weeks before. My insides felt like they were collapsing.

Tears running down my face, I steeled myself as Julie scrolled through her phone until she found a Facebook post taken at a demonstration in Paris the previous week. It had been all over the news, and there was no mistaking the scene: Americans chanting in front of the Eiffel Tower. Only this time, it was Colin and the blond front and center. As Rachel called for me again, I did a rapid calculation: Colin had been in Paris on business and had dismissed my questions about Americans protesting.

I sputtered, "What the hell?"

"I don't know much. The woman in that, uh, sex video, has

been posting stuff about her and Colin all over Instachat, Facebook, and YouTube.

"Who is she?"

Julie put her arm around me and gave my shoulder a squeeze. "Should we sit down?" I managed to shake my head.

"Who?" I repeated in a toneless voice.

"I'm not sure. Apparently Lynetta Larkin is her name. I don't know much, but I did a fast look at 'friends' in common, and she was in the same sorority as Colin's cousin. They all went to college together. All I know is this Lynetta person's been posting and tweeting throughout your entire ceremony. My sister-in-law called Hal during the Justice's remarks to try to tell us. He ignored the call, but she wouldn't stop ringing and texting until he looked at his phone." Julie paused for breath. "I love you, Vic. I'm so, so sorry."

I imagined jumping out a window and running away with Rachel. Obviously I would have to take some action, though I didn't think I could find the energy to walk the two steps toward the door. I used the back of the chair to regain my balance—and remaining shreds of dignity.

I saw myself reflected in Julie's eyes, a woman about to face the guillotine. "What are you going to do?"

My thoughts were spinning. I had to keep it together for my daughter. "Well, now I am going to totally fake it and comfort Rachel. When I say the word, though, I want you to take her back to the chambers, okay? First, tell the guests we're sorry for the delay and we'll be back out shortly. Please don't say anything more." I crossed my arms, fighting the impulse to open the door so I could lunge at my fiancé and put my hands around his neck. "I guess I'll also have to listen to what Colin has to say."

I braced myself and reached for the doorknob. "Coming now," I said, then realized that was an unfortunate choice of words. The worse things got, the darker my humor. Pulling the door open, I zeroed in on Rachel.

"What took so long?" she demanded.

"Sorry, honey. Aunt Julie needed me." I stared into my daughter's eyes, averting Colin's gaze as he stood, arms crossed. I'd heard it said that the line between love and hate was thin. Right now there was no line and no love where Colin was concerned.

"Listen, sweetie," I said to Rachel, doing my best to conceal the pain. "You and I are going to talk a little later. I'm sorry I can't go into details this second, but I want you to stay with Aunt Julie for a couple of minutes."

"But—" Rachel was still clutching the basket of rose petals. Her eyes were wide.

"Everything is fine." I forced myself to lie as my fury and shame rose. I'd have to face the seventy-five nearest and dearest who'd just watched my fiancé in his small-screen debut alongside the blond with the perfect butt. My humiliation was complete. I hoped Rachel couldn't tell how upset I was. "Listen, sweetie. It's okay. When I come out to talk to everyone, promise me that if I say anything that seems strange, you'll keep your questions to yourself until we can speak privately, all right?"

She nodded. "Are we still going on vacation?"

I quashed the impulse to tell her that Colin was a selfish, immoral dirtbag, and I was seconds away from canceling our planned island retreat. "Probably. I'll be out soon, okay? Please go with Aunt Julie, and remember what I said."

Rachel looked like a life-size balloon that was slowly deflating. Her arms were limp and she'd hung her head in a frown. Julie and I exchanged a glance.

"Rach, want to give me a hand feeding baby Maeve? If she's awake, I could use a helper!"

Thank you, Julie. I heart you. I watched them step away as

Colin entered the small room. I heard Julie asking the audience to quiet down.

I turned the knob and heard a click. Colin and I were alone.

"Vic," he began, hand on hip, speaking sharply, sounding almost out of patience. *The nerve.* I stared into the familiar brown eyes I'd loved so much.

"It's not what you think."

How did he know what I was thinking? "What is it then?"

"She, that woman . . . most of that stuff was taken years ago. I can't believe she'd do something like this, it's just so aggressive and crass."

I fought back tears, not knowing whether to call him on the deflecting—blaming someone else for his participation in the wild romp—or pounce on the words he'd chosen, an admission he'd been cheating. I led with my heartbreak. "What do you mean, 'most' of the pictures?"

"Victoria . . . ." He gazed into my eyes with a deep and penetrating look, one that used to melt me, but was now making my blood boil. Selfish jerk. He actually thought he could explain this away.

"It was only a couple of times. You have to believe me. She means nothing. I love you."

"How long has this been going on?" I thought about the clues, things I'd wondered about. Once or twice over the past few weeks he'd canceled last minute, claiming he had to work late. And he'd taken forever to call from his trip to Paris; Orly Airport was so crowded, he'd said. The cab driver had a "no cell phone" rule. And the hotel messed up his reservation. I was worried that something wasn't right, but didn't want to be mistrustful. Yet often Colin had seemed attentive and reliable, taking us to his family's place for every holiday, spending weekends with us, remembering my birthday and Valentine's Day. And he was always so sweet to my little girl, teaching her how to play ball and do card tricks, reading to her. I really thought we were a solid couple. I could never face our friends or his parents again.

"You took that woman to Paris, didn't you?"

I watched as his eyes flickered before he looked away. More tears fell as I realized that Julie had been right about how recent the cheating had been.

"I hope you two will be very happy together." I pushed past him and reached for the door.

"Vic, wait." He grabbed my arm. Our faces were inches apart. I felt like choking him with his silk bow tie.

"Can we please talk about this some more? I love you."

"Right now we have a room full of people who are inconvenienced and confused after watching your YouTube performance. Your girlfriend got all your best angles." I couldn't help getting in one zinger.

I pushed his arm away and reached for the box of tissues someone had left on the corner table. "How could you? *I loved you.* And I let you into Rachel's life. You know how cautious I am about having her get hurt. It's bad enough that every time I close my eyes, I'll be picturing your lady friend's silky blond hair. I don't know how I'm going to live with myself knowing how much Rachel will be crushed. She thought you were her new dad." I wiped my eyes with my fingertips.

"It doesn't have to be like that—"

My fury boiled over. "Yes, it does. And I expect you to back me up when I make my announcement. It's the least you can do."

Colin nodded grimly and followed me into the room where our guests had been waiting. Everyone was instantly quiet when I took my place at the front, Colin slouching behind me. "Um, hello. We apologize. The wedding won't be happening after all. Please respect our wishes for privacy."

I walked back to the antechamber, noticing that the Justice gave me a sympathetic glance as she motioned for the clerk to shoo everyone out. Julie and Hal called the restaurant and told them to donate the party food to a local pantry. Then they texted the band and photographer, and took Rachel to my apartment while I figured out what I would say to her.

I slipped out the back and into the front seat of my car for a good, long cry. I was alone, no parents or siblings; a single mom by choice who'd protected myself against further pain by avoiding intimate relationships and using a sperm donor to have the baby I longed for. There were moments of terror about raising Rachel on my own, but desperation proved to be a great motivator, propelling me through the demands of childcare and my practice. I'd gotten by on my own, never expecting to find someone to build a future with.

Until Colin.

I still couldn't believe he'd been sleeping with that woman all along. How could I have misjudged him, and what was I going to tell Rachel? At least my ten-year-old didn't use social media, so she wouldn't see the sex video. I was grateful for small miracles.

Back at my apartment, I sat Rachel down and told her I'd gotten "cold feet," a phrase that made her smile, adding that Colin wasn't the person I was meant to spend the next fifty years with. Rachel nodded as I spoke, her large gray eyes serious, "Okay, Mom. If you don't want to marry him, that's your decision."

I knew there would be questions when I least expected them. Until then I'd have to get Rachel and myself through the breakup. I blocked Colin's number, and took my daughter on a honeymoon cruise through the Caribbean.

She swam with dolphins and played shuffleboard, while I mulled things over. I was a good mother, my child was doing well, and my psychology practice was running smoothly. But if I was so competent, how had I missed the signs? I was a humiliated wreck; sobbing in our stateroom quietly every night after Rachel fell asleep.

A few days into the trip, I pulled myself together. Where I'd once resisted the typical suburban pilgrimage, I now welcomed change. With memories of Colin and echoes of my recent humiliation at every turn, my first order of business would be vacating the Central Park West apartment the three of us had shared, and in the process, evading the gossips and their judgments. I began to hatch a plan. Kids needed space and a yard. Since the school year was ending, the time was now; instead of squeezing into a tiny one bedroom, spiraling further into a state of shame and desperation, Rachel and I would search out great schools and a tight-knit community.

Julie texted me as we were stepping off the ship. The woman in the video had been Colin's girlfriend during college and after. The details were scant, but Julie had heard he wouldn't put a ring on it. As the ceremony began, the blond live-tweeted and messaged a few of her and Colin's mutual friends and one or two of his family members. What started as a brief flurry of activity took on a life of its own, as guests huddled together over their phones. Within minutes, nearly everyone in the room had seen the lewd video.

Colin had downplayed their relationship. Well, he and Blondie deserved one another, just as Rachel and I were entitled to a baggage-free life. I'd been racking my brain, thinking about what our lives might look like if we started over, when a thought popped into my mind: What about Mayfair Close?

We scrolled through the town's website, Mayfair Memes, which described a rosy, suburban haven. "The village is a peaceful and idyllic community north of the city. Its Victorian houses and leafy streets are home to families drawn by the award-winning schools and lush parks. Exalted former denizens include Felicia

Wynn, first female astronaut, and Butch Calloway, famed journalist and sportscaster."

The town had been on my radar for years. My parents and I spent several summers there when I was a child, visiting Great Aunt Pearl. After Mom and Dad were gone, she and I continued to vacation at the house until I went off to college and she retired to Boca and rented it out.

Aunt Pearl had been my rock, seeing me through high school and holidays, birthdays, and crises. Rachel and I visited her often in Florida, even stopping there after the blighted honeymoon. When the nurse called to say my great aunt had suffered a massive stroke, there was nothing more the doctors could do, all I knew was frantic terror and a disconnected feeling that left my body icy, limbs stiff, and heart crushed.

Except for Rachel, I was officially alone. Again.

My daughter remained stoic when I delivered the news, knitting her brow and concentrating on my face before asking, "Why do people have to die?"

I drew her close and said, "Aunt Pearl was very old, ninety-four. But I'm not going anywhere, sweetheart," I added in response to the unspoken question in her eyes. Tears slid down Rachel's cheeks as her sideways glance told me that she was scared. Me too. And several months after the memorial service, I was still raw. How could I help my child going forward when I was struggling?

Great Aunt Pearl had always been there, saving me in every way. In the end, she'd left me the old Mayfair place with instructions to sell if necessary. Even though I'd known that was her intent, and had notified the tenants and visited the property after the will was read, the timing of her bequest felt like a sign: My aunt was saving me yet again.

We had a house in a suburban town with excellent schools. While I was all in, my "fresh start" was Rachel's worst nightmare.

At the mention of relocating, she'd stamped her foot. "I am not moving to some dumb house and going to a school where I won't know anyone. No!" She stared down, her hands balled into fists.

"I understand, Rach. But I really think you'll like it. You'll have your own room, not a dining alcove like the one you grew up in. There's cool outdoor stuff, and you'll meet nice people."

She'd turned her back on me and glowered at the wall. "I'm sorry you're upset, but Aunt Pearl wanted us to have the house," I said. "And the schools there are supposed to be great. Now that I'm not with Colin anymore, we have to find some place to live, and this is the best choice for us."

Rachel began to cry. "You just talk on the phone with your friends. So what do you care if we move? I don't want to go and leave *my* friends." She wiped a tear with the back of her hand. "This sucks." We sat in silence.

"I guess I have no choice," she finally responded, brushing away the arm I tried to place around her shoulders, barely speaking to me for the week that followed. "At least we'll have a huge backyard," I said, my best shot at a peace offering.

Our new house sat at the end of a shady road in the part of Mayfair favored by bankers and big firm lawyers. Across town was an apartment complex where teachers, piano tuners, police officers and their families resided. There was a busy main drag with a post office, gas station, dry goods store, and sweet shop, and more modern homes too, clustered around strip malls with big box stores.

Rachel and I motored up a long hill, passing an apple orchard, and following a tree-lined path, finally reaching the large white Victorian with a wraparound porch. After we entered through the kitchen, she bypassed the back staircase and butler's pantry in favor of the front parlor. "My room is up here, right?" Rachel asked, taking the steps two-by-two. As her mood lightened, I felt myself starting to relax.

We were standing in the doorway of her bedroom, scanning open spaces and a row of windows that overlooked a trio of rose bushes. "Wow, it's bigger than our whole apartment," she said, smiling for the first time that day. "Can I invite Zoe and Savannah to sleep over?"

She agreed to give Mayfair a chance and I promised to bring her back to the city to visit her friends. By mid-August we were out of the gate and up to our waists in cartons. It felt like I'd come full circle, relocating with my daughter to the home where I'd spent summers in my youth.

I remembered Mayfair as a sleepy town, quiet and serene. I was relying on distant impressions, watercolor memories formed years earlier.

A bell sounded, jolting me out of my reverie. Rachel and I were now at the doorway of Barnum Elementary, trapped in the rush of kids and backpacks. Surrounded by fresh faces, I saw hope: After Aunt Pearl's death and that close call at the altar, we were finally on the other side of our difficulties.

Maybe it was naive. Last spring I would have said that live-tweeting during a wedding was the worst possible use of social media, and that the woman behind the stunt was the lowest form of bully.

But now, living here in Mayfair, I know better.

Two
Mayfair Memes

We entered Barnum Elementary through double doors. The lobby was boxy and nondescript, the sort of place one might visit to apply for a driver's license or a visa for foreign travel; only it was teeming with children and nervous energy.

Rachel spoke over the chatter of children rushing to class. "There are lots of kids." She looked older than her almost eleven years, and at five foot one, was practically as tall as me, the gray in her eyes, accentuated by sandy-colored braids. Though my eyes were a shade darker, they were deep-set like Rachel's.

Meeting my daughter's gaze, I recalled how she'd looked up at me in infancy, studying my face, finding love and reassurance. I felt like hugging her right here in the hallway, but restrained the impulse, searching instead for the right words, encouraging words. But before I could say anything, she strode off, always a step ahead of me.

We were now near the main office. Out of the corner of my eye, I spotted a red-haired girl who looked to be about Rachel's age. As she attempted to readjust the straps of her clunky pink backpack, her floral lunchbox and thermos clattered to the tile floor.

Rachel remained off to the side, pulling out her phone and

avoiding eye contact as a petite girl came into view and motioned for one or two others to join her. She wore a streamlined, black knapsack; a Swedish brand, the kind all the celebrities favored. Watching the red-haired girl rooting around on the floor, they tittered as their ringleader, the kid with the knapsack, threw her head back and laughed.

The other girl was struggling to balance her possessions, dropping the thermos a second time with a tinny ping that prompted additional giggling. I moved closer and glanced at the kid with the knapsack: "Please stop, girls. Be nice," I said in a tone that was more soothing than scolding.

A woman in tennis whites raced over and stood next to the group, her back to me, sweeping her perfectly sculpted arms toward the fifth grade hallway in a gesture intended to herd them toward the classrooms. She didn't even look my way, and with all the chaos in the halls, I got only a split-second glance of her toned physique and the light hair she'd twisted and tucked into her visor.

The knapsack girl shot me a dirty look and moved down the hallway with her friends. The hapless kid followed, clutching her belongings to her chest. Even though I'd lost sight of them, the meanness I'd witnessed would be etched in my mind for some time to come. I'd torn my daughter away from her school and friends and given up the cozy apartment we'd called home. What if moving here turned out to be a mistake?

I glanced around. The mom in tennis clothing was near the main office, waving at someone in the distance, failing to engage with those in her vicinity. As she stepped toward the exit, the other parents parted, making way. This woman was obviously important, and I wondered who she was.

The lobby was quieter now. I prayed that Rachel and I would find a community at school, and I wouldn't run into any patients. I'd recently leased part-time space in town with a view toward building a local practice. But while I'd strategized about how to deal with potential clinical conflicts, living and working in the same suburb wouldn't be easy. People regarded me as a keeper of secrets, a safe harbor in a storm.

Since my Mayfair clients had been seeing me in the city and didn't know I'd moved here, they'd be unnerved running into me in the parking lot or at a volunteer event, and I wasn't too keen on making small talk with them, either. I'd have to go case-by-case and see when to raise the issue, being clear about boundaries, while setting limits and looking halfway presentable—no dropping off in pajamas.

"Don't talk to anyone," Rachel hissed, stepping quickly down the hallway without looking back. My daughter would be fine; it was me I'd have to worry about.

An hour later, I was on the Upper East Side, unlocking the door to my city office. Unlike my personal life, it was neat and orderly. Bookshelves stood near the entrance, and a small area rug abutted the couch. On one side was a black leather patient lounger and footstool, perfectly mirroring my matching chair and ottoman at the back of the room. My diplomas and license were displayed on the far wall above the desk.

The light on my machine was blinking. I crossed the room, recalling how thrilled I'd been fifteen years earlier—a lifetime ago—when I was accepted to the clinical psychology doctoral program at Columbia. I'd finally get to read Freud and see patients in supervision! I smiled at the memory, and pressed the button to play my messages.

Colin's voice boomed. "Victoria. I've given you space like you'd asked. Just checking in again. I'd like to have dinner so I can explain a few things."

Bastard. I hit delete.

There was a second voice mail: "It's been rough . . . . Please give me a few minutes of your time." Colin's persistence had more to do with being at the wrong end of a breakup than missing me. I had no interest in speaking to him, but would have to find two minutes to call and reiterate that he needed to stop contacting me.

The buzzer sounded. Amy was my first appointment of the day. She'd also recently moved to Mayfair and had no idea that I now lived in her town and had a daughter attending the same school as her children.

The session was slow going; my patient was stuck, repeating over and over that the suburbs were "vile, awful, hell on earth." Round and round she went, an old vinyl record caught in a well-worn groove.

I went with one of clinical psychology's most reliable techniques: the gentle nudge. "Perhaps you're not aware, but your thoughts keep coming back to how unhappy you are in your new town. Any idea why you're so knotted up?"

Amy ran a hand through her dark curly hair and tucked her long legs behind her before glancing around the office. Her eyes finally came to rest on a framed photo hanging over the couch: a leafy road wending its way to parts unknown, part of a larger trail, and most importantly, an invitation to speak. She let loose.

"You wouldn't believe how cruel they are, Dr. Bryant. I was out walking the dog yesterday afternoon, and I overheard them in the next yard, laughing. They didn't know I was there." Amy stopped abruptly, shifting from detached observer to down-and-out sufferer. Her face became a silent movie of expressions, showcasing hurt, anger and longing. Her chest rose and fell, and she swiped her hands in an effort to stem the flow of tears.

I smoothed the creases in my pantsuit and leaned forward, wondering what she would say next. After a silence, she continued.

"They were so smug, standing there ripping everyone apart . . . . It was like they were picking through items at a sample sale, scanning, then tossing them back into the reject bin; only they were talking about people. I can't remember all of it, but it was stuff like,

'She's so fat,' followed by their tittering, and 'She has a tic—have you seen it?' Or my personal favorite: 'That one's a real loser.' They had something to say about everyone, and roared with laughter every time someone hurled another insult. I was so shocked; I just wanted to back away, escape undetected. And then I heard them mention my daughter: 'You know the new girl, Lucy? She has zero personality, and no one likes her.'"

Amy wiped her eyes. "It was horrible. I had no idea who they were, except one of them spoke with a twang."

I shifted in my chair. "All of that must have been really diffi-cult to hear, but you have to consider the source. Adolescent girls are known to be mean—they're famous for it. Their sniping says more about them than about Lucy, or you."

My patient sobbed wordlessly. When she finally spoke her voice went flat, and her eyes looked dead. "It was the moms."

Now it was my turn to be speechless. Maybe I had misheard. No, she'd definitely said "moms."

A picture formed: a bunch of gossips, ripping apart the entrails of their neighbors' children, scheming to advance the interests of their own kids, blind to the collateral damage they caused.

Dread sank into my gut. What would women like these do to Rachel now that she was at Barnum?

When I arrived later that afternoon, hundreds of people mobbed the front steps of the school, though thankfully no patients. Nor-mally I'd let Rachel's sitter, Alva, pick her up, but I'd worked a shortened day to get to the classroom by three o'clock in the afternoon.

I'd hoped to spend some more time with my daughter in the coming year and planned to transition away from full-time in Manhattan. I'd started working Tuesday and Friday mornings in

Westchester, and was excited for Rachel's final year of grammar school—my last chance to spend time in the classroom and be one of those moms who volunteered and served on committees.

When the school doors opened, a woman in secretary glasses and overalls announced: "Caregivers and parents, you may now proceed to the classrooms and wait outside in the hall for your children."

There was an immediate charge; I felt like I was at the Running of the Bulls.

I stepped quickly down the fifth grade hallway with the others, eager to get a glimpse of the classroom. They were weaning parents off hovering in preparation for the transition to junior high. By late fall, no one would be allowed in.

I peeked into the room. A group of kids was at the board with the teacher, solving a math problem. The rest were sitting at their desks, working independently. Rachel was biting her pencil and staring at a textbook. She whispered something to the girl next to her, and they giggled quietly. Maybe moving hadn't been such a bad idea after all. Other parents arrived and began to chat as they waited in the hallway for the school day to end.

I was about to introduce myself to a woman who'd just arrived at the classroom when the bell rang. The teacher waved the parents in and smiled, as we filed past, moving around the room to collect our children. "Victoria Bryant," I said. "Rachel's mom."

A small sinewy woman zigzagged across the room and came to stand next to me. I found myself staring at her slender form, bright-blue eyes, and perfectly highlighted hair. "Are you Rachel's mother?" she said.

My work clothes were rumpled and there were bags under my eyes. I glanced at her outfit: snug jeans and red knit top with billowing sleeves. She'd paired the ensemble with dark boots and a matching leather satchel. I wondered how this mom was so pulled together on a weekday afternoon, when some of us looked like we had just come from cleaning out a garage. "Yes, I am. Hi," I said.

"I'm Jess. My daughter is Lexi. She and Rachel had lunch together today—I got a text about it. Rachel is adorable, by the way."

Her eyes were friendly. "Thanks, Jess."

Out of the corner of my eye I thought I recognized the tiny blond girl who'd been in the hallway earlier that day. She stood with one hand on her hip, directing classroom traffic. "We're taking that. Use this one," she said, pointing at a bin of plastic calculators. The other kids obeyed without a peep.

"Hi." A wiry woman with shoulder-length dark hair and fringed bangs had come over to stand with Jess and me.

"You're new, right? Welcome." She was blushing, almost shy. I liked her on the spot. Her openness reminded me of my friends from the city.

I was happy she'd introduced herself. "Nice to meet you. I'm Victoria."

"Sharon. Nice to—"

Jess interrupted. "Sharon's son is in this class. Neil's right over there."

I turned to look at a tall boy who was using his math textbook as a football and pretending to land the game-winning catch while his friends cheered him on. After a couple of seconds, he raised both arms and laughed, revealing a pair of well-placed dimples.

"He's so cute—" I began.

Jess continued speaking: "You live in the old Walker house, right?" She was ignoring Sharon, speaking only to me. "We saw it listed years ago on the Tour of Homes. I've never been inside, but what curb appeal! It's a gorgeous place. And huge! We used to pass by with the kids and make up stories about the family who originally lived there. Did you know there's a book about the Walkers in the village library?"

I hadn't known. Jess barreled on. "My daughter, Lexi, has been dying to meet the girl who moved into that house. It was all she could talk about on the way to school this morning. By the way, what do you do? Psychologist, right? I googled you. I'm glad Rachel is in this class. There are a lot of nice girls. Oh, and I wanted to mention that a bunch of us are getting together in a couple of weeks. Maybe you can come along. We periodically plan a night to blow off some steam, otherwise we'd all go crazy."

"That sounds fun." I glanced at Sharon, whose mouth was set in a hard line, and shivered involuntarily, remembering how Jess had looked through her moments earlier. "Nice meeting you, Victoria," Sharon said, before walking off to find her son.

Just then Rachel motioned from the other side of the classroom where she'd been standing with several other girls.

"Can Lexi and I have a playdate today?" she called to me.

"Sure."

I turned to look as Jess walked across the room and stood in the same area as Rachel, behind a slightly built blond girl with perfect braids. She put her hand on the girl's shoulder. I was starting to figure out who went with whom, and decided that those two were right out of central casting: a gorgeous duo who smiled all the time and lacked any apparent obstacles in life.

As Rachel and Lexi debated whose house was better, the girl who'd just been giving orders about the calculators came over. Like Lexi, she was small and blond, with deep-blue eyes. I didn't get to see much more, though, because the glint of her enamel bangles picked up the fluorescent light of the classroom, distracting me. I recognized the bracelets instantly; a patient had mentioned coveting a similar set, but her husband had said, no way—too pricey.

She strapped on the black knapsack—this was definitely the kid I'd seen earlier—and spoke. "My house, guys."

Lexi nodded. "Mom, Rachel and I are going to Collette's."

Jess laughed at the trio before circling back to where I stood. "Like I was saying, a bunch of us are going out for a Ladies' Night. Hopefully you can join us."

"That's so kind. I'd love to." It was nice to be included, but I felt uneasy, remembering how quickly Sharon had taken off.

Jess was onto the next thing. "Hey, what about volunteering?" she asked. "Lee—that's Collette's mom; you'll love her—assigned all the jobs over the summer, but we'll squeeze you in if you'd like to come to the lunchroom and hand out pizza."

"Sure. I'd definitely enjoy doing something like that on my day off," I replied.

"What's good?" she asked.

"I can do some Fridays."

Jess nodded. "Perfect. I'll put you on the schedule and email you the details." She went to join the teacher, who had waved her over to a wall of student paintings. I smiled at Rachel, who was still chatting with the two girls. Jess came back toward me and paused to answer a text, giving me the "one minute" sign.

In my peripheral vision, I noticed a couple of moms looking over in our direction. One woman wore her hair in a short brown bob. I turned full circle and made eye contact, but she looked away. The woman adjacent to her had sporty transitional glasses that changed color for sunlight. I couldn't see her eyes because the lenses were adjusting to indoors, but thought she'd whispered something. It was hard to know in the chaos of kids' conversations, parent sign-ups, and teacher greetings.

The two of them motioned for their kids to wait, then approached Jess and me.

"Hi, I'd love to be a cafeteria volunteer," the one with glasses said.

Jess finally looked up. "Oh, I'm so sorry. I just gave the last spot to Victoria. She's new. Have you met?"

"Hi." She nodded at me for a split second before addressing Jess. "I emailed you. Several times."

"Gosh, I didn't get anything from you—better check my spam. Like I said, we're good on lunchroom volunteers. But next time, for sure." Jess went back to her phone messages.

The women glanced at one another and walked back toward their children. "I've got the girls," Jess said, quickly stepping to catch up with them as they sped down the hallway. "Text you my address later. Want to pick up Rachel at five thirty?"

"Is that okay, Rach?" I called.

"Yes," she answered, turning around to smile at me. "Bye!" she called out before running to catch up to the others.

Rachel seemed to be making friends. Phew.

Turning to leave the classroom, I passed the whispering moms.

"Hi." I tried to be friendly. "Nice to meet you. My daughter just started here." I scanned their faces. The one in glasses nodded slightly; the bobbed-haired woman barely looked up. And what was with the whispering? I'd made sure there were no clinical conflicts when I registered Rachel; the principal had been helpful and let me look at the class lists when I explained the situation, no names, of course. And though I had two patients, Maureen and Amy, who had kids in a different classroom, I wasn't treating either of the women standing in front of me. No issue there.

Even though some of the people seemed clique-y, I wasn't going to dwell on the classroom situation. I'd understand the landscape better when I got to know all the players.

Sharon came over on her way out. "Let's have lunch one day."

"That would be great. May I take your number?" I asked, entering it into my phone as she dictated.

I was grateful for the offer. It would be nice to have a friend who could fill me in about Barnum.

Walking out of the school building, I paused to make a note—my upcoming stint at the cafeteria was a few weeks out—then, looked up into the sun and breathed in. The move seemed to be going well, while the parent personalities and classroom dilemmas were what I called "problems of the worried well."

Three
This Old House

I was lying on my side, half-awake. Rachel had crawled into my bed at 2 o'clock in the morning, burrowing in beside me, cocoon-like.

Life's road bumps had taught me to be grateful for the smallest blessings, like the warm skin and gentle breathing of my lively ten-and-a-half-year-old. In my years of practice, I had seen countless families struggle as their children suffered with school problems, mood disorders, and serious eating concerns. Recently, a physician colleague and I had to hospitalize a teenager who ate nothing but sugar packets. Her parents huddled in my office, the mother weeping as her husband stared mutely into the ether. Sometimes raising a child was like trying to manage your own private tsunami.

I floated in and out of sleep until Rachel shook me.

"Mom, wake up." Rachel's tone was serious. I opened my eyes immediately. She sat surrounded by pillows, her gray eyes wide and earnest beneath yesterday's messy braids, her hand resting on my arm.

"I have to ask you something."

I managed to locate my glasses. There were still thirty minutes before I had to get up for work.

"Are you listening? Mom?"

I braced myself for the worst. She'd been at Barnum for a little over a week. Was something wrong?

She shook my arm. "Can I get an Instachat? Everyone at school has one. And pierced ears."

Earrings I could handle; it was all the other things, like social sites, that were harder for me. They meant Rachel was growing up, but I wasn't nearly ready, despite knowing all along this day would come. Separation was inevitable. I'd read that in a textbook, or maybe it was written on a message inside of a fortune cookie. Either way, I'd have to let go. At least she wasn't asking for a tattoo, not yet.

"I'll need to approve it," I said, rubbing my temples. "Snaps" were supposed to disappear. But recipients found ways around their transience, and teens were routinely caught in compromising situations. "You know you can't message strangers or send anyone photos of yourself."

"I'd never do that."

"Okay." I sighed. "In a few minutes we have to start getting ready. We'll talk more about Instachat and earrings later." I was torn about breaking up our slumber party. Oops, there I was again, cataloging my feelings.

Good or bad, compulsive or not, feelings had always been my focus. That was why I became a clinical psychologist, to understand them. I learned to handle life's challenges without becoming overwhelmed by emotion. Losing both parents at once at the age of twelve, my grief was so bad it felt like I was going crazy. I'd see others laughing at school and feel cut off, alien. The days blurred, and everything was muddled and bleak. I finally figured out how to compartmentalize and get through the long hours, the loneliness. *Doctor, heal thyself.* Except for barely dodging that bullet at the altar, I'd mostly done okay.

Rachel fell back to sleep and I tried to snuggle a little more. But my mind had started going and I could no longer relax.

Shoving the sides of my pillow inward in the manner of a crazed accordion grinder, I sat up and rolled back down, vertebrae by vertebrae. But nothing I did seemed to have any impact. At least my abdominal muscles were getting a workout.

My left eye insisted on peeking at the clock again: 5:48 a.m. I gave in; why rest when you can fret until dawn?

I made my way downstairs, thinking at least I was enjoying the house. I loved the polished oak floors, wide curving stairway from entranceway to second floor, and gracious landing that gave way to a large parlor. Outside, there was even a sprawling veranda. *Veranda.* That was a fun word to say.

But the good times ended there. The porch was elegant, but dilapidated, just like the rest of the place. The roof leaked, and the plumbing was shot. We couldn't afford to do any major renovations. Rachel and I had figured it out, though. We would be okay as long as we didn't run the shower and wash our clothing at the same time.

Coffee beckoned. I made my way through the darkness, down the old staircase, noticing the feel of worn brocade under my toes. There was a rustling in the wall next to me, and my heart screeched to a halt. Hopefully there were no mice or other vermin here—that was all I needed. I inched forward into the kitchen, picturing Stuart Little on the counter, balancing on hind legs, waving a welcome sign. As my hand brushed the worn piece of lace covering the windowpane above the sink, I told myself that worrying about mice was ridiculous, and flipped on the light switch.

A small spotlight shone beneath one cabinet, casting a single beam from countertop to floor, yet still leaving most of the room dark. Perfect. I could see enough to press the button, but still awaken gradually while the coffee brewed. Early morning was my time to think. I listened as each inky drop hit the glass carafe, and kept returning to the same thoughts: I was alone in the world with my wide-eyed pre-adolescent who was dependent upon me for survival. We had moved to the same village as two of my patients who had kids in the school that Rachel now attended, and which, according to one of them, was a place where a band of moms ran around committing all sorts of social atrocities.

I wondered why I was so bothered by Amy's last session and her *Hunger Games* view of life in town. Everyone I'd been meeting seemed nice; maybe she was exaggerating—or there was more to the story. Still, my patient wasn't the only one who'd warned me about Mayfair. My daughter and I would eventually learn the truth.

It would be fine. Rachel was lively and resilient; my helicoptering was the last thing she needed. I pictured her the weekend we'd moved in, friends visiting from the city. As I unpacked in the bedroom, she called upstairs: "Bye, mom. We're riding bikes."

There was a cacophony of sounds: a thumping, sneakers on wood mixed with peels of laughter. "Don't forget your key—and you still have to do some unpacking!" I'd yelled over the din, but a resounding thud from the front door silenced my pleas. Peering out a window I watched as Rachel and her friends rode off over spotty crabgrass and patches of brown that had appeared where lawn was supposed to be, their Yankees T-shirts and baggy shorts fading into tiny blue dots before disappearing altogether.

There were now percolating sounds emanating from across the room. The scent of hazelnut began to engulf me, slowly, sensuously; the potent beans causing my nostrils to vibrate and desire to grow until that first sip was all I could think about. It was a welcome respite from patient conflicts and worry about my child.

The coffee pot beeped. Finally. Time to hit pause on the self-analysis and fight the shrink within.

I crossed the floor, tiled in an ornate pattern of white and black. The rest of the room was limited to painted white wood cabinets and light tiles above the counters. My aunt's improvements were surface-level, but elegant. I sipped and smiled as I heard the sound of bare feet above me.

After drop off, I drove into the city, parked, and walked to my building. Ten minutes later, when my first appointment was scheduled, I opened my office door, noting the waiting room was free of occupants, human or otherwise. I got busy, filing paperwork and sorting through the mail.

More than halfway into the hour, my patient, Maureen, sailed in, having commuted from Mayfair. I wondered if she knew that we were now neighbors whose kids attended the same school. She strode across the room, flipping her straight dark hair out of her eyes and smiling in my direction.

Lowering herself into the patient chair, she began to speak. "I signed up to volunteer at a soup kitchen. Everyone around me is so focused on shallow and material things, like improving their tennis serve or lowering their golf handicap. I can't wait to see my speech therapy friends after this. They're doing good work, and I miss being part of that. Oh, and sorry I was late." Maureen had quit her job as a pediatric speech pathologist when she'd moved out of the city.

"Sounds like you're saying you'd like to get involved in something more meaningful," I commented.

"Well, yeah. People where I live are mostly brain-dead idiots. I love my friends, and some of the other women in town are fun to go out drinking with, but they aren't really aware of the larger world. I miss helping people."

Maureen was deep in thought. "I'd like to go back to work, but all the hospitals and clinics have eliminated part-time positions to cut costs," she finally said. "And since we can't afford live-in help, I have to deal until the kids are older."

"You sounded happy when you mentioned volunteering."

"Yes. Last week, my friends asked me to serve as the cochair of our town's Newcomer's Committee. It's the most important part of the PTA, helping new families assimilate into the community. I'll be working with Lee DeVry, and that's a big deal. Have you heard of the family? They're charitable people, very successful. Their home is magnificent: over 11,000 square feet, on a private lake with two docks, floor-to-ceiling windows and—this blows my mind—no two walls the same size. It was in an architectural magazine, a huge spread. Lee's husband, Jack, is a financier. He told Bob he's building a helipad on the property."

Lee? That sounded familiar. I thought back. Jess had mentioned her when we met in the classroom.

Maureen glanced at the clock and continued. "I've known Lee since sophomore year; we were in the same sorority. She's a natural blond with a perfect body, a true southern belle!" Maureen laughed. "All good, unless you piss her off. One time she blackballed a cheerleader who went after her boyfriend. It got ugly." She paused, furrowing her brow. "I forgot why I got onto this. Oh, right, the Newcomer's Committee. Like I said, I'm glad to be working with Lee. She's, like, the most popular woman in town. Our daughters are best friends, and our families are really close."

"That's nice to hear," I said.

Her phone buzzed and she took it out of her purse. "Lee is in the city and wants to meet up. My speech therapy friends will have to wait." She glanced at the clock. "Okay. I see it's that time."

I always found it interesting when patients told me it was time to end. I knew that for Maureen, this probably had to do with wanting to know when she should rein in her feelings. She had a lot of self-control, and valued her ability to compose herself.

I also found it interesting that Maureen was going to make her speech therapy pals wait until after she got together with Lee. I had a nagging feeling that maybe my patient wasn't the Eleanor Roosevelt she made herself out to be.

She stood up. "Almost forgot to mention, I googled because

I was going to leave a message, and saw that you also have an office in Mayfair. If you're new to town, it's my job to welcome you on behalf of the Newcomer's Committee. But I can't show you around. Obviously that would be weird."

Obviously. I was sweating as she stood up and walked to the door. This boundary stuff was going to be tougher than I realized.

"Maybe we should switch it up, meet in Westchester next time. I'll call you about that. Either way, see you next week." She turned and threw me a parting grin, and I was struck by how pretty she was, by the friendliness in her smile. It wasn't hard to see why Maureen had so many friends, and why she was head of her town's welcoming committee.

After she left, I grabbed a sip of water and glanced out the window onto the busy city street. Maureen, official town greeter and soup kitchen volunteer, was standing next to her car, ripping up a summons and shoving it into her purse. She'd parked in a handicapped spot. Perhaps we would talk about that next hour.

This session had me thinking about Maureen and other women who felt hamstrung by the maternal role. So many seemed to be struggling to understand who they were now that their kids were a little older and they had more time on their hands. It was the moms whose primary source of identity was derived through parenting that struggled the most.

I was pleased when my phone pinged. It was Sharon, one of the women I'd met in the classroom, inviting me to get together: *"Would love to meet up. Next couple of weeks, crazy, but after that?"* *"Sure! Love to,"* I responded, and we signed off.

〰〰〰

Rachel and I began to settle into a routine. We had breakfast together and I dropped her off and headed to work, leaving pick-up to Alva, our sitter since Rachel's birth. The two of them were close. Knowing what it was like to feel the void of loss, I was thrilled when Alva agreed to work in Westchester.

"Can we have eggs today?" Rachel was asking. We'd make it to school, but if we didn't leave in the next few minutes, I'd have trouble getting into the city on time.

"Sure," I said, glancing at my watch. "You'll need a big meal to get through school and unpack all of the cartons in your room."

She stomped upstairs. "It isn't fair! I should be allowed to keep my room the way I want."

I cracked the eggs, thinking that being a mother was hands down more difficult than seeing clients.

As we were getting ready to leave, I walked past the powder room and noticed a small puddle where water was leaking. The place was in disrepair with antiquated plumbing and loose tiles everywhere. A team of construction workers would barely make a dent, and I had no idea how to stop a toilet from running over or fix a sink. Where was my old super when I needed him? I imagined calling him in an emergency; maybe he would come over for a repair, or if it snowed. Come to think of it, I still hadn't purchased a shovel. Better get on that before I wound up trapped in a huge drift.

Rachel gulped down her breakfast and we drove to school. She accepted my apology for being short-tempered, and promised to start on the boxes later that day. Through the rearview mirror I took in her fitted V-neck, cropped jeans, and the Adidas sneakers she'd lobbied for—the ones all the Mayfair girls were wearing. For the majority of the ride she stared down at her phone, fingers moving across the screen. I asked how everything was going.

"It's fine. Everyone's nice. I like the teacher." I'd hoped for more, but knew better than to probe. Once we arrived, she barely waited until I'd stopped the car before opening her door and catapulting out, knees bent, like a parachute jumper. "Bye." Her departure told me everything I needed to know: The classroom and peer group were fine.

Since we'd gotten through drop-off ahead of schedule, I parked and headed for the Starbucks by the station platform. The place was packed, a magnet for commuters from several towns over. Inching my way in, I noticed that it reeked of too-potent coffee beans and vibrated like crazy whenever a train approached. Spending time there was like supping at the base of a live volcano.

There were a few women, including Jess, at a small café table across the room from the counter. While queuing up, I looked over a few times and tried to wave, but Jess was deep in conversation.

After my cappuccino was paid for, I grabbed it and squeezed through the crowd, stopping at her table to say hello. She and her friends were in yoga clothes, sipping hot drinks and laughing. "Hi," I smiled. "How's everything?"

"Good," she nodded, as I glanced around at the group and smiled. One of the women was telling a story. The others were focusing on her and didn't meet my eye.

"Just thought I'd say 'Good morning.' I'm on my way to work." Jess waved briefly before turning back to the others.

I made my way toward the door, wondering whether it had been a mistake to go over. She hadn't introduced me to her friends, but wouldn't it have been rude for me to leave without saying hello? There was a catch in my chest. Something was wrong.

A fast search of my pockets told me I'd misplaced my cell phone. Pivoting quickly, I failed to notice the tall, dark-haired guy who'd been resting against the wall, coffee in one hand, Kindle in the other. I bumped into him, tipping his cup and spilling dark liquid onto the floor.

"Excuse me," I said at exactly the same moment he apologized.

"Good reflexes. Did I burn you?" He was smiling.

I shook my head. "My fault. I'm sorry I spilled your coffee."

A train rumbled its approach. "No worries." My pulse quickened as he held my gaze for several moments until a buzzing sound—my phone!—pulled my attention toward my purse. I dragged my eyes away and dug around as a surge of commuters moved en masse toward the doorway. When I looked up, the cute guy had vanished.

Too bad, but he was probably married.

Four

A Visit

I was straining pasta over the sink—not exactly groundbreaking from a culinary standpoint, but it would have to do—when Rachel burst in from soccer practice. She was muddy, red-cheeked, and full of news. "Collette's coming over tomorrow. We're going to do homework together. Can she stay for dinner?"

"Of course." I motioned for Rachel to take her cleats off and leave them by the door.

"Let me know what you want to eat, and I'll ask Alva to get the ingredients." I was glad our sitter had agreed to do more of the housework and cooking now that Rachel was older and needed less in the way of childcare.

My daughter was nodding along, vigorously. "Something fun, like tacos?" she said, bending down to begin the process of untying. "Can Collette and I make popcorn and watch *The Voice*?"

"Sure." After seeing that kid in action, bossing everyone around in the classroom, laughing at the red-haired girl, even giving me a dirty look, I wasn't a fan. But I controlled my impulse to comment. Rachel had the right to choose her own friends.

The following day after work, I walked in as Alva was leaving. We said a quick hello as I set my car keys and purse down, opened the refrigerator, and grabbed a container of orange juice. I'd just

finished pouring a glass and shoving the carton in the compartment inside the door, when Alva raced over.

"My refrigerator," she laughed, grabbing the container and
moving it to the top shelf as she debriefed me. "Rachie is having
fun," she said, buttoning her sweater. "I'm glad she has a friend.
They were chatting up a storm today! They're in her room now."

I said goodbye to Alva and tiptoed upstairs to peek into the
bedroom. The girls sat side-by-side on the bed, putting on lip-
gloss, taking selfies, and joking around. Rachel's laughter sounded
pressured; more like a strange cackle than the giggle I was used to.

"Don't post that." I heard Collette say. "Delete it."

Rachel nodded, her face red.

I tiptoed down the hall and headed downstairs to empty the
dishwasher. Julie called, and I filled her in on the new school and
Rachel's classroom.

"You know, Vic," she said, "things may work out for you after
all."

We laughed as I took in the meaning of her comment. Instead
of being the woman who was humiliated at the altar, maybe I was
poised to live a comfortable and happy life with my daughter. Dare
to dream.

"I've been meaning to ask you. Rachel hasn't talked about our
aunt or Colin. I'm not sure how to help her process her grief and
all the other changes."

"You know what to do. Follow her lead. And why don't you
try to have a little fun for a change? Take a risk; you're too tightly
coiled."

She knew me well. "What do you suggest?" I cradled the
phone between my ear and shoulder as I reshelved the previous
night's dinner plates.

"What about bungee jumping?"

"Ha. Ha." After a brief silence, Julie spoke more gently.

"Rachel will be fine. Let's work on you. Have you met any women you might want to hang out with, potential friends?"

"There was one mom, Sharon, who seemed nice. She reminded me of Sam. Remember Zoe's mother?"

"That's your friend who went back to work, right?" she asked at the precise moment there was a large clatter and some screaming on her end of the line, followed by a noise that sounded like a slap: "Work sounds good." Julie's tone was dry. "Maeve grabbed a container of paint and dropped it on the dog, who is now a hideous shade of magenta. Carly hit her on the back, and Maeve is crying, so I have to go."

"You know you're not allowed to paint in here—" was the last thing I heard before the call cut off. It was hard enough keeping up with a preteen; I had no idea how Julie managed two on one.

It was time for Rachel's favorite show. I called up to the girls, who informed me they'd watch on their laptops. Why would I think they'd come downstairs and hang out with me? Growing up I'd sat in the living room and viewed my parents' or aunt's selections. I shook my head, contemplating the end of family time.

As I was surfing channels, I heard the sound of gravel in the driveway and peeked out the living room window. An army-size SUV pulled up and its driver alighted. He rounded the car and opened a rear door, and in the headlight beams, I spotted a woman walking up the path. Even if Collette hadn't been over, I'd have known instantly it was Lee, the PTA president I'd heard so much about. Just as everyone said, she had arresting blue eyes and perfect cheekbones.

Staring at her toned physique, I was pretty sure she was the woman in tennis clothes that everyone had cleared a path for that first morning in the lobby of the school. She hadn't seen me, but her daughter had.

I opened the door. "Haiii. You must be Victoria." She eyed me up and down, "Look at you, tiny little thing; Jess said you were adorable," before charging past. "May ah come in? Ah've just been dying to see your place. My mother's parents had a home like this, down South."

"Really, where did they live?" I asked as she raced into the foyer, ignoring me. "Mah stars! This place is huge."

"Please come into the kitchen. I have some iced tea or Perrier."

Lee followed me, scanning the joint like she was looking to buy. She didn't miss anything, not a crack in the ceiling or a chipped tile. I handed her a glass and an old joke: "Maid's day off. And the construction staff has gone fishing." She looked confused. "There's so much I want to do around here, it's . . . well . . . ."

Her eyes came to rest on the sink. I'd wrapped a thick ribbon of gray duct tape over the faucet to patch a leaky gap. She stared at my makeshift repair, and then turned back to me. "You just need the right crew and interior designer, honey. Let me ask Jack, mah husband, for names of contractors."

Lee and her friends were so wealthy; I didn't want the contact info for her designer or crew. With the rent of two offices and Alva's salary, I could barely pay the hefty real estate taxes, let alone renovate.

I pushed aside my insecurities and smiled. "That's nice of you. Would you like to see the rest of the house?"

"Sure."

For the next ten minutes, Lee ooh'd and aah'd about square footage and antique beams, mentioning as we climbed the stairs, that she'd designed her home and built it "from the studs up." She surveyed my room and the master bath, and I became acutely aware of several loose tiles and a drip. Lee told me she'd spent nearly a month selecting faucets and hardware.

Now we were passing the bedrooms. She waved at the girls while I walked on. Hearing giggling, I relaxed a bit; Rachel was having a good time. We were finally at the end of the hallway and began descending the stairs, where mercifully, our tour concluded where it had begun, in the front hallway. I asked if she would like another Perrier, or wanted to sit down in the living room. "I'm sorry I can't; I have *got* to run. Collette! Come on!" The younger DeVry appeared at the top of the landing. "Let's go, sugar. Say thank you."

"Thank you," Collette parroted, as she advanced down the staircase in this moment's jeans and sequined high tops, Rachel following on her heels. When they'd reached the bottom of the landing, Collette looked at me and whispered to her mother. Lee raised her brow and glanced over. I focused on my daughter. She'd shed her favorite fleece hoodie in favor of fitted clothing, and now seemed to prefer hanging around on Instachat to riding her bike. As I was contemplating these changes, Lee moved to where I'd been standing and kissed each of my cheeks before leaving with her daughter.

Rachel glanced at her phone as the door closed behind them. "Lexi just texted. There's a basketball interest meeting next Wednesday night. Her mom's driving; can I go?"

"Sure!"

"Guess what else! Collette and I made a joint Instachat account." She grinned and held out her phone so I could see.

"That's great, honey," I said, hoping that new friendship wasn't a bad idea.

Jess and her friend Audrey followed up on the ladies' night. As members of the Newcomer's Committee, it was their job to reach out to Mayfair's recent arrivals. The plan was for us to meet the following Tuesday at the Mexican place by the harbor.

I was parking in front of the restaurant, when Jess pinged that she and Audrey had already been seated and Lee would be joining us. I glanced down at my jeans and white cotton blouse. Hopefully I'd dressed properly. It was supposed to be a casual evening.

As soon as I opened the door, I spotted them on the opposite end of the room. While Jess was small and blond, Audrey was tall and dark. A huge red chili pepper was suspended from above, and swayed in time with the piped-in mariachi band. The place was nearly empty.

Jess wore leggings, a fitted T-shirt and ballet flats; Audrey had gone for a black trapeze dress and yin-yang pendant. They'd chosen to sit on the same side of the banquette. As I slid in across the table and started introducing myself to Audrey, her phone began to ring. "Babysitter," she mouthed to Jess, shaking her head as the caller spoke: "So what? That's just too bad." She ended the call and caught Jess's eye: "Jagger refuses to shower. I've about had it with that kid." Jess pointed to the menu. "Who'd order a mole? Sounds disgusting." They laughed and read through the rest of the entrées together.

I was starting to feel awkward, like I'd crashed their dinner, when, as if to make my point, Audrey reached for a laminated card featuring specialty drinks, while Jess peeked at her phone.

It was obviously up to me to start up a conversation, and I was wondering why no one else was joining us, but didn't want to say the wrong thing. "I haven't been to this place before."

Jess nodded. "Do you like Mexican food?"

"Yes. How about you guys?" I smiled across the table. Jess started to respond, but was distracted by the buzzing of her cell. She glanced at it, showed Audrey a message and turned back to me. "Lee's running late. She doesn't usually make time for these dinners, but she did say that she wanted to come tonight to *personally* welcome you." There was a slight edge to her voice.

Wishing there were other moms present, I glanc
of entrées as my companions spent the next few mi
down at the cell phone; burrowing in like scientists over a micro
scope, acting as though they were Watson and Crick unlocking
the mysteries of DNA.

"Everything okay?" I asked.

Jess pulled herself away from the screen. "Lee went to a gala in
the city last night. She's been posting photos on her blog."

"Look at that dress." Jess sighed, handing the phone to Audrey
and smiling briefly at me before turning her attention back to the
screen. "Wow. I love those shoes!"

I was still at a loss about what to say, when the door to the
restaurant opened and Lee stepped inside. "Well hiiiiiiiiiaaiiih."

I stared at her chocolate brown nail polish, russet mini, and
flowing camel-colored cape. The garments rolled into one another,
rising to an elegant silver fox collar that crowned her shoulders
like an exotic necklace. The outfit screamed couture—haute couture. I managed to tear my eyes away from her accessories and
return her greeting: "Hello."

Lee took her place at the head of the table.

The waitress approached and asked if we wanted to order
drinks.

"What's good?" I asked, glancing around the table.

"The drinks are mahvelous," Lee told me, as the others nodded
along. "Margarita please, frozen, no salt," I ordered. Then it was
Lee's turn: "The three of us will each have a Skinny Girl Margarita, please."

The waitress asked if she should bring over some chips and
salsa. Lee shook her head, motioning between herself, Jess, and
Audrey: "Thanks, but we're gluten-free."

"I'll have their gluten," I told the server. She snorted and
moved toward the front of the restaurant.

"How old are your kids?" I asked Audrey.

"My daughter, Katie, is in the same class as Lexi and Collette."

"Mine too. Her name is Rachel."

She nodded. "I heard."

"So, how long have you all lived in town?" I asked glancing around the table.

"Long enough to know who to avoid," Lee shot back. "Ah could tell you stories; there are some real losers here. A bunch of gals haven't opened a *Vogue* magazine since the nineties." She glanced at my blouse as Jess and Audrey snickered.

Just then Lee's phone buzzed with an incoming text. "Will you look at this?" She said, displaying a photo of a willowy blond who was arm-in-arm with a chestnut-haired man in large, dark-rimmed hipster glasses. "She's almost twice his height." The three of them laughed until the waitress came over with our drinks.

While the waitress was serving us, Jess squinted at the screen. "Phoebe looks good."

"Yes," Lee interrupted. "But check out Bart's glasses." I sensed they were intentionally leaving me out, and felt like an audience member watching a play.

"Peter and I are having dinner with them next week," Jess began as Audrey and Lee raised their glasses and sipped. "I can add you guys to the reservation," she said as Lee recoiled in horror, causing Audrey to laugh so hard, she almost choked on her cocktail.

Lee was obviously the group's Mother Ship. I was tempted to ask how late Jess and Audrey were allowed to stay out, but got sidetracked when two other women came into the restaurant and started waving in our direction. I decided that with matching brown ponytails, red SoulCycle tanks, and tight black exercise pants, they looked like Thing One and Thing Two; identical, except Thing Two had a slightly larger nose.

They came over to the table and began kissing and hugging Lee, Jess, and Audrey.

Lee smiled at Thing 1. "Stacey, haiiiah. Sorry we couldn't be there tonight. How's it going?"

"It's going," Stacey said.

"This is Victoria," Jess said, exchanging a seventh grade glance with Audrey as Lee examined her manicure.

Why had they joined the Newcomer's Welcoming Committee if they didn't like newcomers? These women were less welcoming than Torquemada during the Spanish Inquisition, and by this point, I'd had it.

As the hostess approached with take-out bags, Stacey bent down to kiss everyone goodbye. "Don't worry about tonight," she told Jess, placing a hand on her shoulder. *"I know you owed Lee a favor."* They grabbed their food and headed toward the front of the restaurant. "Nice meeting you," one of them called as the door was closing behind them.

So I was the favor? Were Lee and her friends really that bitchy? I was about to invent a headache and leave when the server brought our fajitas.

While we were eating, a family from school showed up. Their daughter looked to be a little older than our kids and had a pronounced lisp. Audrey noticed it too, and asked Jess in a stage whisper: "Why wouldn't they get that kid some help. It's beyond."

I recalled hearing she was a pediatrician who worked part-time, and Jess had been a teacher before having kids. *The two of them were professionals and they were trashing an impaired child and her parents?*

Lee leaned across the table. "You'll soon find that there are the right people and the wrong people to be friends with in Mayfair," she told me.

"I'll keep that in mind," I said, "though I tend to find something interesting about everyone." They cocked their heads and stared as I forced a smile.

Lee raised a hand like a school crossing guard stopping a line of cars. "Spare me the psychobabble, Victoria. I'm definitely not your target audience."

"I wasn't looking for an audience, just a friendly dinner," I said, as Lee leaned back, crossing her arms over her chest. Hoping to lighten the mood, I turned to Audrey. "So, why did you study medicine?" Given how insensitive she and the others had been, my curiosity was genuine.

"My dad was a doctor and let me hang around the office when I was in grammar school. My interest grew from there."

I nodded and asked Jess about teaching. "I've always liked books. My mother worked a lot when I was little, but we read before bedtime." Lee broke in: "It's true. This gal always volunteers at the library and runs herself ragged chairing the book fair, bless her heart."

Then my dinner companions all zeroed in on me at the exact same moment. "Are you divorced? Does Rachel see her dad a lot?"

I shook my head.

"Why do you live here if you work full-time in the city?" Audrey was asking.

"Do you ever get to see your daughter?" Lee locked eyes with me.

My pulse was racing, and I affixed a hard smile on my face: "I'd heard great things about the schools. Moving here was a no-brainer. I'm very fortunate. In my practice, I can work part-time in the city and have a local office here." I allowed myself to make one small dig. "It's really the best of both worlds."

I was furious and my jaw ached from all the fake smiling. This had to be the tensest dinner since President Bush threw up on the Prime Minister of Japan, and I was dying to get out of there.

We finally settled up and left the restaurant. Sliding into the driver's seat of my car, I inhaled deeply and tried to shake off the tension. I had no idea why Lee and the others were acting like junior high school kids imposing a bar to entry in the popular group.

Surviving in Mayfair wasn't going to be easy. I thought about Rachel and the girls she'd been hanging around with. If they were anything like their moms, it was best to advise her to steer clear, or at the very least, broaden her horizons.

Five

Carpool

The basketball interest meeting was about to begin. Everyone had gathered at Barnum in a large basement room that was used for afterschool programs. On the beige tiled walls were posters advertising various clubs. There were metal picnic tables and benches clustered up front. A group of kids was seated at the tables, listening to the coach's remarks. Parents stood at the rear, waiting to sign a set of participation forms.

I was standing in the doorway waiting for the coach to finish, when Lee appeared, blocking my path. "Victoria. A word please."

Her tone made me uneasy. "What's up?"

"Ah just have to tell you Rachel really hurt Lexi and Collette's feelings, running off with Katie like that. Dance with the one that brung ya, I always say."

My heart hammered in my chest. "Rachel left with Katie?" I worried they were wandering the school grounds, alone in the dark.

Lee's look was impatient, like I was slow on the uptake. "They're right over there," she said, pointing toward the front of the room.

I spotted Rachel on one of the benches, next to a girl with a thick brown ponytail, and relaxed. "Sorry, I'm not following."

"The carpool. Rachel rode here with Lexi and mah Collette.

And then she dropped them. She's sitting with Katie, and going to her house later. Collette came over and told me all about it. She was surprised and upset." Lee tilted her head and waited.

"Oh. I had no idea. I'm sorry Rachel hurt Collette's feelings." Had this woman just ambushed me about my daughter's choice of seat and decision to change cars? That was absurd.

Lee bared her teeth. "We can't have Rachel in the carpool if she acts like this. You drive her home," she said, tossing her hair and walking off.

I was stunned. Lee's reaction, the entire incident, seemed overblown and petty. Rachel was just a kid, and still learning. Wouldn't the mother of an eleven-year-old understand this? I pushed my anger to the side. I'd speak to my daughter later.

The coach was asking parents to line up and sign waivers. Rachel and her friends walked the perimeter of the room, giggling and looking down at their phones. Lee and Jess stood off to the side, laughing and chatting. Since they were the only moms I recognized, I situated myself at the end of the parent queue and tried to smile.

Seconds later my phone pinged.

"You get 5 points extra on the math test if you wear a football shirt. I'm going to Katie's house to borrow a jersey. Her mom is in the parking lot and will bring me home right after."

"OK," I responded. *Don't forget to thank Katie's mom. I met her yesterday, by the way."*

Rachel texted *"K,"* and started to walk toward the door with the ponytail girl, who was obviously Katie. They waved and I felt a momentary pang, remembering when my daughter and I talked instead of exchanging electronic messages.

When it was finally my turn, I was relieved to see that Lee and Jess had already left. After introducing myself to the coach and signing the forms, I headed out to the car and drove home.

As I was putting dinner on the table, I heard gravel crackling under the wheels of an approaching car. The kitchen door opened.

"This is it," Rachel announced, holding up a child-size version of a Giants jersey while stepping inside. "I told you we get five points for wearing this type of shirt."

"Sounds good," I said, taking a seat at the table. "Are there events for Spirit Day? Or is it just about the clothes?"

"It's really for the high school football game." She slid into a chair and grabbed her fork. "We just wear stuff that promotes spirit."

I watched as Rachel devoured her turkey burger. "Mrs. DeVry told me you rode over with Collette and Lexi, but planned to leave in a different car?" My question sounded ridiculous, overinvolved.

She looked up from her plate. "It wasn't like that. When we were driving over, Lexi and Collette told me to wear a jersey and laughed when I mentioned my softball uniform. Only losers wear baseball clothes on Spirit Day. They FaceTimed Katie, and she offered to lend me something as long as I picked it up right away. We decided I'd leave with her."

"That makes sense. Did you sit with Katie and not the others?"

"No, we were all near each other. Why are you asking so many questions?"

"Sorry." I thought back to Lee's words: 'Dance with the one that brung ya.' "Mrs. DeVry said Collette's feelings were hurt because you planned to leave with Katie."

"I told you, I only went in Katie's car to get the right shirt so I could wear the same thing as everyone else and earn points in math. Collette knew and she didn't care what car I went home in." Rachel grabbed her plate and utensils and stood up. "I don't want to talk about this anymore." She crossed the room and deposited her dishes in the sink.

After she'd gone upstairs, I sat alone, contemplating. Lee had spun things in the worst possible way. I wondered what innocent thing she'd misinterpret next.

And then there was the fact that she'd kicked Rachel out of the carpool. Dictating who was in and out was nothing less than social engineering. Lee had shaped the group, and then played me. And I was sure it wouldn't be the last time.

mmmm

It had been a long couple of days, plus roadwork on the parkway, which meant extra travel time. I was happier than ever about my no-commute Friday, and looking forward to picking Rachel up and hearing about school.

I'd parked in the rear and gone to stand in the designated waiting area in back, when I spied the fifth graders in the outdoor yard behind the building. I watched as Rachel approached a group at a picnic table and sat down with them. From afar it looked like Lexi, Collette, Katie, and a couple of others. One by one, the girls got up and walked off, leaving her alone. My heart cracked in two.

I longed to race over and comfort my child. But the school had a strict rule: Parents were not permitted on the premises until the final bell. Or were they? Lee was striding over and speaking to Rachel. I watched as my daughter squinted into the sun, nodding from time to time, and my anger rose. What was this, some kind of inquisition?

I stepped away from the other waiting parents and began to cross the small patch of grass that led from the back of the building to the play yard. Before I knew what was happening, a tall man in a blue uniform appeared and held up one hand. "Sorry, no parents." I was about to point, when I saw Lee retreating toward the rear entrance of the building. I nodded at the man and returned to the area where everyone was waiting. Rachel still hadn't moved, and remained red-faced and alone until the period ended and the class went back inside.

What exactly was going on?

Once we were in the car, I waited for her to bring it up. After watching her stare at her phone, I tried to speak calmly. "How was school, honey?"

"Fine."

When she didn't look up I pressed on: "I was early for pick-up and saw you sitting at the picnic table."

Rachel stiffened. "Uh huh. The girls were being mean. I'm going to text them later and ask what was up."

I nodded. "That's a good idea. Did someone's mom come over?"

"Collette's mother. She's always around."

During the school day?

"I didn't know that was allowed," I said, trying to sound nonchalant.

"She's got some important job at the school, so I guess she gets to come to our class when she wants to. That's what Lexi told me."

"May I ask what you guys talked about?"

"I don't know." Rachel was blushing.

"Rach?"

"Well, she wanted to know if I liked our house and going to Barnum. Stuff like that."

"Anything else?"

Rachel picked at a cuticle. Something told me Lee had crossed a line.

We were silent. Rachel seemed to be making up her mind about whether to speak. "She asked who else lived with us, and wanted to know where my dad was."

I was stunned. She'd asked at dinner but I'd failed to respond. So she'd put Rachel on the spot.

Rachel must have sensed my displeasure. "I told her I didn't want to talk about it, so she walked away."

"Good for you, honey," I said. "You don't have to discuss anything you don't want to, especially things that are personal."

▒

The subject of Rachel's father wasn't something we discussed much. As a first grader, she'd been riveted by *Miracle on 34th Street*, telling me: "That girl doesn't have a daddy." I knew she was talking about herself. Keeping it simple as experts advised, I'd said, "Your father is in California, but we're not in touch." She'd searched "The Golden State" on our desktop before insisting she had no further questions, and wouldn't discuss her dad after that.

When my daughter was turning ten, I started seeing Colin, and didn't want there to be any secrets. Where my romantic life hadn't been an issue before—I dated some but had flown mostly solo, preferring to be home with my girl—it now made sense to tell her the story of how she'd come into the world.

We were at the kitchen table having breakfast. "Honey, there's something I've been waiting to discuss." She stared down at her iPod touch. "Please look up. No videogames at the table."

Rachel barely masked her annoyance. "Yes?"

"Well . . ." I breathed in. "I wanted to talk about your father. Around the time I was finishing grad school, I wanted very much to have a child, and chose a path that wasn't the most common one. I used the services of a sperm donor."

Rachel's brow furrowed. Was she upset? Single parenting had been my choice. I could have waited to have a baby the traditional way, but I felt ready, as though I didn't need a husband or boyfriend to complete the picture, and went for it. Would a child her age understand that? Or would she be sad or angry with me?

I was sweating now, feeling like a defendant about to receive sentencing.

"Molly was born in a test tube," she said, referring to assisted reproductive technologies. I breathed in and waited. "Leo doesn't have a dad either. And Amanda told me her moms had a donor."

"Do you know who my dad was?" she wanted to know.

"The file said he was really smart and finishing graduate school, and was fairly young and healthy. His identity was kept confidential."

Rachel nodded and looked to the side, digesting. When she finally spoke, her voice was matter-of-fact. "Other kids don't have a dad." I waited for more questions, like why I hadn't gone the traditional route of marriage before kids. Instead, she told me she had to meet friends at the library.

And now, more than a year later, the worries persisted. My almost eleven-year-old had already faced many adult situations, and that made me sad. After she'd gone to bed, the floodgates opened. I'd pushed for the move, tearing her from her friends and bringing her to a small town where the girls were blowing hot and cold, and the Queen Bee clearly disliked me and was now giving us a hard time.

I did this. And I'm ill-equipped to deal with the situation. My guilt rose until I could barely breathe.

A few days later I pulled up to the house, and saw Alva on the side by the entrance to the kitchen, closing the recycling bin.

"Hi," I said. "I'm glad to catch you alone. How do you think things are going with Rachel?"

Alva shook her head. "She's been very unhappy, quiet."

"She'd been socializing at first," I said, as Alva nodded. "Has she mentioned anything?"

Alva shook again. "Not really. Maybe you can make a playdate for her? Take some kids to Friendly's?"

"Good idea. I'm going to speak to her right now." As we

walked in together through the kitchen, I spotted Rachel at the table doing homework. Alva grabbed her coat and waved goodbye, closing the door behind her.

We heard the engine first, and then the sound of steel drums fading as she drove off.

"How's school going?" I asked.

"Okay."

I took a chair next to hers. "We never got to talk about what happened after the girls left the picnic table. Did you ever text them?"

She tapped her pencil against the edge of her notebook. "It's fine."

"It doesn't seem fine." Rachel looked down. "Believe it or not, I was a teenager once. I know how hard life can be. And cell phones and social media have made things exponentially more difficult."

She softened. "What do you want me to say? It sucks, okay? Lexi and Collette and those girls are kind of mean." She wiped a tear with the back of her hand.

I put an arm around her shoulder, not knowing where to begin. "I'm sorry about the girls. If you give it time, it'll all blow over." Rachel shrugged and sat stiffly staring into her lap, as tears ran down her cheeks. My non-hovering policy went out the window. "I had the impression that Collette and Lexi were friendly to you."

She immediately shook her head. "I just told you. They're not."

Hadn't they just had playdates? The shift was as abrupt as whiplash. "It sounds horrible. Can you explain what they do that's mean?"

Rachel eyed me warily. "I don't want to talk about it. They have their group. That's it."

"I know this is upsetting," I spoke carefully. "And you prefer not to get into the details. But I'd like to help, and I don't understand. Are you're saying that the girls in your class don't have room for a new friend, like a taxi that's full?"

She rolled her eyes. "You spent like five minutes in the classroom—you don't have any idea what it's like. There's one girl, Maya. No one likes her. And there's Lexi and Collette and Katie and a few other people; they've been BFFs since pre-K. They're family friends. Their moms went to college together, Lexi told me. They do everything in a group. They all went skiing in Idaho last spring."

I pictured them, perched at the top of a mountain, wearing brightly colored puffy jackets and pants and dotting the white horizon as they descended gracefully, their daughters gliding behind in tandem.

"Try to branch out," I offered. "There must be some people who'd like to meet someone new. Not everyone can be part of the same group. Isn't there a nature club?"

Rachel was grinding her teeth.

"I could call Zoe's mom, Sam. Drive you into the city."

She stomped her foot. "Stop! No!"

Rachel's phone pinged, and she smiled at me. This kid was definitely not one to hold a grudge. "It's Zoe," she said. "She wants to FaceTime." As my daughter headed for the stairs, I thought back to the picture she'd painted: local girls and their moms skiing en masse, navigating together the world's snowiest peaks and valleys.

So that's how it was. In Mayfair, the adult's friends dictated who their children's friends would be. Well, I had a lot of catching up to do. These women had nailed down the members of the clique while their daughters were still in the womb.

Six

MIA

It had been a long day listening to patients, and I was ready to spend time with my little girl. Closing up the office for the night, I deliberated about whether to stop on the way for ingredients so we could do something fun like bake cookies, but went straight home, peeking into Rachel's bedroom only to find her MIA.

I noticed a text from Sharon as Alva was walking by with an armload of laundry: "Let's try for early next week." I sent a "Yes!" and smiley face emoji in response. A friend sounded good right about now.

Alva waited until I'd hit "send." "Rachie's in the crawlspace," she said. Before she could get the rest of her explanation out, I was halfway down the stairs.

"Honey?" There was no response.

"Not now, Mom." I heard a sniffle.

I burrowed in next to her, hoping I wouldn't meet any rodents. Something brushed against my arm and a slow prickle spread over my skin. "Can we crawl out now?" I asked. The silence was protracted. "Rach?" She was still quiet. "Let's get out please. I need to know what's up with you."

We shimmied through the opening, me feet first. Her eyes were red and swollen, her face covered with dust and tears. I felt my pulse quicken as we arranged ourselves on the den floor, eyeing one another.

Rachel finally spoke: "Collette and Lexi had a party yesterday, and they invited all the girls in our class, even Maya." She choked the rest of the sentence out. "Everyone, but me." Her voice sounded small and sad.

My stomach dropped. "Are you sure?" I asked.

"Yes, I saw it on Instachat. They all posted." She started to cry.

I spoke gently. "What do you mean, everyone? All the girls in the grade, or the ones in your class?"

"Out of the nine girls in my classroom, eight were there." Rachel choked back another sob.

People in the city had made a point of including all the girls in a class, especially when there was a small number like this. Even if the moms disliked me and their daughters had cooled on Rachel, the snub was harsh. "Maybe you were invited and it was a mistake?" I asked.

"I wasn't. It was a sports party. Katie told me in gym. Collette and Lexi's moms dropped off special Frisbee-shaped invitations at everyone's houses. They said they didn't have our address."

My pulse was beating so rapidly, it was almost like a message in Morse code. *Didn't have our address?* Lee certainly knew our house well enough to barrel in and take a personal tour. And as for finding the street number, I was pretty sure Jess had access to the school directory; in fact, I think she'd compiled it.

I breathed in to steady myself. "That's awful! It must have hurt your feelings, honey." I pulled Rachel close and she buried her face in my shoulder and sniffled.

I couldn't think straight, I was so angry. "Let's plan something fun this weekend. Maybe after your team practice we can go to a movie or do some shopping?" Rachel looked miserable, but nodded.

My fury mounted as I went downstairs to warm up dinner.

There were no dirty dishes or food remnants, and I assumed Rachel hadn't eaten. Thirty minutes later, I went back up to Rachel's room with a bowl of mac and cheese. She was in PJs, under the covers of her bed, staring at her cell.

"Rach?"

She didn't look up, but shoved the phone under the covers. "Please have a little dinner." She got out of bed and sat down at her desk to take a few bites. "Give it some time. You'll find other kids who'd love to be your friend—I'm certain of that. Good night. I love you." I kissed her on the head and extracted a promise she'd brush her teeth and head off to bed.

That night I slept fitfully, waking up on the hour until I gave up and stared at the ceiling. Certain moms were in charge, deciding what kids were in the carpools and invited to the parties. My child hadn't made the cut.

Another week passed with Rachel mostly silent and spending more and more time in her room. We were driving to school, and I'd been planning to use the ride to check in about the girls, but now had a more immediate concern: we were trapped in the carline and moving so slowly, I was afraid I'd miss the entire workday. I cursed myself for foregoing the shortcut because it was too muddy. Mayfair's lack of busing was already driving me crazy.

As the traffic inched forward around the circle, I checked out all the kids who'd gathered near the building, waiting for the doors to open. There was a group from Rachel's class, standing under the leafy umbrella of a copper beech. I spotted Lexi and Collette, who were chatting with some boys I didn't know, and watched as others moved in and out, bumping into each other and giggling, their preteen hormones on display. A girl I didn't recognize walked up and joined them. She had wavy brown hair, and looked windblown. Collette glared and turned away, and I felt uneasy just watching from afar.

A couple of minutes later, we finally pulled up to the front of the school. Rachel was still looking down at her phone.

"We're here, hon."

She raised her head slowly, and then spent a few moments, zipping her jacket and gathering her books. Several car horns later, she opened the door and gingerly lowered her legs, first left and then right, onto the curb. There was more beeping.

"It's getting late!" I said, blowing her a kiss.

Rachel made no movement toward the door handle.

"Is everything okay, honey? The girls are over there."

Rachel rearranged her backpack and slid out in slow motion, placing both palms on the car door like a perp headed for line-up. She shoved the door slowly, grudgingly.

I watched through the rearview mirror as she stepped slowly toward the fifth grade group, situating herself at its edge, and staring down at her phone, her right foot tapping.

Rachel had seemed to retreat overnight into a whisper of her former self. I didn't believe in hovering, but since her self-confidence had been plummeting, I wanted to help. And with what I'd learned about our new town, I knew that meant reaching out to some of the moms. I'd blocked off the morning for paperwork, but decided instead to head inside and mingle. My dread rose at the thought of seeing Lee.

There was congestion at the school doors. Parents on their way out and stroller gridlock as tiny siblings held on to their mothers, with one toddler stepping slowly, her lost Cheerios paving a path to the building's front door. There were latecomers too, even a UPS delivery guy.

It was silly to inch along and push my way in. So I turned

around, bumping immediately into Lee. She didn't even attempt to conceal her irritation at running into me.

I tried not to stare at her leather trousers, sky-high pumps, and cell phone case, all a matching plum color. Her sole piece of jewelry was a moonstone ring, worn on the third finger of her right hand, an enormous globe surrounded by rubies and opals. She brushed her fingertips against her hair. It had been pulled into an up-do, contoured perfectly, and secured with tiny barrettes adorned with gems identical to those on her ring. I wondered whether the hairdresser went to the DeVry home before drop-off.

There were fewer people now. As Lee stepped toward the front office and approached a pair of passing women, I hovered in the vicinity. "See you tomorrow night, ladies. Be sure to bring all your ideas for the mixer," she beamed. They nodded and waved as she faced me again, her smile tight. "Yes? I'm kind of in a rush. Jess and I are about to head into the city to do some shopping." She smirked. "I'd invite you to come along, but you probably have to work."

"I do. Work really gets in the way of my shopping."

"Funny." Lee was unsmiling. "I've got to go." She walked toward the double doors.

A line of young kids, maybe first graders, snaked by. I heard their teacher's voice: "Single file. That's right. Hands to yourself, Jason." It was only 8:40 in the morning and already she seemed ready to collapse.

I knew just how she felt. The guilt and worry about Rachel were constant, and I was feeling drained. All of our current difficulties—the strained interactions and awkwardness, Rachel's misery and growing isolation—were my fault. I'd have to keep plodding along until I figured out how to make things better for her.

I glanced around the main hallway. In my peripheral vision, I noticed a group of moms who'd gathered around a table at a sign-up of some sort. I went over and saw a handwritten sheet and a printed poster: "Colonial Fair! Call for Volunteers!"

I waited until the crowd had moved on. The woman behind the desk had a black T-shirt with the word "zen" spelled out in white letters down each arm. "What kind of help do you need?"

"Well, Lee DeVry and her cochair have already assigned most of the big jobs. But we could use people to clean up after the feast."

The Fair was scheduled for a Friday in June, yet they were looking for volunteers on October 1? Wow, Lee ran a tight ship.

"Sure." I wrote down my name and email.

"Sharon mentioned you," The zen woman began. "She and I have kids at the same preschool. I'm Anna."

"Nice to meet you."

"You're a psychologist?"

I nodded.

"So what do you think of Barnum?" she asked.

"Um, it's nice," I said. "How do you like it here?"

Anna rolled her eyes. "It's great—if you like vanilla."

I laughed as she paused to hand a pen to a woman who'd made her way over, dragging a small boy in an Elmo shirt.

"Hey, Anna." The mom with the toddler began signing her name on the volunteer list. "Did you hear they're trying to get the local police commissioner to do a talk on cyberstalking?"

"Yeah, well, we need it," Anna responded. "Some lunatic was all over a bunch of kids' social media pages, posting and chatting and viewing everyone else's posts. This was at a private school," she said.

That was alarming. "How do you know?" I asked.

"Lee told me about it at the School Board Foundation fundraiser. She's putting the whole program together, researching experts on cyberstalking, finding speakers."

Cyberstalking adolescents? Between that and the social engineering, I couldn't believe what went on these days. I waved good-bye to Anna and left.

⊞

I was gasping for air and coughing. Rachel and I were trapped in the crawlspace. Lee had blocked the latch with a two-by-four, and the opening was getting smaller and smaller, its sides closing in.

I sat up, bathed in sweat. My sheets and pillowcase were soaked. Sipping water from the bottle on my night table and breathing in to steady myself, I cursed Lee for invading our lives and my mental space.

I'd been assuming that Rachel's social problems were transient. But now I wasn't so sure.

Things were fine initially. Left to their own devices, the girls had included my daughter in playdates and carpools and interacted with her on social media.

Something else had to be going on.

I thought back to Lee, how she'd questioned Rachel on the playground, kicked her out of the carpool, and invited all the girls in the class, but her to a party. Things had gone downhill after Lee had gotten involved.

But a few isolated incidents didn't explain why Rachel was continually being left out. What was I missing?

I recalled the playdate: Collette whispering to her mother, and the two of them glancing over at me. I'd obviously offended them by telling Collette to leave the red-haired kid alone. My mind flashed back to the schoolyard: Collette and the others, walking off as Rachel tried to join them at a picnic table. Lee had already made known her dislike for me.

Putting two and two together, I began to realize that Rachel's social difficulties had everything to do with Lee's actions behind

the scenes and her palpable dislike for me. Once the PTA president lead the charge, her friends and their daughters followed suit,
making it impossible for Rachel to fit in.

My heart was hammering in my chest. If all of this was true, and
Lee had been using her influence to ensure that Rachel was shut out,
it could only mean one thing: Lee had been bullying my daughter!

I'd have to stay on top of the situation: figure out how to stop
the PTA president in her tracks, stand up to her more firmly, and
find ways to help Rachel assimilate. I buried my head in my hands
and gave into the tears that were starting to fall. I needed to fix this
before it was too late.

The phone in my city office was ringing. I spoke into the receiver,
"Dr. Bryant," I said, making my voice go up at the end.

"Victoria? It's me."

Colin. "Why are you calling? I've told you not to contact me."

"I was hoping you'd hear me out. I'd like to take you to dinner
so we can talk." I said nothing and glanced at my watch.

"Victoria, are you there?" His tone was almost a whine. "I've
been having a hard time and I want you back. I even found a
therapist."

There had to be a catch. Colin had no interest in looking
inward.

"I went twice. She told me I didn't need treatment." *That was
the Colin I knew!*

"Good for you." I said in a rah-rah voice, as though he'd scored
a goal or made a great catch.

"Yes. I'm ready for us to try again."

"Sorry you've had a hard time, but our relationship is over. You
need to move on, so please don't call me again."

We hung up. I wasn't about to waste any more energy on my ex-fiancé. Rachel needed me, and I had to save my strength.

A couple of days later, after running home from the Westchester office during a break, I came upon my daughter in her room. She was upstairs, sitting at her desk, her back to the door. "Hi, honey. How are you?"

She snapped her laptop shut as soon as she heard me. Her posture was stiff and tense.

"Rach?"

When she finally turned around, her face was streaked with tears. I froze.

"Yes?" Her tone was clipped, miserable.

"What's going on?" I asked.

"Nothing. I have to study now." She turned back around and stared into a book, and I breathed in. This wasn't over.

About a half hour later, she went to take a shower, and I headed straight for her room. The computer was right where she'd left it, but this time the cover was up, open to her Instachat feed.

Rachel knew that access to social sites was contingent upon my occasional monitoring of her accounts; it was what the authorities advised. I wasn't crazy about looking over her shoulder, but in this case, I felt I had to.

I peered at the screen. Her profile photo showed her smiling, wearing a hoodie. Her bio was the words: "Yep, still me," followed by soccer ball, microphone, and dog and cat emojis.

I scrolled down, looking at her posts. In one, she'd put up a picture of our house and written "#MovingDay." She'd posted on the day of her first soccer practice, and again a bunch of weeks ago at our house while on a playdate with Collette. There was a photo, their hands extended, nails polished in matching shades of blue. That must have been the picture Rachel had mentioned posting on their joint account.

I scrolled down to the most recent thing. Rachel had put up a photo of herself and several kids from her former school, writing "Besties and Onlies." The girls in the picture had commented, "Wish you were here," and "Miss you."

Did that mean the kids from the city were her only friends? I forced myself to read further. Lexi, Jess's daughter, had commented: "So go back!" And Katie, Audrey's kid, had echoed that sentiment: "No one wants you here."

Though Zoe and the others from the city had made nice comments, they hadn't made much of an effort to get together, even when I'd offered to drive. Zoe's parents were embroiled in a custody battle and Savannah had practices and travel games. I wasn't sure if they were really busy or if they'd moved on.

Rachel was now turning off the shower and heading down the hall. After she'd thrown on a pair of pajamas and sat down on the bed, I kissed her wet head. "Please talk to me about what's going on."

"Why? It's not like you can do anything."

"I want to know what's troubling you. As long as you talk about problems, they can be fixed. Please tell me, so we can figure this out together."

She looked up, pondering. "Well . . . ."

She teared up and described the biting comments, and her fear that other kids would join in and everyone would laugh at her.

"What should you do if anyone taunts you or makes mean comments?" I asked.

"Try to ignore it and not show they were getting to me. Just like you told me."

"Right. If they don't get a rise out of you, they'll move onto something else. I've also said that I think you should find some different people to sit with at lunch and recess."

For some reason this part of the equation was proving difficult for her to navigate. "I don't have that many choices really." She slumped forward looking weary, and showed me how to remove

the comments—just a simple right click: "One and done, Mom."
Not so fast. While the hateful words were gone, the sentiment that
she was not wanted remained and continued to burn.

I'd been on the receiving end of something similar at the
Newcomer's dinner. I'd yet to see a mom at Barnum who made
decisions for herself—with the exception of my patient Amy, and
she was ostracized. I thought again about how all moms followed
Lee, and how their thought process filtered down to the kids. It
was like a "groupthink" experiment gone awry.

Things had been easier in the city. Here in Mayfair, everyone
was similar in terms of education, profession, ethnicity, and financial position. There was only one group—you were in or out, and
the pressure to conform was extreme.

I glanced over at Rachel. "There must be other kids, Rach."

She shook her head.

"Please explain why you haven't tried to spend time with . . ." I
racked my brain, "What was her name? Maya! She's in your class,
right?"

Rachel looked at me with tearstained cheeks. "Lexi and
Collette don't like her."

I nodded.

"That's it. If they say someone isn't cool, and you hang out
with that person, then they'll think you're weird."

So Barnum was a poisoned well. If the "in" girls didn't like you
or your friends, you were tainted.

"I understand that hanging with 'the group' is important to
you. But isn't it better to look for people whose company you enjoy
than push in with kids who aren't friendly? Just find one nice person—who cares what Lexi and Collette say?"

Rachel sniffled and buried her face in her hands. "It doesn't
matter what I do or don't do. Those girls make it very hard. And
they're very popular. If they say bad things about someone, everyone believes them. And if they tell people not to hang out with

someone, everyone listens. If I hang out with Maya, all the girls will make fun of me."

So Collette and the other girls were now picking on and excluding Rachel.

Lee's enmity for me had spread like a virus, afflicting my child, and making it impossible for her to have any kind of social life in our new town.

Seven

I'll Never Do Lunch in This Town Again

The first thing I noticed was the smell: ammonia burning its way through my sinuses, searing every tissue in its path like that potent Japanese mustard I hated. How could the kids stand this place?

I had no interest in seeing Lee or any of her friends. But I wasn't letting them steal volunteering out from under me, not after finally being able to spend time at school after years of full-time work. There was no way I was canceling.

After getting a pass in the front office, I headed for the cafeteria, where the word of the day was "drab." Cinderblock walls, steel picnic tables, and hard wooden benches as far as the eye could see. Multigallon trash canisters lined the room's perimeter, their wide-open jaws awaiting the latest haul of pizza crusts and goldfish discards. The aides seemed miserable, and I couldn't blame them.

I introduced myself to the other volunteers, two moms whose daughters were in the second grade. One of them asked me if I'd heard the district had been awarded first place in the state's orchestra and strings competition. And did my child play in the band? I told her that Rachel had briefly taken a turn at the recorder, but decided to quit when several of our former neighbors called the doorman to report that a wailing sound, possibly the cries of an injured animal, was emanating from our apartment.

They laughed, and then it was time to ready the tables for the first group of kids.

Moments later, the room began to buzz with entering students. The kindergarteners walked in two-by-two, their colorful lunchboxes swaying, as they skipped to their seats. Two girls began giggling over mac and cheese and smiley-face cookies, as the boys across from them broke out into a sword game with their milk straws.

The girls clapped and slapped hands. I broke into a smile. "Miss Lucy Had A Steamboat." I hadn't heard that one in years. The girls were face-to-face, like they were the only two kids in the room, mirroring each other's delight. On the other side of the cafeteria, several boys in football jerseys who looked to be about eight, laughed and threw Cheetos at one another. The buzzer sounded and they lined up in two messy rows, snaking out of the cafeteria and up the hall.

The upper grades made their way in, and it became a war zone. I was on high alert wondering how the girls would treat Rachel. I hoped that seeing them in their element would give me some ideas about how to strategize with her, help her meet different kids.

Turning to the task at hand, I set down greasy paper plates of pizza in front of the children. Rachel sat quietly at the end of the table of girls. The others were chatting, interrupting one another and laughing.

Suddenly, Lee appeared in tennis whites, her shapely legs on display as she approached one of the tables. "Excuse me, Ma'am." An aide was running behind her, flagging her down. "You need a pass from the main office."

"You must be new," Lee snapped. Turning her back on the woman, she handed several takeout containers to Collette.

I was hoping Lee would stay across the room, but she strode over to me. "Jess said you'd be here today." She stared, waiting for a response. Before I could formulate one, a woman in a roomy college sweatshirt headed straight for us.

"Lee?" Her voice cracked. Lee smiled mouth only. "You rang?"

"We met at a rec game last spring. I'm Robin." She paused and cleared her throat. "I'm here to drop off Ally's EpiPen. Anyway, I came over to talk to you in person because I, uh, tried to text you."

Lee frowned. "What did you want to speak about?"

Robin looked over at the closest table of kids, who were busy debating whether Nicki Minaj or Cardi B was a better rapper. "Well, Ally's been asking for a playdate with Collette. I was wondering if we could get them together one day after school?"

"Let me get back to you, okay?"

Robin nodded and lowered her eyes. For a second I wondered whether she'd bow and back away. Instead she sped out and down the hallway.

Lee scrolled through her phone. "There's no way mah Collette would spend even fahve minutes with her loser daughter," she muttered, before looking up at me. "Why are you still standing there?"

I felt like making a snarky comment, telling her I'd come for the collaborative atmosphere, but the secretary cut me off. "Mrs. DeVry?" she called from the doorway.

As Lee was leaving the room, a screeching sound drew my attention back to the tables, where the red-haired girl I'd seen that first morning was digging her heels into the floor, squatting to push the bench backward and stand up. Lee's daughter, Collette, had used wooden chopsticks to push a small container of soy sauce to the edge of the table, where it tipped over onto the redhead's lap.

She managed to stand and wipe her pants, and was slowly making her way over to the trash bins. Collette and one or two others giggled, and the rest of the group ate their pizza, business as usual. I felt a catch in my throat, glad Rachel was at other end of the bench and temporarily out of danger, though I couldn't shake a feeling of despair. Kids could be so cruel. I really hoped it would get better for Rachel and the redhead.

I ignored the impulse to go over—volunteers were not allowed to interact, just hand out food—and made my way to another table, where I served a pair of twin boys in identical gold LeBron James jerseys, and then the rest of the group. On one side was a kid with a cleft chin, next to a curly haired child in a bright blue T-shirt bearing the image of a large smiling dog. "I Love Poodles," the caption read. Suddenly, one of the twins elbowed the poodle kid hard, causing him to fall off the end of the bench.

Physical danger crossed a line, and just as I was about to intercede, a tall aide pointed at the kid with the cleft chin, who appeared to be the ringleader. "You have been warned, Jake. Leave Lucas alone." Jake and several others snickered. Lucas moved to the other side of the table, focusing intently on his lunch tray.

My stomach lurched. No wonder people repressed their childhoods.

I'd made my way over to the other volunteers and was about to ask if they wanted to go out for coffee, when Sharon texted, asking me to join her for lunch. I accepted, grateful for a friend.

We met at the Organic Hub, the new health food restaurant close to the station. It was a tiny place, next to a frame store, a small wooden room with a few bistro tables, chairs, and a counter. Sharon stood up when I walked in and gave me a kiss on the cheek. "So glad we could do this," she said, pushing her dark bangs out of her eyes. "How are things going? Does Rachel like school?"

"Moving in fifth grade hasn't been easy."

Sharon nodded. "Why did you choose to do it now, as opposed to next year when they'd be in middle school?"

I wasn't sure if I should tell her about my great aunt's house. I didn't want to sound showy, and I definitely wasn't going into the scene at the altar, though I wanted to be authentic with her. I compromised, "It was a good time for us to leave the city, and the house came up."

"How long have you guys lived here?" I asked.

"Seven years. I can't believe that it's been that long. We came here for the schools when Neil was turning four. My job with the planning bureau required city residency, so I had to quit. The first few months I was isolated because the pre-K was two towns over. That was brutal. But once Neil started kindergarten, I met people."

"And you like it now? It stinks that you had to give up your career."

Sharon was about to speak when the server came over with a smoothie. "Can I get you anything?" she asked me.

I glanced at the menu. "Everybody around here seems crazy for avocado toast. What do you think? Is it as good as they say?"

Sharon laughed, "Let's do it!"

"Two orders of avocado toast," I smiled at the server. We were seated next to a window. Two women in matching black yoga pants strolled by. Didn't anyone wear street clothes anymore? They were walking in step with their identical wheat-colored dogs. I said, turning back to Sharon, "I was interested in what you were saying, about moving and having to quit work."

"I was with the real estate department. It was a lot of paper-work. And then our first year here, my husband, Michael, and I decided that it made sense for me to go back to school for graphic design."

"How has that been?"

"I like it, and I can structure my hours around the kids' sched-ules. And you?"

"Psychologist. I love my job; people are fascinating."

"Especially around here." Sharon leaned forward. "Some of the girls' moms are interesting. They can be pretty clique-y."

"I think you mean bitchy."

Sharon looked like she didn't know whether to laugh or give me a sympathetic shake of the head. "Neil had some playdates with a few of the girls in kindergarten. Some of their moms were insufferable."

I nodded. "Still are. I've been trying to steer Rachel toward some of the other girls, but she seems afraid to befriend the ones who aren't in the right crowd."

Sharon nodded. "Their grade has a bunch of snotty moms and kids. But there are some nice people, promise."

I nodded, remembering my silent vow to stand up more firmly to Lee. I still wasn't sure exactly how to do that without making things even worse for Rachel.

Sharon was speaking again. "Does Rachel play sports? She'll meet kids that way."

The food came quickly, and although it didn't rise to the level of the religious experience everyone had promised, the toast was filling. We paid the bill and promised to get together soon.

I was making my way to the car, thinking how Sharon had said that some of the girls' moms were "insufferable," when a dark SUV sped past. As I registered the vehicle's insignia, a symbol resembling a chrome peace sign, something brushed my leg. It was a third buff-colored dog, the latest iteration of the hypoallergenic mix that was favored by Mayfair's cognoscenti. No need for an identifying marker on *his* rear.

Watching the pup retreat, I slid into the front seat of my compact car thinking: In Mayfair, kids were "popular," dogs, blond, and cars, black and roomy.

mmmm

The fifth graders were gearing up for the upcoming basketball season, practicing on Saturdays. Rachel had been randomly assigned to a team with Lexi and a couple of others from class. To my relief, Collette was on a different squad. I hoped playing in the rec league would be a good experience for my daughter. Today was her first preseason scrimmage.

We were at the gym. While Rachel went onto the court, I took a seat in the bleachers, planting myself next to a tall, lithe woman in fashionably ripped jeans. I thought I recognized her from the classroom and also as the woman Lee had displayed the photo of at dinner. "Hi," I said, "I'm Victoria. I think I saw you at pick-up. Our daughters are in the same class."

She shook my hand, "Phoebe. I heard a new girl had moved in." I was about to ask who her daughter was, and if she'd played basketball before, when Lee and Jess walked into the gym with their girls.

Phoebe stood up immediately. "Excuse me," she said, stepping down a few rows until she reached the one where Lee and Jess were now seated. I watched, pressure rising, as she positioned herself next to them. I guess I didn't rate when the Star-mothers were around.

There was the same in-group/out-group nonsense I'd heard patients rant about. I felt like leaving the gym, but wanted to watch the scrimmage, and pulled out my phone, hoping my email messages would distract me.

When I wasn't dodging the PTA clique, I was trying to block out the conversation of two men who were seated down the row from me, watching the kids warm up. "That one has a good shot, though it needs work. See how she doesn't put enough movement in the wrist?" I rolled my eyes. His companion offered an opinion. "See how that one moves. Now she's a ballplayer." Rating players on athletic ability and promise, these guys sounded as though they were scouting for a professional draft.

I glanced down at my phone, noticing out of the corner of my eye, that a tall man in a knit shirt, dark jeans, and suede loafers had appeared at the top of the bleachers. Before I knew it, he was sitting down next to me. "What are you doing here, Colin?" I hissed, while scanning the room. Hopefully no one was watching.

"Rachel posted on her Instachat that preseason was starting." I made a mental note to have her block him. "I told you—"

He flashed a big smile at me and spoke a little more loudly than I would have liked. "I thought that talking in person might make a difference." A few people glanced over.

"You had no right to show up here," I whispered, noticing that Lee and Jess were now staring. "Your presence will only confuse Rachel. Please go."

"Fine." Colin stood up. "But I think you're being precipitous." I glared at his retreating back until the whistle blew.

The girls were now running up and down the court, in the action. Rachel was dribbling the ball, passing to the others. After the first quarter had gone by with her taking several tries to score, she caught a pass, set her body into position, and made a basket, scoring three points. "Go, Rachel!" I hooted and applauded, along with the coach. Rachel gave me a look, so I sealed my lips and watched the rest of the game without a peep.

Whenever Lexi, Collette, or Phoebe's kid scored, Lee and company shouted and clapped, but only for their daughters and those in the chosen group. I wondered if Rachel was aware of this. There were other parents too, but I didn't know them. A couple of women had taken seats a few rows behind the contingent, and also screamed only whenever certain kids made baskets.

A few parents were more diplomatic in their show of support, but only a handful. I decided that Jess, Audrey, and Phoebe, were like members of a college sorority, striving to fit into Lee's group, no matter what cruelty ensued. The clique was their oxygen tank.

While we were driving home, Rachel played on her cell phone. "Any nice girls on your team?" I asked.

"It's the same people from school," she said without looking up. "Can we have pizza and watch a movie in bed?"

"Sure."

It turned out to be fun; giggling at Will Ferrell's portrayal of an elf come to earth, while eating our slices. It was nice to see my daughter smiling again. But given the situation with the moms and kids, I suspected that our good cheer wouldn't last very long.

It did not. After waking up the following morning with my mind pinging like a pinball machine, from Rachel's misery to Lee and the other mothers, and back, I couldn't sit still. Getting out of the house would help.

"Come on, let's go for a run," I said, trying to rouse Rachel from her phone.

"Nice sweats, mom. Where'd you get them, the Knicks uniform archives?"

They'd looked kind of cute when I grabbed them from the sale rack. "They're yours anytime you want to borrow them," I said as Rachel slid into the back seat of the car.

I parked on a quiet street and admired the changing leaves as we headed to the track. She went around once, then played Candy Crush in the stands while I huffed and puffed my way through a few more laps. Man I hated jogging. My motto had always been, "Don't run unless someone's chasing you."

I told Rachel we could grab a frozen yogurt after doing a few errands. We quickly did the grand tour: pharmacy, dry cleaner, and shoemaker. Thirty minutes later, we were sitting at the counter of the sweet shop. "Tell me about school, honey?" I asked as she swiveled on a tall stool.

"It's fine."

"What did you do in science this week?"

"Nothing much. We did a lab on butterflies. Right now the larva is at the stage that's called a pupa." She busied herself with the cell. "Look, I made it to the ninth level."

"Bet I can beat you," I said.

"No way. You can't even get to Level 3."

I had never tried this game. "We'll see about that. Winner gets an extra scoop and sprinkles."

I managed to coax a smile, but couldn't help feeling sad. Once again Rachel had made no mention of anything social.

A few hours later, we were sitting on the sofa watching a sitcom about a family of witches and warlocks, when Rachel grinned and invited me to look at her phone. Since she rarely bestowed confidences these days, I was eager to see what she was sharing.

It was something the kids called a "Tribute," a flattering post on her Instachat feed. Rachel had written: "Happy Birthday Mom. Thank you for everything you do. Love you!" Above the words was a photo of us hiking in one of the upstate parks we'd discovered last summer.

My heart fluttered. My daughter didn't find me annoying—at least some of the time! Glancing around the old room at the faded grass cloth wallpaper, wishing real time had a pause button with which my happy moment could be preserved forever, I reached over and hugged Rachel. "This is beautiful. I love you too, sweetie. Why don't I make a special breakfast for my birthday tomorrow?"

The next morning I made the pancakes, arranging strawberries in a half-circle smile with two fat blueberries for eyes, and a glob of whipped cream at the top. Julie called, and she, Hal, and Carly sang "Happy Birthday" into the phone, while Rachel giggled.

The mood changed quickly while we were eating. Rachel showed me her phone. Katie, Audrey's kid, had posted a vomit emoji, while Lexi added a laughing face. Rachel deleted both comments.

Another day, another bully. The kids were just as bad as their moms, and it was getting to me.

A little bit later when Rachel suggested we get the first Harry Potter book and read it together, I felt a tiny surge of hope: we were a team and together we would conquer the girl problems. Then Alva came to drop Rachel off at school, and I headed for work, still feeling burdened, but making time to grab lunch at a salad bar close to the train station.

It was the type of place that had lots of sustainable products and smoothies made with kale. In the back, I saw my patient, Maureen, chatting with a woman. They were hunched together, whispering.

I'd have to be quick. Holding utensils and filling a plate with greens, chicken, and vegetables—apparently they mixed everything together at the counter—I'd passed by the drink line and ordered a tea to go. Grabbing a giant chocolate chip cookie in Saran Wrap and sticking it between my lips, I turned and promptly bumped into Maureen, who had gotten up to get a cup of coffee. We nodded and smiled. I broke into a sweat, resting my purchases on the counter, and handing the cashier my debit card.

When I was in the doorway putting on my coat, I heard the cashier ask her about the new yoga studio that was opening up in the next town, but raced out without stopping to hear the answer.

I finally made it to my office feeling like a goldfish, or maybe a canary, whatever the trapped and cornered creature was. *Let your psychology practice distract you.* It's easy, I told myself, all you have to do is focus on work.

But wait—these people were my work.

Eight
Lunch Ladies

My phone lit up with an electronic reminder: another tour of cafeteria duty. My dread rose; though I wanted to help Rachel and check in on her, handing out pizza with Lee and her acolytes was the last thing I wanted to do.

As soon as I arrived, there they were, clustering by the kitchen area, pulling on rubber gloves, and stacking cheese pies and paper plates. I hovered in the doorway, wondering if she or any of the others felt awkward, but they didn't seem at all concerned.

Jess raced across the room to kiss my cheek and pet my faux pony tote bag. "Love your purse," she purred. Why she was acting like we were pals when she'd recently left Rachel out? I felt like slapping her manicured hand away, but managed a hello before moving toward the table where the pizzas were.

It was excruciating, being trapped in a room full of PTA phonies and forcing myself to be civil. I heard a clamor as the kids began to take seats. "You get that one." Jess was pointing, directing me to work the third grade table.

Once the littler ones had left, Rachel's group marched in. I saw her sit at the end of her bench next to a brown-haired girl I didn't know. She gave me a look that said, "Keep away." After I'd served the other tables, the brown-haired girl waved me over. I stood behind her and Rachel, straining to hear because she was speaking so softly. "I was supposed to get two pieces," she said, pushing her thick brown hair away from her eyes. "Sure, Maya," I said, noticing the name on her water bottle.

As I was walking to get another slice, I noticed that the woman with the short bob, who'd wanted to volunteer that first day, was delivering her son's lunch. I tried to catch her eye and say hello, but she put the lunch down and left. Her son went back to trading Pokémon cards with his friends. I wished his mom would stop nursing a grudge.

Before I knew what was happening, Lee and I were face to face. "Well, if it isn't Victoria. What are you doing here, defending the rights of the downtrodden, ostracized, and misunderstood?"

"That's it. You let me know if you need an advocate." I nodded briefly and stepped away.

Scanning the tables, I recalled how the kids had made disturbing Instachat comments and shook my head, disgusted that this was even an issue, disheartened that volunteering had long ceased being enjoyable.

Just as the hour was ending, Sharon texted, asking me to meet her at the local teashop.

Once we were situated with our steaming drinks, she dove right in. "How's it going? Neil usually tells me nothing, but he did say that some of the others have started giving Rachel a hard time." My kid was the talk of the fifth grade? That made me cringe.

She put a hand on my arm and continued. "When I asked why, he said he didn't know. But if he mentions anything, I'll tell you." She shifted in her seat.

"My exterminator sold me a pest control package to address my vermin problem. Too bad it extended only to the actual mice."

Sharon giggled. "Oh no."

"It's worse than I thought, the way these women act. Sometimes I'm afraid Rachel will be scarred from all the exclusion and nastiness."

"You're referring to the girls' moms? Lee and Jess, and the rest of them?"

I nodded as Sharon sipped from her steaming cup. "They're the worst. They don't do much except work out and stop on the way home to pick up a rotisserie chicken for dinner."

The image was so specific it made me laugh. I almost choked on my tea.

"Rachel will be okay. After this year, they'll mix up the classes. She'll meet some different kids, even though we're stuck with the same people through the end of twelfth grade." Sharon shifted in her chair. "Any time you want to talk, I'm available," she added, gathering her purse and jacket. "Sorry, but I have to go home to take a call, a new client. But, I did want to mention, there's a school benefit coming up right after the break. It's a karaoke night; we should go."

"Sure," I said. "Maybe you can introduce me to some of your friends who aren't in the bitchy clique?"

"Of course," Sharon laughed.

A week later I was in the Westchester office when Amy buzzed in and sat down. Pulling her wavy black hair into a loose bun, she described how a group of PTA moms repeatedly ignored her, while their girls told Lucy there was no room in the afterschool class. "How can that be possible? Everyone else who signed up got in! Then the girls laughed when she showed up at the meeting and tried to join. I heard about it after work."

She balled her fists. "I hate them—especially the mothers. They're like a bunch of junior high school girls, planning parties while someone who isn't invited listens in. They're just so small-minded. I went online last night and checked all of their social media accounts: Facebook, Instachat, Twitter, every last one. And

I looked at the kids' accounts too, the open ones. I didn't post, just figured out who the key players were, parents and kids. Information is power, you know."

I felt the hair on my arms rise. Reading a bunch of preteens' social media posts, trawling the internet, and checking up on people? That was creepy. I couldn't see myself doing that. But I understood her frustration.

The next morning after the last bell had rung and all the stragglers were racing past, we were parked in front of the school. Rachel was refusing to get out of the car.

"I can't go today. Can I go back to bed?"

I turned off the ignition and got out to join her in the back seat. "What's wrong, honey?"

"My stomach hurts." She was crying now. "All the girls are going to be emojis together. Even Maya—who they say they don't like. They got costumes online, and the DeVrys are making a big haunted house in their yard for Halloween in a couple of weeks. They were talking about it at lunch yesterday."

Rachel turned to face me and took a deep breath. "Mom, I don't know if I have any friends." She buried her head in my shoulder and sobbed. The sadness filled my chest.

"Sweetheart," I stroked her head. "Everybody feels like that sometimes."

"Can I stay home alone?" she asked.

"I guess you can today, but you'll have to go back tomorrow."

"I'll just go in," Rachel's tone was glum.

"We'll try to figure this out when I get home from work, okay?" I was kicking myself again for moving to Mayfair. We were stuck—you didn't just give up a mortgage-free house in a top school district—but since the same kids would be together in middle school and beyond, something had to be done.

Watching Rachel enter the building, head down, I no longer

cared about rules concerning parents in the classroom and PTA hierarchies. I needed to act, but instead headed to work, where I spent the rest of the day making inroads on everyone's problems, but my own.

Hours later, I'd just locked the door to my office when it hit me: Why not look at Guardian, an independent school with small classes? Perhaps sending Rachel there would solve our problems.

Guardian was the only private school in the area that offered a number of scholarships. And it was convenient, halfway between the city and our house. The website said the application deadline had passed a couple of days earlier, but I had an idea.

After composing an email to the headmaster, introducing myself and referencing a mutual friend, I asked if he could see me on an admissions matter, and hit "send." When he replied, saying I was free to stop by, I headed out the door and into the car. The school was just south of Mayfair on the highway, a complex of stone and more modern buildings surrounded by meticulously maintained sports fields.

The office was in an old Tudor house close to the entrance of the campus. After passing through a huge wooden door, I found myself in the tasteful beige admissions office, standing next to a black rocker with the word "Veritas" on it.

"Hello," I said to the receptionist, smiling to mask my anxiety. "Victoria Bryant. The headmaster is expecting me." She spoke quietly into the phone, and before long, a lanky man in a tweed vest was striding across the carpet.

"Dr. Robert Lacanne. What can I do for you?"

Lacanne hadn't even crossed the room, and he was already finished with the introductions. My best hope was to turn on the charisma. I stepped forward to shake, but tripped on a bump in the thick carpet. As the headmaster moved to steady me, I pumped inadvertently, shaking both hands at once, managing to turn a routine introduction into a full upper-body activity. There was only one thing for me to do: get a rocker that said "Klutz."

When I regained my composure, I said, "Hi. My name is Dr. Victoria Bryant."

He nodded. "You asked to see me?"

Ugh, this wasn't going to be easy. "Thank you for meeting with me on such short notice.

The headmaster just nodded. A Jehovah's Witness would get a warmer welcome, but I barreled on.

"I'd like to discuss my daughter, Rachel Bryant. She's a fifth grader at Barnum Elementary."

"What did you want to discuss?" He glanced at his watch.

"Uh, well, I'm considering enrolling her, and I came to pick up an application."

"Our deadline was October 14th. At this point, there's nothing I can do. Thank you for your interest." He stepped towards the receptionist's desk.

I kept talking to overcome my growing desperation. "She's so excited about studying here. So is there any way you can give me an application?"

The Headmaster glowered. As my panic rose, another man came out of the back of the office. He was tall and athletic with a masculine jaw and strong forearms, and something about him was familiar. Now the new man was also staring at me; I was starting to feel like a zoo animal.

"We make clear on our website that deadlines are final. No exceptions." The Headmaster looked at his watch again. "Our meeting is concluded," he said motioning toward the door.

My anxiety level surged. This was not only just plan B, but also C, D, and E.

"Wait. Please." My voice sounded high-pitched.

He turned to stare. "Sir, I'm a practicing psychologist with over fifteen years experience, and my credentials are impeccable. I could help out, provide services . . . ."

A nerve pulsed in his cheek. "We have several clinicians on staff, Yale-trained."

I'd googled, and was well aware of the staff's pedigree. "Is there anything I can do to help my daughter's chances?"

"Miss Bryant . . . ."

Had he intentionally demoted me?

"Guardian does not tolerate requests of this sort, which raise the specter of favoritism and sully the admissions process." He walked toward me and took my arm. "And now I must advise you again that our meeting is concluded. Good Day," he propelled me toward the door and disappeared into a back room.

I checked out my reflection in the glass door. Who was that red-faced and exhausted-looking woman in a pencil skirt and heels? My long brown hair was disheveled, and I had a run in my pantyhose. I was battle scarred and humiliated—and it was a new low.

I bolted to the exit and sat down on a bench close to the front of the property. In our town and at Rachel's school, the playing field was not level at all. How was I going to protect my child? Tears began to pool in the corners of my eyes.

"Are you okay?" Someone was speaking to me. It was the guy with the forearms—and though crying had made my vision blurry, I could tell his shoulders and pecs weren't bad either.

I sniffled. "I'm leaving. You don't have to call security."

He smiled. "No, it's fine. This is nothing we haven't seen before. It's been a parade of anxious parents around here lately," he said, rerolling his sleeves. I wiped my eyes and quietly checked him out: pressed pants, blue button-down shirt, and plain loafers—solid and understated.

My new acquaintance continued with his story. "Yesterday a

woman showed up with a $30,000 tote from Paris. She made a show of putting the big orange box on Lacanne's desk and telling him how much his wife would adore owning the 'it bag.'"

"Seriously?" I asked with a small smile. He was kind, but I still wanted to run home and hide. "Well, thank you. I guess I should be going now," I said, standing up.

"You might try Lakeshore Academy. They're still taking applications, I hear."

"Unfortunately, I don't have an extra forty grand lying around and it's too far from our house. That's why I was so excited about Guardian. This location and scholarship program are ideal."

The man extended his hand. "Jim Reilly. I'm Head of the Lower School." We shook briefly. His palm felt nice on mine.

"Victoria Bryant."

Jim looked at me and smiled, his eyes crinkling up at the sides. He seemed compassionate and was very handsome, although he was taller than the guys I usually liked. "Didn't we run into each other at Starbucks?"

Of course! This was the guy I'd bumped into when I was rushing to work.

"Yes. Sorry again about your coffee." He held my gaze as a warm blush deepened across my cheeks. Handsome as he was, I wasn't sure what else to say and stood up to gather my things. "It was nice to meet you, Jim."

"Victoria, wait." My pulse picked up.

"You look like you've had a long day. Would you like to get a beer with me?"

I tilted my head. "Do you have drinks with everyone who tries to elbow their way into your school?"

"Only the unsuccessful ones. I can't go out boozing with the mothers of my students. That would be inappropriate."

I laughed. Five o'clock might be a little too early for beer, but a cup of coffee would be okay. There was still time before Alva had to leave.

Had he just asked me out? Was this a date? I felt a pounding in my chest, but quickly pivoted. Given the fact that nothing had ever stuck, Colin was my first and only long-term relationship, dating seemed ill advised.

"I—"

"It's only a beer." Jim's tone was playful, sparking tiny waves of excitement from within the dark recesses of my chest. As he stood there, smiling down at me, I felt my resolve beginning to waver.

"Sure," I said. "Why not?"

Nine

Mayfair Memes 2

I texted Rachel that I'd be home in a couple of hours, then forced myself to shove the Lee and school situations to the side, at least temporarily. Jim drove us to his favorite sports bar. It was one town over in a quaint village with a stone church and tiny main street. We waited to be seated, watching out the front window as stressed out looking commuters hurried past us, away from the train station toward their parked cars.

A man peeked out from the kitchen and told us to take any table we wanted.

Jim chose a booth near one of the giant flat screens, motioning for me to switch sides with him. "I'd rather talk to you than watch the game," he smiled. "Do you like baseball? My dad used to take me to Yankee Stadium. We even went to Florida for spring training one year."

A quick glance at the screen told me which team was playing. "I do. Sammy Sosa just made a diving catch. The crowd is going nuts."

"How do you know so much about the Cubs?" he asked, his eyes expressing curiosity.

"My Dad had season tickets years ago when we lived in Chicago. He was a huge fan."

"Tell him I forgive him." Jim's smile was teasing. He held up two fingers. The bartender brought over some water and two glasses of whatever was on tap. We sipped and smiled, feeling at ease.

I liked that Jim was confident and playful, and decided not to disclose the fact that Mom and Dad were no longer around. I might not be a rock star at dating, but even I knew that my depressing early history was a bit much for the small-talk phase.

"You're kind of quiet," he observed.

His interest was flattering. "Just used to being the listener, I guess." I couldn't stop staring at his deep blue eyes and the perfect curve of his jaw.

I recalled the saying that dating was like riding a bike; I was never much good at that either. "So tell me about yourself," I smiled.

"Not much to say, really. I'll give you the Cliffs Notes version."

As we talked, I glanced at his physique. His shoulders were muscular, fanning out in the shape of a V. I traced a path with my eyes down to his waist.

Jim spoke about his grandparents, how they'd owned a series of canine retrievers with names like Chauncey and Winston. I imagined what his skin would taste like and how his lips would feel, and lost myself in his eyes and the rich, masculine timbre of his deep voice.

Then he began describing his parents: "My mom and aunt were with me during the week because my parents divorced when I was six, and my dad, who was a lawyer, worked all the time. I spent most weekends with him and tagged along on a couple of business trips when I got a little older. Those were fun."

He shrugged in a self-effacing way that was adorable, and I decided then and there that I'd faint if he waited much longer to kiss me. He was absolutely dreamy. I smiled and nodded as he spoke, encouraging him to go on.

"I played a lot of sports growing up. Like every kid in America, I wanted to be a professional baseball player. Played Division 1 until I tore my meniscus and ACL sliding into third. And that was that. I went into teaching, then administration. And you know the rest."

Hardly, but this was an interesting start. I was glad he'd shared his story. "Wow! You played at that level?" Jim reddened "I guess we can add modesty to your virtues," I added.

"And voraciously hungry." He'd changed the subject, but I could tell he was pleased by the way he sat a little taller. His humility was endearing.

Jim was now smiling at me. "Why don't we have dinner?"

Even I knew that the suggestion of a meal meant things were going well. The little waves of excitement I'd been feeling returned. I breathed in and sat on my hands, being sure to offer a composed response: "That sounds great."

"Is red okay?" he asked, opening the wine list. I was back to looking at his mouth. It was smooth and soft.

"You choose," I said, feeling like a damsel batting her eyelashes. "But I can only have a little. I'm driving." Jim got the waiter's attention and asked for two glasses of Chianti. Then we ordered our entrées. I was glad not to have to be in charge for a change, and relaxed into the banquette with a big smile.

"You're in a good mood," he commented as the waiter arrived with the wine.

"Well, you're more fun than my regular end-of-the-day appointment, a divorcing couple who are at each other's throats."

"So I am more fun than two people who hate each other's guts? That's high praise."

I laughed. "By the way, I was interested in what you were saying. Where'd you play baseball?"

"Boston College."

I'd heard how selective that school was. Everyone who studied there had to maintain a high GPA.

He must have read my thoughts because he said, "Lucky for me, we were expected to keep our grades up; no free rides for athletes. I had to study, which meant I could finish my degree and get a master's."

"I figured you were a good student."

"I ambled along, Ms. PhD. Where'd you go to college?"

"University of Illinois, which was great because grad school was so expensive."

Jim was easy to talk to, and his responses were kind. "I'm sure, but obviously worth it," he said. "Which grad school?"

"Columbia."

"You have an Ivy League degree? Impressive."

My cheeks felt hot. "I should warn you. I can't take a compliment," I said.

"It's cute." He shifted in his seat. Was I imagining it or had he moved closer? "How'd you do it, going to school, working, and having a daughter all at the same time?"

It was really hard. "It wasn't that bad. I had Rachel when I was finishing up the licensing requirements, working at one of the big hospitals. I've always had a great sitter."

"Were your parents psychologists?" he asked.

"No, they had a bookstore just outside the Chicago city limits, not too far from our house. They worked long hours and fell into bed."

He leaned in. "So it was just you, then? No brothers or sisters?"

"I was an only child. I spent a lot of time playing by myself. And I was always close with my great aunt. She was a book editor."

"All the reading and studying is genetic, I guess."

I smiled. "And your family?" I asked.

"I'm an only child too. My mom's in Florida now; she plays mahjong and canasta. And my Dad's out west with his second wife. They're on the bridge circuit, and she's into quilting."

That sounded deadly. I nodded as Jim spoke with a shrug. "Not my speed, but it seems to work for them."

We were definitely on the same wavelength about cards and quilting. He touched my hand as the waiter arrived with our plates. "Since the regular season is over and you like baseball so much, why don't I try to get seats to a playoff game?"

"That would be great," I said, feeling another tingle of excitement.

Jim bit into his steak. I was so excited I could barely eat mine.

"A story for another time, but my ex hated everything about sports."

So Jim had an ex? That was interesting.

He didn't seem to notice my mind had started calculating. "My friend Jack has tickets he doesn't always use. I'll look into the game." He smiled, and my stomach flipped so fast and hard, I had to avert my eyes.

After dinner, Jim drove me to my car, which was back at the school, and we chatted about the chillier temperatures and falling leaves. I was having trouble concentrating because all I could think of was whether he would kiss me. I kept remembering his lips and how he'd leaned toward me at dinner. By the time we made it to back to the lot, I felt like I was about to explode.

"This was fun," he said, drawing me close as I stood on tiptoe until our chests were touching. I took it all in: the feel of his cheek, his citrusy smell. And then I forgot where I was, as his eyes closed and lips moved slowly over my mouth, making my whole body come alive.

After a minute, I forced myself to pull away. "I'm sorry, but I really have to go. It's getting late, and my daughter is waiting for me. I had a really nice time."

We kissed once more before I got in and drove off, waving through the window.   Driving home, I couldn't stop grinning.

Even my time with Colin wasn't like this. It had been years since I'd had this much fun.

The following evening Rachel and I were at the kitchen table eating fish tacos. Though she hadn't reported any new slights, her recent fears about having no friends had stuck with me. "So, how's it going?"

She shrugged. "Same."

"I know it's been rough with some of the kids, but why not ignore people like Lexi and Collette? Maybe ask some other kids in your class to come over for a movie night?

"Stop! I already told you. No! That's not how it works."

What had happened to make my child become so cynical? "Okay. Then please tell me how it does work."

She shot me a "you're so stupid" look. "They're all a big group. You don't just ask Lexi and Collette's friends to get together! Those girls have to ask you." I'd suppressed the rules governing middle school cliques, but our conversation brought it all back.

Since private school wasn't an option, we'd have to make things work in town. I'd encourage Rachel to branch out while I figured out how to be strong and stand up to Lee.

I gritted my teeth and tried again. "We'd talked about your trying a new activity. Has basketball made things any better with the girls?"

Rachel shook her head.

"What about signing up for something else? Chess?"

"I'll think about it." We'd finished eating and carried our plates to the dishwasher. After Rachel went upstairs to do homework, my phone buzzed with two texts from Jim.

"You know what I'm thinking of? . . . Derek Jeter."

I was figuring out what to write back when Jim buzzed again: *"Where do you stand on PDA's?"*

I felt my heart pounding. Someone that smart and cute was

actually flirting with me! I really liked his sense of humor. *"Would the PDA be with me or Derek?"*

"I think you know the answer to that," he wrote.

I was wondering if I should write back when another text came in: *"Storming any schools tomorrow?"*

"I've retired from that life." He LOL'd and signed off, reiterating his promise to see about tickets.

The following morning, Rachel and I took the shortcut, parking behind the school. I watched her walk through the doors and hoped she wouldn't get any more stomachaches.

Jim texted as I was driving to the station. *Try not to spill anyone's coffee.*

The train was crowded, but I managed to find a seat. *Not making any promises I can't keep,* I wrote back as we pulled out.

An hour later, I was in my Manhattan office sitting face-to-face with a young urban couple that was struggling with infertility. In a cart-before-the-horse moment, I recalled that Jim had said he'd just turned forty. I wondered whether he wanted kids. Even though I was open to the possibility of giving Rachel a sibling, I was thirty-nine and had no idea about my fertility—that could be a deal breaker if Jim did want kids.

I reminded myself to slow down. Despite all the texts and calls, I'd been on exactly one date with the guy.

When I got home, Rachel told me that Collette and the others had continued to give her the cold shoulder. But it was fine, because she'd eaten lunch with Maya and Sharon's son, Neil, and they'd asked her to work on a group project. Since Rachel was feeling happier, I thought I'd earned another night out with Jim.

On the evening of the game, he picked me up at the office and we headed to the Bronx. Our seats were right on the third base line. Jeter had recently announced his intention to retire at the end of the season, and we immediately fell into discussing his illustrious career (.310 batting average! 260 home runs! Lifetime RBIs: 1311!), as we watched the Yankees pummel the Orioles 8-2.

Jim pulled me close and kissed me straight on, right there in the stands, in front of a whole bunch of strangers. My heart was pounding so hard, I was sure the beer-swilling guys to my left could hear. I glanced around. What if we were on the JumboTron and my clients saw me on TV kissing a strange man? And what would Rachel think?

"Let's get out of here," he said, pulling me toward the exit as the final out, a foul ball, cracked off the bat and popped into the catcher's waiting mitt.

He held my hand on the drive home, and told me about his ex, who thought it was funny to hide his keys just as it was time to leave for the opening pitch. I was dying to hear more, but bit my tongue. It was too soon to tell him my sad backstory. I listened and joked. When we paused at a stop sign and he suggested a nightcap, I was tempted, but what I said was, "I would love to, but I have to get home to Rachel. He nodded and seemed to get it.

Our conversation turned to books, and Jim told me his favorites were *Vanity Fair* and *Middlemarch*. My pulse sped up; I loved the classics. I remembered a story one of my friends had told me: When she and her boyfriend had first met, he'd fed her a bunch of white lies, telling her he loved rom-coms and organic restaurants. As soon as they were an item, he said no to any movies that didn't involve a car chase or explosion, and refused to set foot in a health food place. I suppressed a laugh. For all I knew, Jim read only comic books. I liked him so much I wouldn't care.

"I haven't met too many people who like nineteenth-century satire. Besides me, I mean," I said.

"I'm a sucker for biting social commentary, I guess. It reminds me of the families I see at school. I'm also perfectly happy reading the *Post*. And I've been through all of the Harry Potter and vampire books, whatever our students are into."

Score one for Jim.

We were now in my driveway. He turned the ignition off and pulled me close. My pulse quickened as the windows disappeared under a cloud of steam. "Guess it's good night," I said burying my face in his shoulder, "but I don't want it to be." Jim hugged me and promised to call later that evening. I watched him drive off with a tug in my chest.

As I was hanging up my coat, Rachel called to me. She was upstairs getting ready for bed. "Can you be the class parent on the trip to the American Museum of Natural History? All you have to do is email the teacher, and she'll put you on the list."

Based on what I'd heard, the PTA president decided. I had a greater chance of starring on Broadway than being chosen to chaperone Rachel's class trip, but maybe meeting Jim signaled that our luck was about to change. I'd think positive. Perhaps I'd get the go-ahead for the outing and the girls would ease up on my daughter.

Later after dinner, I went upstairs and found her snuggled in bed with a book. "How 'bout I read to you tonight?"

"No thanks. It's faster when I read to myself. I want to know what happens." I kissed her on the head, pleased at the lightening speed at which she was developing, but sad that as my daughter was becoming independent, our time together was slipping through my fingers.

"Time to turn out the lights now." I went down the hall, changed into a nightshirt and got into bed. Consumed with racy thoughts of Jim, I fell asleep, smiling and hugging my pillow.

Ten

Benched

It was Saturday, and Rachel had a game in the school gym. I didn't feel like mingling. So while she warmed up on the court, I plopped down in a corner at the top of the bleachers and pulled out a book.

Rachel's team won the tip-off. As usual Lee and her pals cheered for their kids, while the rest of us tried to make up the difference.

My daughter had been sitting on the bench for the first two quarters. I glanced at my watch. Would they put her in? Jess's husband was the coach, and I was starting to wonder whether the dads were as bad as their wives, when Rachel was rotated in.

Our team was up by six. Rachel was dribbling, trying to get close enough to the basket to take a shot. I clapped and cheered, watching her move down the court. Suddenly she pitched face-first onto the floor. My heart stopped, but I made my way down the bleachers, passing Lee and her crew along the way.

"She's clumsy, that one," Lee tittered as Rachel stood up and rubbed her head.

My fury rose as I made my way down. Hopefully Rachel wasn't badly hurt.

"No parents, Ma'am." The ref was coming toward me, motioning for me to sit down. I planted myself in the front row to monitor the situation. Lee raced over with an ice pack—being PTA president obviously guaranteed a blanket security clearance—and then Dr. Audrey swooped in. To my relief, she made a thumbs-up gesture.

Rachel was now speaking to the ref. "I don't know. I just tripped."

I spent the rest of the game employing mental gymnastics, desperate to manage my racing thoughts. It was important for kids to learn to solve their own problems; they needed room to fail—unless, as in this case, the playing field was stacked.

After the game, I raced down to the court, and while motioning for Rachel to come over so we could leave, nearly bumped into Lee, who was laughing with Jess and her husband. Lee and I locked eyes as he stepped back with a look that screamed no female drama.

Rachel had come over and was standing next to me. "Let's go," I said, steering her past Lee.

"Cat got your tongue?" She called after us.

"Not at all. But I *am* wondering, don't you have anything better to do than laugh at a ten-year-old who's tripped and fallen on the court?" I guided Rachel toward the door without waiting for a response, noticing out of the corner of my eye that Lee and Jess were beginning to whisper.

Once we were in the car, Rachel ignored my questions about her head and refused eye contact or conversation. "Why would you say that to Mrs. DeVry in front of the whole team, and the moms and dads? Now everyone will be even meaner than they are now." She was screaming by the time we pulled into the driveway. "I hate it here. And I hate you." I was about to apologize, but she'd gotten out of the car and slammed the door.

I watched her let herself in through the kitchen, worrying that I'd finally done my best to stand up to Lee, but had only made things worse.

My fears were borne out a few days later. Rachel told me she'd gotten ten points off on an in-class math exercise because she hadn't been able to measure the base of an isosceles triangle. Some kids—she assumed Collette and Lexi because they'd been whispering and laughing—had taken her pencil case and ruler. She told me when I got home from work.

It was typical fifth grade hazing, but I was concerned. Rachel obviously wasn't fighting back. That evening I joined her at the kitchen table where she'd been doing her homework. "Maybe you could sit with other people and avoid those two?" I suggested.

Rachel's eye roll told me everything I needed to know. "That's impossible. We're all in the same class," she curled her lip in a show of preteen contempt.

"You can push back a little."

She looked skeptical. "I guess."

I moved on. "I found this," I announced, stepping toward the sink and pulling one of Rachel's long-sleeved T-shirts from the cabinet underneath where I'd stashed it.

The garment had been shoved at the bottom of the kitchen garbage that morning and was definitely worse for wear with macaroni noodles pasted to the front, and carrot peels dangling off one of the sleeves.

Rachel said nothing.

"Did you throw it away?"

She gave me a pleading look. "Collette said that she's the only one that can wear shirts with French sayings on them."

My anger rose, and I wanted to tell Rachel that she shouldn't let another kid dictate her wardrobe, but bit my tongue, knowing how intimidating Collette could be. "Okay. No more French sayings. But let's donate this so some other girl can use it." I added the shirt to a pile of dish towels I was about to wash. Rachel nodded and picked up the book she'd been reading about Pocahontas.

The ruler and T-shirt incidents told me that certain girls had turned out to be exactly like their moms. Their clique-y behaviors and the group's sheer numbers, all went against Rachel's ability to stand her ground.

I had a lot on my mind, like the call I'd gotten several hours earlier from the school nurse, the second one that week.

"Anything you want to tell me?" I asked, as she climbed into bed.

"No." She twirled her hair and looked off to the side.

"What's wrong, honey?"

She was quiet, and my anxiety rose. "Did something happen at school today?"

"This girl Francesca, the one with the red hair, was crying at recess. Some of the kids took her phone and sent texts from it to a boy, pretending to be her, writing stuff like, 'Will you go out with me? I like you.' It was really mean."

My body tensed. The stolen cell phone story was cruel and made me realize that aside from a few early warnings about texting with strangers and making friends online, I hadn't had the full "internet safety" talk with Rachel. Now was as good a time as any. "What they did to Francesca sounds awful. Did it upset you?"

"I guess."

I saw my chance. "I've been meaning to go over something. If someone you don't know texts or contacts you on social media, what would you do?"

"How would a stranger get my number?"

I sighed. "Say he or she somehow gets your number and starts bothering you. Or posts on social media. Then what?"

"I'd tell you." Rachel shrugged.

I gave her a thumbs-up. "You have Facebook and Instachat. Anything else?" She shook her head.

"Just an FYI," I said, "First thing this weekend I want to go through all of your social media accounts."

Rachel stiffened. "I showed you when I made them."

"And I told you that I'd be checking periodically." I didn't have the energy to look at her phone right now, especially since we hadn't gotten to the nurse issue. "I'm glad you told me about Francesca. I think it's terrible that she's being picked on." Rachel nodded. She shrugged, and I took a deep breath. "Which brings me to my next question. Was there something else that happened today?"

I waited as Rachel shifted uncomfortably. "I went to the nurse's office."

I was about to hug her, but stopped short. It was better to let her speak. "Why? What were you doing there?"

"There was too much drama in the cafeteria, and I had a stomachache. The nurse let me lie down on her cot."

If Rachel had gone to the nurse's office during lunch, things were getting even worse. "How many times have you gone there?" I ignored the flutter in my chest and forced myself to sound calm, as though I was asking whether she'd remembered to put her homework in her backpack.

"Uh . . . I ate there today, and yesterday. And a few times last week I went to the library."

"I thought you were eating with Maya."

"Sometimes."

"Why didn't you tell me about the lunchroom, sweetie?"

Rachel looked down at her hands, and my butterflies turned to anger. The nurse's messages indicated that there was no fever, and said that she'd been sent back to class. But even if there was nothing physically wrong, my child clearly needed help.

I'd given Rachel time to transition, and had been unsure if I should contact her teacher. But the time had come.

After kissing Rachel good night, I fired off an email:

"Hi, Ms. Franklin,
This is Victoria Bryant, Rachel's mom. I'm writing today because I am concerned about something and would like to speak tomorrow. I will be at work, but if you let me know what times are convenient, I'll call you when you are free. Otherwise, you can reach me on my cell.
Thank you.
Victoria

The voice on the answering machine was reassuring. It was Ms. Franklin, Rachel's teacher. "I'd be happy to speak during my lunch hour if that time is convenient for you," she said.

I called at the agreed-upon hour. She was soft-spoken and sounded kind. "You said you're concerned about Rachel? Tell me what's going on."

Shouldn't she know? I pushed my annoyance to the side, and focused instead on the fact that she'd made herself available so quickly. "She's been quiet and anxious lately, keeping to herself socially, and going to the nurse's office at lunch."

"I wasn't aware of that. By the way, Rachel is a lovely girl. She works hard, and is very bright. And from what I've seen in the classroom, she's doing well. As far as socially, Rachel often sits with another girl during small group time. Do you know Maya? And she's gone over math problems with Neil. So I haven't seen any major red flags. As teachers, we don't usually witness what's going on in the lunchroom or on the playground, but I will discuss it with the aides. I agree, Rachel shouldn't spend her lunch period in the nurse's office."

She started to say goodbye, but I pressed on. "Thank you for looking into this and for speaking with the aides. May I check back with you about this?"

"Of course. Anytime." We hung up.

Ms. Franklin sounded like she cared about the students, but my doubts still nagged. It seemed odd that Rachel's teacher wouldn't have picked up on anything. She had to be missing something. Two knots pooled in my shoulders. It would probably be up to me alone to deal with my child's problems.

As soon as I'd placed the receiver in its cradle, the phone rang again.

"Hey," Jim said as I picked up. I loved how deep his voice was. "How 'bout dinner Friday night? Someplace quiet, so we can talk."

"Sure. That sounds great." A third date!

"I'm glad you're free."

After we hung up, I left word for Alva, asking her to please stay late on Friday. Then with Rachel's troubles continuing to weigh on me, I counted the hours until my date with Jim.

Eleven

Hooky

Barnum's number was displayed on my caller ID. I immediately broke my no incoming calls rule. "Please excuse me. It's an emergency," I told the couple I was seeing.

Stepping into the office's tiny kitchen area, I closed the door and answered the call. "Dr. Bryant. I'm calling about Rachel's absence. When she's out sick, we ask you to call first thing in the morning."

"Absence—are you sure?" Panic gripped my chest. I'd dropped my daughter off and watched her walk toward the building.

"I'm certain."

My hands shook as I promised to ring her back and dialed Rachel's cell. It was a relief when she answered on the first ring.

"Are you okay? Where are you?"

"Home."

I waited. "I had another stomachache. So I went to the parking lot. Some mom offered to give me a ride home."

My head was spinning. Who takes a ten-year-old off school grounds without checking? "What mom?"

"She said her name was Leslie. I didn't know her."

"This is serious, Rachel. You played hooky and got in the car with a stranger. I know you've been getting stomachaches, but leaving without checking in is not okay. DO YOU HEAR ME?"

Her voice was quiet. "I won't do that again."

I told her we'd talk later and warned her that I'd be taking her phone for the next week, and would increase the punishment, if she ever pulled a stunt like that again.

I went back into the session and apologized to my patients. When I got home that night, I went straight upstairs to her room. "Let's go back to this morning, Rachel," I said, sitting down on her bed.

"I know it was wrong. Don't you ever just need a break?"

I crossed my arms and waited. "Okay. I know I'm punished," she said, handing me the phone.

A knot of anger pooled in my chest. "It's not about the punishment. What made you leave school?"

"I just saw them all standing and whispering, and it really did make my stomach hurt. I wanted a day off. I'll go back tomorrow and hang out with Maya and Neil. I'm just sick of those girls."

"Try not to let them get to you. Life isn't static, and things won't always be this way."

Rachel was twisting a strand of hair around her pointer finger, her forehead one big crease. Watching her puzzle over the school situation reminded me of another serious talk we'd had years ago. She'd furrowed her forehead and twirled her hair then too, asking why people would want to hurt dolphins.

And now Rachel's mannerisms told me she was thinking long and hard about what had happened that morning outside of school. When she finally nodded and said "Cutting school was stupid. I'm sorry," I knew she understood the gravity of the situation. We could move on.

I leaned in to hug her. "Love you. Good night."

"Do I get my phone back now?"

"Not a chance." I turned the lights out and closed her door behind me.

The next morning Maureen buzzed into the Mayfair office. I knew what was coming.

She sat down in the patient's chair. "So, you have a fifth grader at Barnum?" she asked. "How come you didn't just say that when I asked that other time?"

I did my best to remember the response I'd prepared, one that acknowledged reality, but left room for my patient to react. "I'd be glad to answer. I'm just wondering if you'd be comfortable telling me why you're bringing this up right now."

"I heard a while ago that you moved across town and had a girl the same age as my daughter, Hannah. I meant to bring it up but forgot."

She had me. The best way to handle it was to reaffirm her perception of the truth and then ask her to explore what she imagined.

I nodded in response to her question and tried to dampen down my feelings of annoyance. Maureen was the last person I felt like discussing my child with. She certainly had it easy, being best friends with Lee, and her Hannah not having to endure any of the loneliness and exclusion my daughter had faced. I had the urge to tell her that so far I really wasn't impressed with her clique-y friends and their daughters, but kept it professional, allowing her to react. I said, "That's true. I do live in Mayfair and have a fifth grader. Any feelings about that?"

"I don't know. It's weird to think of running into you at meetings and open houses. Your daughter is in Collette's class. That's what I heard. We won't see each other on parent/teacher night."

Maureen was picking at a cuticle. "You've been helpful, and coming here has made things better. So . . . I want to tell you something. It has to do with Lee." She shifted uncomfortably.

This couldn't be good.

The air in the room felt heavy. Was the PTA president so powerful that the tides shifted at the mention of her name?

"I don't know if I should say this . . . ." Maureen crossed her arms over her chest and then unfolded them again. "So, uh, she's my friend and all, but there was an incident when they lived in New Jersey, out in horse country."

Before I could process what Maureen was saying, she barreled on. "This was when their older daughter was in fourth or fifth grade, something with texting or maybe Facebook. Lee was accused of making destructive comments about a kid in town, someone her older daughter didn't like. After Lee was done with that girl, she, the kid, was distraught, cutting herself on the thigh, talking about suicide. She had to be hospitalized. It was a terrible situation. She's okay now, I heard. And Jack got the charges dropped, but they had to leave the school. That's when they moved here."

So Lee had been accused of bullying a ten-year-old in another town, and that kid had become suicidal. It was a sad story, but not a total surprise.

Maureen leaned forward in her chair. "I'd watch out for Lee if I were you. She doesn't like you. And in case you're not aware, there's a Mayfair Moms Page on Facebook. Lee runs it, and decides who can join. There are maybe ninety or one hundred of us; I've lost track. She's been posting, warning about her plans to 'put someone in her place.'"

My heart was hammering in my chest. The warning was concerning. I'd deal with that after I ran through the clinical conflict issue.

Arguing in public with one patient, then discussing it in session with another was an ethics nightmare. The silver lining was that I was in familiar territory. If a person made a specific threat toward a known person, psychologists were required to break confidentiality and file a report—it was the law. I almost hoped Maureen would say that Lee had threatened to come after me. Then I could call the police.

Instead of addressing the boundary question head-on, I took

the safe route, parroting her words: "Put someone in her place?" I asked, sounding like a caricature of a bad therapist.

"Yeah. She never said who. Obviously, this could all be just dumb talk. Lee loves to exaggerate." She shifted in her chair and regarded me with a steady gaze. "So I thought I'd mention all of this, since you went off on her . . . ."

As Maureen continued, exploring her wishes to protect me, I felt myself beginning to panic. Lee was after my daughter and me. And she was dangerous.

It was becoming hard to listen to my patient. My mind had started to spin. Maureen said that Lee bullied a girl who'd become suicidal and that she was the type to get even.

Rachel had already developed stomachaches and played hooky. What else was Lee planning, and how much lower would she go?

When Maureen's session ended, I left Julie a voice mail, filling her in about the warning and last weekend's game, asking when she could give me some peer supervision. Since Julie was also a licensed psychologist, consulting on cases was allowed as long as everything was above board—no names or identifying information.

I waited for a call back, breathing in to steady myself, trying to slow my mind. I'd left time between appointments to do paperwork, but that could wait. There were now more pressing concerns. Lee was only human (or so I assumed). Finding out about her might put me on a more equal footing and calm me down.

I opened my laptop and googled. The results were nothing out of the ordinary. Listed were charitable foundations, boards, and public works she and her husband had endowed, along with photos of the two of them, arm-in-arm at benefits and galas. I scrolled through the causes she supported: dolphins, political candidates, and orphans. I was about to close the laptop when I noticed something interesting on page seven: a photo of Lee and a bunch of women, all in navy sweatshirts emblazoned with a yellow M for

University of Michigan, which was Colin's alma mater. That was an odd coincidence.

Julie finally called.

"What's up?"

"It's too much, living here in small-town hell, being stuck in Westchester with Opie and Aunt Bee. When I inherited the house everything happened quickly. I didn't look through my caseload or speak with each person about potential conflicts. Although I did make sure the principal didn't put Rachel in a class with the children of patients. Since a woman I've been seeing for years has also recently moved out here, it's only been a matter of weeks that any overlap has occurred."

Julie was sympathetic, and offered to help me refer Maureen and Amy out, though we agreed that Amy was fragile and an immediate switch was fraught.

I was ready to hang up and go home, but she wasn't letting me off so easily. "We need to talk about Lee. What the hell, Vic? I get that she's an uber-bitch who has gone after Rachel, but you can't antagonize the PTA president in public. It'll tarnish your professional reputation. I think you should apologize."

"What you don't know is that a patient warned me not to start with Lee and told me Lee was accused of bullying a girl in another town. That kid was hospitalized for suicidal thoughts."

Julie sucked in her breath. "That's awful. But as far as Lee being a threat, you have no concrete proof. Even if she allows her daughter to exclude yours, this kind of thing happens—no matter how much it sucks. I think you should write her a quick note of apology. Please don't make comments or antagonize her again, especially in public. You'll only make things worse." We hung up, agreeing to touch base the following week.

I sent a short email to Lee, apologizing for my comment at the basketball game. She responded immediately: "So glad to clear the air. Hoping Rachel is all right." Give me a break. Our détente went no deeper than the characters on the screen, and I'd never trust a thing she said.

That night I slept fitfully, knowing Lee tended to get even and wondering what her next move would be.

It had been a trying week, and I couldn't shake my fear that Lee would come after Rachel and me. The thought persisted into Friday evening. I tried to act normal, baking brownies and smiling when Rachel insisted on licking the mixing spoon, even though she'd refused to eat the chicken Alva had prepared.

After my daughter had gone into the living room to watch TV, I grabbed my slinkiest dress and strappiest shoes, and took the quickest shower in history. Alva was staying late, and Jim was taking me to a romantic place near his apartment, a restaurant housed in a building that had once been an old carriage house.

They seated us in a quiet corner and a server came by with a tray of hors d'oeuvres.

"Escargot?" He extended a silver tray toward me. I smiled and shook my head, and he backed away.

"I don't really like snails," I whispered.

Jim was a head taller, even when we were sitting. He looked down at me and took my hand. I felt a familiar excitement in my chest as the server came back to ask if we had any questions about the menu. "Not yet, but please bring us a bottle of this," Jim said pointing. I thought about how comfortable he was, ordering wine and asking for more time.

As we sipped rosé, Jim smiled at me and moved closer. I leaned in and started kissing his neck and earlobes, and he put down his glass and whispered, "If you keep that up I'll never be able to stay long enough to order dinner."

The wine was starting to make me giddy. "Promise?"

Just then another server arrived and began refilling our water glasses. After he moved away, Jim laughed: "That guy's timing is the worst," he said, grabbing my hand again. "So, I've been meaning to ask, what do you think of Mayfair?"

"Believe it or not, some of the places are landmarked, and even older than this building. George Washington once stopped on our road so he could feed his horse and have some bread, or so the story goes."

Jim bit into a roll and grimaced. "I think this piece came from the same loaf as George's." I giggled and had to bite my lip when our waiter came back to ask if we needed anything.

Jim told me about work, and I entertained him with a story about my commute the day before, how a train conductor had argued with a drunken passenger. He poured some more wine and we nibbled on the bread. All I could think about was that I couldn't wait to get out of there.

Jim played with my hand, holding my fingers as he curled and uncurled his grip. And before I realized what was happening, he'd left the servers some money, grabbed his jacket, and steered me down the street. We were at his building.

The elevator ride took forever, but as soon as the door to the apartment closed, we embraced and found ourselves in a tangle of arms, legs, and skin. I couldn't see much in the dark—bookshelves, an area rug, and large leather sofa—not that I cared.

Jim scooped me up and brought me to his bedroom. With anyone else I would have said that carrying me over the threshold bordered on cliché, but in this case I hardly noticed.

He kissed me slowly at first, then more insistently, before depositing me gently on the bed. As he cupped my chin in his hands and raised my lips toward his, I felt a slow heat spread across my chest and down into the rest of my body.

We kissed over and over, until Jim reached for my thong, rolling the fabric between his fingers. I moved his hand and snapped the lace gently, smiling as he groaned.

We moved together quickly and deliberately, and time stood still. We were lost in each other, and I knew then that nothing would ever be the same again.

After we'd made love, I touched the crinkles around his eyes, tracing each tiny line softly, following a gentle path to his temples.

"When we're together, it's like an electric current," Jim said, kissing me again.

I knew what he meant. I was falling for him, and didn't even try to stop myself.

We kissed again slowly. After a few minutes, he turned on the nighttable light and said, "So tell me about your new house." He was leaning on an elbow and looking down at me.

"It's fine. The extra rooms are great, and the yard is nice for Rachel." Noticing that his apartment was small, I was uncomfortable talking about the home's large proportions, and felt myself freezing up.

"Did I say something wrong?"

Note to self: never play poker. "Not at all," I kissed his cheek. "I'm censoring my X-rated thoughts."

He pulled me in close. "X-rated is good. But I was interested. How do you really like Mayfair?"

It was too soon to go into the school situation. "It's convenient and the schools' academics are great, overall a very nice town. Do you know it?"

"Actually, I grew up there."

As Jim adjusted his posture, I searched his face, wondering if he'd say more.

We lay quietly on the bed, Jim leaning on one elbow, looking down on me. I snuggled next to him. "So, how about you. Do you like living in Northfield?" He nodded slightly, and I barreled on. "What made you choose it?"

"You know," he shrugged, "all the usual reasons."

I resisted the impulse to ask additional questions, like did winding up in the apartment have something to do with his ex, and what was it like growing up in a small Westchester town? But he had a few for me. "You always tell me about Rachel, and often mention your aunt. What about your parents?"

I exhaled. "I lost them when I was a teenager."

Jim stroked my cheek. "That's terrible. It must have been very hard."

"It was awful, but my aunt saved me in every way. And you? How long since you broke up with your ex?"

He shifted slightly and began kissing my neck. I was excited, floating, but aware my questions still hung in the air. He slid down on the bed, kissing my thigh, and working his way across my hip and up over my waist, before looking up.

"Evasive maneuvers?" I asked, being sure to keep my tone light.

Jim laughed. "Okay. You got me. My ex, the apartment, those are fifth date stories. So I guess we'll have to go out a couple more times."

We hugged and kissed until my watch buzzed, breaking the mood. I didn't want to leave—though I was eager to chew on his fifth date comment. After another buzz of the wrist, I groaned. "It's after nine thirty. I have to leave now. Babysitter's rules."

He kissed me again while I was grabbing my clothing from the floor by the bed. I felt a familiar tingle, and could barely shake off my excitement, the intrigue of the entire night. I pulled on my clothes. He wrapped himself in a towel, and hid behind the door as I opened it. I allowed myself to be drawn back one last time when he pulled me close. My watch sounded again. I'd never have made it out of the apartment if the thing hadn't gone off.

When I was about to start the car, Rachel texted: *When will you be home?*

"Soon! What's up?"

"Nothing." She went silent, probably resuming whatever activity she'd been involved in. I tried a little back and forth when the cars in front of me stopped at a clogged intersection: *"How was school?"* But she signed off. *"Fine. Biiiii."*

I used the rest of the ride home to consider my romantic situation: hot, smart, funny guy who seemed really into me, and I definitely liked him. Great sex, too. Our relationship was picking up steam, and that was terrifying. Caring and getting attached meant being vulnerable, which I definitely was.

I was really into Jim, but he seemed guarded about his past. There was definitely something he wasn't telling me.

Twelve
Pilgrim's Progress

The three-hundred-year-old canoe was long and intricately carved. The fifth graders stood on tiptoe, staring at the markings, a few reaching to touch the ancient wood. They'd been energized all morning, bouncing from one exhibit to another, laughing and jostling as they made their way through several of the great halls to the displays depicting life during the earliest settlements.

But it was the whale that had mesmerized them. We were making our way through the main floor, passing rows of cases that contained preserved animals: cheetahs, lions, other big cats. The kids were looking up at the crustaceans dangling from above, when they spotted it, and all conversation stopped. We were descending the steps into the dark hall of ocean life. I shivered. The room was dark and deep like the middle of the Atlantic. We marched ahead, staring into the blowhole of an enormous blue whale that had been suspended from above. I was enjoying myself. I hadn't been to this museum in years.

It was a surprise when Ms. Franklin called to say she'd be delighted to have me chaperone. On the morning of the trip, she immediately pressed me into service on the traffic circle, recruiting me to help students find buddies, form a line and assign numbers to each pair, then count as everyone boarded the bus. When

I wasn't telling kids to turn off their cell phones, I was stealing glances at Lee and Jess, who were also along for the ride.

Collette's voice floated through an open window, "You have to move."

"No saving seats," Ms. Franklin announced from the front row.

It was too late. Rachel and Maya were already standing up. I watched from the curb as they shuffled up the aisle and situated themselves closer to the front. We moms boarded last. I sat near the teacher, while Jess and Lee climbed in back with the cool kids.

As the kids were leaving the area with the canoe, they asked the guide about the carvings and wanted to know how the vessel was able to float. The guide chatted about this as we walked to the dioramas that depicted life in native America. While the class was studying the TV-size displays, one of the boys raised his hand. "I heard they didn't really eat turkey."

"Correct, Dylan. They were mostly vegetarians." Ms. Franklin smiled her approval.

As the class chatted about the earliest settlers, Rachel and Maya stared at a scene: a group of men in pelts rushing at a group of Europeans wearing dark-colored pants, white shirts, and buckled shoes. A young warrior led the charge, bow raised and arrow pointed.

"What did the Indians do when they captured someone?" the same boy was now asking.

The museum guide made a stop motion with one hand. "Native Americans would be a better term." He had the adults step to the side so all the kids could gather in the front of the largest display, asking them to imagine life back then. "The Native Americans had been on the land for centuries, taking care of it, not overusing resources. How do you think they felt when these new people came along?" the guide asked, pointing to the scene of a group of men hunting bison.

I felt Lee's eyes on me. She'd been standing to my left, regarding me with amusement.

Collette raised her hand and the guide called on her. "They probably didn't like having new people bother them. It was their turf."

Lee was smirking now.

"And what did the natives do when the European newcomers arrived?" the guide was asking as Ms. Franklin sped off towarda group of boys who'd taken out their phones and began drifting across the room.

Lee whispered for my benefit only: "Why they scalped them, of course."

I raised my hand. "Actually, I read that the earliest settlers and Native Americans coexisted peacefully and learned from one another. It was their descendants who were thought to be the troublemakers," I said as the kids tittered at my use of the word. "Guess they raised their children to be unwelcoming."

The guide nodded. "What you say is true. The pilgrims were welcomed with open arms." Now it was my turn to smirk. A tiny victory was better than none at all.

As we rode back to school, Alva texted that she had the flu and would be out for the next few days. Sitting on the bus, I couldn't shake the thought that even though I'd put Lee in her place, something was about to go wrong.

My fears nagged me into the weekend, receding only when Jim took me to the batting cages he liked to visit. "This is a test," he teased, as we passed through the glass entrance into the reception area.

"Should I be nervous?" I asked.

Actually, I wasn't. I had played softball in high school, and didn't mind the airport hangar-size facility or its high-testosterone patrons.

"I'd be if I were you. I only date women who hit .300 or better."

I was about to make a joke about my knuckleball, when the owner approached us. "So this is where you bring a girl? And they say romance is dead." He punched Jim in the arm.

I laughed as Jim blanched. "Victoria, this is Rocco. Rocco, Victoria."

We shook hands, and Rocco walked off to deal with a broken vending machine.

"I like it here," I told Jim, as we headed toward the cages.

"Me too. I'm helping out while we hire someone to coach, keeping the kids' skills up all winter so they will be ready when official practices start this spring. I've been bringing the school team here to practice on Saturdays."

Aww. He spends time with the kids on the weekends too.

He set the machine to pitch at 35mph. I managed to hit a couple, and did a little palms-up celebratory dance.

"We could use you on the team," he laughed.

"I played girls' softball growing up, but not competitively." I swung my hips as I waited for the next pitch.

"Now that's distracting," Jim was grinning at me. "I probably shouldn't reveal all my secrets, but whenever I get all hot and bothered at the wrong times, the best way to clear my head is to think about baseball." He leaned on his bat. "It'll be hard to forget the image of you wiggling around in your jeans like that, so this little outing may have killed the baseball strategy for me."

My pulse sped up, and I jumped out of the cage as the next pitch flew out of the mechanical arm. Baseball could wait. Jim's flirting was the only contact sport I needed. "Does this mean that you'll always think of me as the one who ruined the MLB for you?" I asked, taking off the batting helmet and moving to stand near him. "That's a lot of pressure."

He grabbed my hand. "I never know what's going to come out of your mouth. It's always interesting." I smiled at him. "Does Rachel like sports too?"

"Yes, she's a good softball player." I pointed a finger at him. "Hey," I said, narrowing my eyes. "I know what's going on here, so quit stalling. It's your turn. Come on, let me see that swing."

Jim laughed and put on a helmet before heading back into the cage. I was glad he was focusing on the ball because I'd never seen him in shorts before and couldn't stop staring. His quads were so hard and muscular, it was like someone had carved them out of Italian marble.

He asked me to go back to his apartment, and looked disappointed when I said I didn't feel comfortable leaving Rachel alone for so many hours. And though he said he understood, I felt low. What if my lack of free time became too frustrating for him, or he met someone else?

As I drove north through surrounding towns, passing rows of stone houses and white fences before heading up the hill to our home, I thought about how much I liked Jim, and how hard it had been to find weekend time with Rachel sitting home alone.

The thought of introducing them had crossed my mind. But Rachel didn't need another unknown in her life, not now when things were so difficult for her.

There was one bright spot. She and Maya had started shooting baskets with the boys during recess, and had volunteered to feed the principal's turtle one afternoon a week. Plus, she'd been Face-Timing again with her city friends. Since Rachel seemed happier, I relaxed a little.

Alva was back in action and agreed to work a few extra hours, and with the school situation improved, at least temporarily, it felt okay for me to meet Jim after I had dinner with Rachel. Over the next few days, we spent a couple of evenings watching World Series games and stealing kisses in a booth at the sports bar in town. It was easy enough to meet up in his neighborhood or mine.

I'd been trying hard to pace myself, and not jump in feet first. But as my feelings began to deepen, it was harder and harder to stop myself. Then it happened. Rachel was invited to sleep over at Zoe's place in the city. It felt like the stars had aligned.

After I dropped her off, I met Jim at the rotating hotel bar atop Times Square, where we had champagne and watched through curving windows as city lights drifted past. Sitting shoulder to shoulder, looking out the skyscrapers and sky, it was starting to feel like love.

Floating above it all, talking about our favorite books and bands, I wanted him right then and there. I figured a one-time splurge would be okay. "Let's get a room. Want to?"

Jim was built. I was reminded of this fun fact after we'd slipped between the high-thread-count hotel sheets. I moved up and down his body, exploring firm biceps and broad, hard, muscular shoulders. I'd never felt so alive. He kissed me again, and I lost myself in his embrace.

I still couldn't believe this intense connection was happening to me, although I needed to figure out something for overnights and weekends before our romance began to fizzle.

The following Monday, I opened my laptop and scrolled down, choosing carefully before requesting gift-wrap and hitting "enter."

A couple of days later, I was closing up the office when Jim texted: *"For me?"*

I sent a kissing emoji and waited. He called immediately. "Thank you, but I don't think it's my size."

"I can be there in ten minutes," I said, shoving papers in my bag and grabbing my keys.

"I'll be waiting."

My gift was lingerie, black and skimpy. I had no idea what to call it, though my great aunt might have used the word "corset." Labels were inconsequential; my suggestive package had done its job. As soon as I arrived at the apartment, I found Jim waiting, door open and wine uncorked.

He kissed me and went over to pour the wine. I slipped away, grabbing the garment from the arm of the sofa before ducking into the bathroom, where I changed quickly and dabbed a bit of perfume behind each ear.

I'd barely taken my first step into the bedroom when he grabbed me and started kissing my neck and shoulders. We held each other for a few moments, and, before I knew what was happening, we were in bed, moving together. Time slowed, and for the precious moments that followed, all that mattered was that we were alone, our bond stronger than ever.

After we finished making love, he kissed me over and over, and I didn't want it to end. When Jim walked over to grab the wine, I slid back into my skimpy thing, grabbing a blanket and joining him in the living room. As we settled into the brown leather of the sofa, I gazed up at the photographs on the wall.

Shots of beaches, waterfalls, fjords, and boats were on display, all moments and images captured during the course of his travels. "These are really beautiful. I don't know if I ever told you, I like the décor," I said, scanning the walls.

Jim arched an eyebrow. "Did you think I'd hang a poster of dogs playing poker?"

"Ha, ha." Whenever we were together, it was great, except the night I'd asked about his apartment and ex, and he told me those were fifth date questions. I was still wondering about that.

He pulled me close. "You look beautiful," he said, eyeing my lace straps and handing me the wine. I felt myself blushing as Jim sipped from his glass. "So you can send X-rated lingerie through the mail, but you can't take a simple compliment?" Just as I was about to make a joke, Jim got serious. "Vic, this has been great. But hopefully we can spend an entire night together—or a weekend. I want to be with you for more than a couple of hours after work."

I put the wine on the coffee table and moved in closer, kissing his neck. We'd grabbed every possible moment for weeks; the logistical difficulties were frustrating for me too. "I agree. It's just hard with Rachel mostly home alone on weekends. When that changes, things will be different for us."

We sat together quietly for a few moments before he spoke again. "I have another idea. I could come over one night and meet her, then we'll be able to hang out at your place."

I imagined introducing them. It would probably be fine. But as nice as Jim was, the relationship was still pretty new. My body tensed. What if Rachel got attached and he changed his mind?

"What's wrong?" Jim asked.

"It's just a difficult time. Rachel's become friendly with one girl, but the transition's been tough, and I still haven't really figured out how to help her get out of the hole."

Jim sighed as I hugged him. "I'm sorry," I said into his chest. "I'm doing what I can to get her through this. I want to make sure she's okay, and when things get a little better, I'd love for you to come over." I looked up at him. "I mean it, Jim."

"I know."

An idea popped into my head. "I could stop by and visit you at work once in a while; maybe meet you for lunch. Would that be okay?" It was an olive branch, but the best I could do.

"As long as I'm not in an interview or a meeting, I'd love to grab lunch. Just touch base one morning when you know your schedule. You can come to the school lobby and tell the secretary you're there to see me."

I took his openness to meeting in the lobby as a good sign. If he weren't into me or was dating other people, he'd discourage me from visiting work. Things with us were really falling into place. At some point I would have to take the chance and let him and Rachel meet.

Jim kissed me again, and I forgot everything but the softness of his lips and warmth of his skin. Just as I decided he was perfect, life did a handy 180.

Lee was about to intervene.

〰

I'd reread the text so many times, I could recite it word-for-word: "Can you have cocktails Saturday at six? Let me know." Jim was taking me to his club. Did this mean we were a couple?

I stressed out about what to wear. Suit or skirt? Work clothes or cocktail dress? I hadn't been to many country clubs . . . scratch that, . . . to *any* clubs. I finally settled on my favorite dress, a black sheath I had grabbed at a J. Crew sale a couple of years ago, and paired it with a scarf and my great aunt's pearls, my best attempt at looking elegant. Whenever I wore the ensemble, I felt confident.

I wanted to look my best for Jim and all the other people from town I expected to run into. I stood in the back of my bedroom in front of my aunt's antique, full-length mirror, brushing my hair and slipping on a pair of heels, before racing for the door.

We met at his place and drove together. Heading down the small main road, passing the quiet residential area where streets lacked sidewalks and homes hid behind mile-high trees, we followed a long drive, past an enormous tennis bubble and dark green sign with white letters spelling out, "The Oaks, 1899." I hoped I wouldn't run into any patients—or PTA presidents.

We walked up the clubhouse steps and through the main doors. I spied her, standing next to a tall grandfather clock and laughing at something an elderly man in cranberry red pants was saying. Lee gave me the once-over and bent down to whisper something to another woman who was seated on a nearby leather sofa; Jess, of course.

The two of them were in identical tennis whites. I gazed down at my formal dress. Maybe it was too much for happy hour? Jim was in a blazer and khakis, so I relaxed a little.

He led me past the bar to a cream-colored room that overlooked a lake and golf course. "Let's grab a spot here," he said, stopping near a high table with a white cloth and no chairs, one of several situated around the room, grabbing a handful of nuts before excusing himself.

"Wine, okay?" Jim called over his shoulder, as I nodded and pulled out my phone. As soon as he walked off, Lee appeared. "Pretty, isn't it?" she said, motioning toward the floor-to-ceiling windows that overlooked the course. There were outdoor lamps strategically placed around a small lake and window lights twinkling in a few homes in the distance. After a few moments, Jim was back, bending down to kiss Lee's cheek. "Hey, I was hoping to run into you."

Jim knew her? A sudden, intense surge of fear made its way from one end of my chest to the other.

He moved closer and put an arm around my waist. "This is Victoria. She has a daughter Collette's age."

"Tricky, aren't you?" Lee drawled, leaning toward him, "Keeping your new friend all to yourself." Her voice was syrupy as she eyed me. "Poor thing. We thought he'd *never* get over Tonya."

Who? I glanced at my nails. They were too blunt to puncture Lee's carotid artery. Pity.

"We've met," I told Jim. My lips felt tight.

He nodded. "Barnum's a small school. I figured you might already know one another." He turned to Lee, "Way to keep it light."

She smacked him on the shoulder.

"Is Jack here?" Jim asked.

"I'll send him right over. See you later."

Lee started to walk off. Just as I heard her whinny a "Haaaaayh," and kiss someone in a golf skirt, a flash of light drew my attention toward the other side of the room. Jess was arm-in-arm with two friends, posing for photos at a smaller bar by the windows.

I wondered who Tonya was, and was dying to find out how

Jim knew Lee, but kept my lips glued shut. He grabbed my hand and the tension melted away. "Don't mind Lee," he said. "She's harmless." I knew better.

Jim continued. "I want to introduce you to a few of my friends tonight. You'll probably recognize some of the people here." He gestured across the room, "That's Jack, Lee's husband. He's a friend of mine." Jim lowered his voice. "They are also very generous, and on the board of The Guardian School."

I tried to cover my shock, though Jim was onto the next thing, lifting his glass, composing his words, "Victoria, I'm glad you're here." The intensity of his gaze made me forget all about the DeVrys. "Cheers," he said, bending over to kiss me briefly on the lips.

Seconds later, Jack came over. "You must be Victoria?" As we shook, a man I recognized from the school gym walked up to the group. He was Jess's husband, and also Rachel's coach. "Peter," he told me, extending his hand. "We've seen each other at games but haven't formally met." He was shorter than Jack with a shaved head and the brightest blue eyes I'd ever seen.

"Yes. She's new to the sport, but enjoying herself. Nice meeting you," I smiled.

Basketball aside, it was a lot to digest: Jim friends with Lee and her husband, and both of them on the board of his school. I was glad Rachel hadn't applied; last thing she or I needed was to wind up in another milieu where Lee ran the show. I filed away the comment about Tonya, assuming she was Jim's ex.

"Earth to Victoria . . ." Jim was staring into my eyes. Jack and Peter had finished chatting and were now walking over to where Lee stood, leaving Jim and me alone. He put an arm around me and raised his chin toward the bar. "That's Bill. He blew a couple of us off for golf last Sunday, and we had to play with a teenage stand-in who could barely hit the ball. Want to walk over with me?"

Out of the corner of my eye I saw that Lee and Jess were now chatting in a group with their husbands. Lee kept glancing over in my direction.

There were a lot of moving parts. Lee had put Rachel through a terrible time, and continued to mess with her while acting chummy with Jim. It was all too much. Suddenly, my breathing felt shallow. "Actually, I'll run to the ladies' room. Go torment your golf buddy." Jim leaned down and brushed his lips against mine before we parted ways.

Inside the restroom, I crouched inside a closed stall as the tears started to fall. Lee had infiltrated every area of my life. My heart was racing and I couldn't breathe. She'd turned the girls against my daughter. And it made sense that she'd now come after me. What would she do next? I breathed in a few times to steady myself before going back into the large, wallpapered room, sitting down at a vanity table as she and Jess barged in.

"Haaaiii again," Lee drawled. "Ah didn't know you were seeing Jim."

"He's adorable," Jess added.

Both of them were standing over me. Lee continued, "Since September I've seen you at events, interest meetings, games . . . but never with Jim."

"You could be my biographer," I said, rubbing gloss on my lips.

As I stood up to leave, Jess and Lee began discussing the local housing situation. "You know the attached homes on the other side of town?" Jess said. "Ever notice how everyone who lives in them drives an enormous Escalade?"

Lee chimed in: "You mean the condos? Maybe they come with a Cadillac as a consolation prize."

When I left the restroom, they were still tittering. I made it back upstairs just as the cocktail hour was ending. Jim asked if I could join him for dinner, and after checking with Rachel, I agreed to stay. We were walking toward the windows, taking in the view, when a woman waylaid Jim. Had he heard a cyberstalker had targeted Guardian?

As he opened his mouth to respond, Lee came from behind and placed a hand on the woman's shoulder. "Come now, Trish. We're planning a big educational program. Let's not worry too much about this. I'm sure it's just some silly kid."

Jim held my hand as we walked to our table. I really liked him, but he was friendly with Jack and Lee, and I was hard-pressed to imagine a future with that intolerable woman in it.

Thirteen
Back at the Cafeteria

I did a double take. Had they scheduled me again to hand out pizza? Recalling an email—for various reasons a couple of moms had to stop volunteering—I decided not to cancel, even though Rachel was at home with a cold. Getting a sub and switching shifts was time-consuming, and meant I'd have to move patients.

I made a big pot of soup and brought it to Rachel, who took only a couple of spoonfuls. Alva texted that she'd come in a little early, and then I was ready to drive to school.

The routine was familiar. I greeted the other volunteer, a woman named Joelle, who had a fifth grade boy, kindergartener, and toddler in daycare, and began the process of setting each place with a paper plate. No Lee today so that was a relief.

Once the kids were seated, they knew to raise a hand, indicating who had preordered. Some brought bag lunches, but most got pizza. The hungrier ones knew to make a V with their fingers, indicating, "two, please." It was also the sign for peace, although there wasn't much of that going around.

When the older grades arrived I passed out slices and took in the carnage. It was choice day, and the fifth and sixth graders could sit with kids in different classes. A few minutes into the meal, the red-haired girl I'd seen the others pick on, sat down at Collette and Lexi's table. Joelle filled me in. "That's Francesca. She'd been a part of their crowd until a few months ago."

I thought of the story Rachel had recently shared; how they'd stolen the poor girl's phone. If something bad happened to her under my watch, I'd be sure to get an aide. Collette and Lexi made faces behind Francesca's back while everyone else at the table egged them on, then Collette made a slight adjustment to her posture and stance. Lexi mirrored her, and like a choreographed routine, each girl followed, one after another, rotating like dominos collapsing. They jerked their faces sideways and flipped their hair up in a perfectly coordinated dance of rejection. They stopped when all backs were upon the hapless Francesca. After looking at the human wall, she gave up, lifting and carrying her tray, stopping at the end of a nearby bench.

As soon as Francesca sat down, the girls in the new table turned *their* bodies slightly, until they were also facing away, leaving her alone, with nothing to do but stare at the floor. I started to go over, but Joelle reminded me that parents weren't permitted to involve themselves in the kids' interactions; only aides could intervene.

There wasn't much anyone could do. Francesca sat alone, red-cheeked and frowning, staring at her watch. My heart broke as I witnessed the very public and final stage of the collapse of her social standing. Why had she become an object of scorn and derision? Joelle said there had been an incident during preseason volleyball this past summer, and that had landed the red-haired girl on Collette's bad side. "It's virtually impossible to come back from a DeVry grudge," she whispered as I tried not to cringe.

I looked and finally found an aide who walked over and asked Francesca if she was all right before going back to supervise a table of boys. I walked over and offered her another piece of pizza. She met my eyes and said, "No, thank you. I'm okay." We both knew she wasn't.

For the rest of the day, I thought of the bullying. After work, I managed to grab a quick drink with Jim. We were at his favorite place again, the sports bar near his apartment. We sat side-by-side in the booth, legs touching and hands intertwined. "Work was so crazy, I didn't even get a break this afternoon. Be right back," he said, striding toward the restroom. Watching him walk off, I thought again about how handsome he was. I settled into the booth, anticipating a happy ending to the evening, when his phone lit up with a text from Lee.

The good feelings disappeared. How often did she write to him, and what if the text was about me? I'd have to be careful so she couldn't sabotage my relationship with Jim.

While he was gone, the image of Lee's name lighting up on his phone kept running through my mind. I sat, staring at the titles on the jukebox, trying to ignore the tightness in my chest. Finally Jim appeared in my line of vision.

He slid in next to me and I pointed to his phone. "I think you have a text."

"Oh, Lee." I'll read it later. I have other things on my mind now." He pulled me close and kissed me, right there in the center booth in front of all the regular customers.

I stroked him under the table. "You're dangerous," he whispered, putting an arm around me. "Can you come over?"

Five minutes later, we were in his bed, moving together. It was only the two of us and the heat of our bodies. After we'd made love, I had to pry myself away so there'd be time to see Rachel before she went to sleep.

As I drove I asked myself over and over why a married woman was busy texting my boyfriend. Playing by the rules hadn't helped my daughter. Taking the high road hadn't allowed her to make friends or afforded me access to Lee's modus operandi. There had to be something I was missing.

I was on Mayfair's main drag near the post office when an idea popped into my head. It was twilight and there were a few minutes left before the skies went dark. Pulling the car over and taking a few deep breaths, I grabbed my phone from its place in the console between the front seats, and scrolled through the school directory, plugging an address into the mapping app and driving.

I felt a strange tingling as I passed CVS on my left and made my way up the long hill to the modular homes. Dusk had settled in and there was no better time for gathering info. I could see well enough, while still blending in.

The rest of the ride was smooth. Passing tree-lined streets and a small park, I took in my surroundings until my phone began to flash with the red stickpin icon.

Turn back. This is a bad idea. No way. Lee had toured my home, put Rachel on the spot, and excluded her. I wasn't sure exactly how, but it seemed like gathering information would help me find ways to level the playing field.

The cul-de-sac was bursting with outsize Tudors and stately Colonials. My eyes followed the street to the end, settling on a home so large and modern, it was unlike anything I'd ever seen.

My heart was beating as I stared at the monstrous house, imagining Lee inside, and wondering what she was doing.

The place was certainly distinctive: jagged corners, a slanting roof on one side, flat along the back, no two walls the same size, just as Maureen had said. I recalled the PTA chair mentioning it was all her design. *Don't quit your day job, Lee.*

There were several cars parked on the side of the home in front of a white stable-like edifice, each stall fronted by a separate driveway. The first two enclosures housed matching sports cars. I couldn't quite see the plates, but they were custom, something like

LDV and JDV. There was a footpath leading to the garage. It was lined with small white rocks.

The front of the home was flat, and immediately behind it, stood a mile-high structure, rectangular with long glass windows. There were short, separate wings leading to the back of the home, where a light illuminated one of the rooms as an enormous chandelier dangled and shone through the windows of the rectangular part of the house. A staircase ascended from behind the entranceway, remaining visible through the tall set of windows. I idled outside, watching as a woman in a uniform raced up and down, carrying trays from one level to the next.

Suddenly the lights popped on, illuminating the rooms in front. Before I knew it, the front door was opening. I panicked and started the car, driving off before anyone could spot me.

My heart raced as I sped away. Fortunately I'd made it out of there. I'd be more careful next time I checked up on Lee.

The next day Rachel went to Neil's for dinner, and Jim and I met at the same sports bar, sliding into a booth just like last time. Once we'd ordered a round of drinks, he put his arm around me.

I was happy to see him, but he seemed off. "I'd ask what's on your mind, but there's nothing more annoying than that question."

Jim's smile was preoccupied. I ruffled my hand through his hair. "You look a little tired. Have you been up all night texting and snap-chatting with your middle school students?"

He shook his head. "Thankfully, no. They have to make an appointment if they want to speak to me. There are other things I like to do at night." He squeezed my hand and I moved into nibble his ear. That usually got a response, but he sat quietly, giving my shoulder a squeeze as I slid closer. "What's going on in there?" I asked massaging his temples with the tips of my fingers.

He shook his head and smiled. "Just tired." He wasn't usually this distant. Was there something wrong?

I took off a shoe, put my bare foot on his, and worked my way up his leg. He stroked my hand and told me my foot felt "nice."

Jim was speaking more softly than usual, and his vibe was distant, reminding me of his guardedness in bed when the subject of his ex had come up. I'd never gotten to the bottom of that either.

I must have looked concerned. Jim gave my shoulder a quick squeeze. "I have a lot going on with work," he said, kissing me on the cheek. "You know how that is."

I didn't know, but wished he'd enlighten me.

We decided to go to Jim's place, but his reticence was confusing. I'd thought about inviting him to the house and having him meet Rachel, but tabled that idea.

By the time I got home, she'd returned from Neil's. We watched preteen Disney, and during the commercials I asked some questions.

"Did you have fun at Neil's? What's the news?"

"Nothing." She shrugged, pushing a strand of hair behind her left ear.

"Come on, honey. You can do better than that."

"Not really," she said, retreating to the tiny powder room.

Later on while Rachel was brushing her teeth, the phone pinged.

"Rach, someone texted you."

She mumbled something through a mouth full of toothpaste. I glanced as the cell buzzed a second time: "So transfer back!" It was Zoe, and the words startled me.

I scrolled to the beginning of the exchange with Zoe, glad Rachel's old best friend was back in the picture. *"Hate school,"* Rachel had texted, adding a squinting devil emoji. *"It sux."*

"Y do u hate it?" came the response.

"Everyone is mean. Clique-yyyyy!!" I was glad Rachel could confide in her, and relieved they were still in touch. Zoe's mom, Sam, had let me know her work schedule and custody situation

were making it difficult for the girls to see each other, so at least they still texted and FaceTimed.

I focused on the screen. *"I was popular but they all ditched me."* Rachel had written. *"Now I'm not friends with any of them."*

"Ask your mom if you can transfer back here?"

If only it were that simple.

Just then the humming of the electric toothbrush ceased, and I returned the phone to the nightstand. Rachel came in and climbed between the sheets. I sat down on the edge of her bed.

"Everything okay?"

"I guess." She bit her lip and refused to look at me.

"It doesn't look okay. Please talk to me."

"I just miss being at school with Zoe and my other friends." She rolled over and turned toward the wall.

"Did something happen today?"

Rachel wiped a tear from the corner of her eye. "We were on the playground during recess. Collette asked me if I wanted to play basketball, HORSE, with Katie, Lexi, and this other girl, Chloe, so I said okay. They all passed only to each other and laughed whenever they threw the ball over my head. Chloe filmed the whole thing and sent it out to a bunch of kids." She was crying now.

There were seven months left of the school year. Before this pattern became ingrained, she needed to fix it. "Rachel, don't give these kids so much power. Focus on other people, like Maya. Where was she?"

"Absent."

"Let's invite her over for a playdate." Rachel stared at her phone. I tried again. "Please don't look away. I just want to know how you are doing."

Rachel shrugged. "Okay. I just wish I had more people to hang out with."

It was frustrating. All my years of schooling and practice, of helping other people solve their problems, and still I didn't have the right words for my daughter. I gave her a hug and turned out the light.

Seeing Rachel endure months of bullying had left me drained and desperate for advice. When I got into bed, I finally broke down and called Jim.

"Hey, was just going to text you," he said.

"How do you feel about free advice?" I blurted out.

He laughed. "Is this an old joke? What's the punch line, something about how you get what you pay for?"

"Probably, but this time you'd be giving the advice," I said.

"Ah. Then I'm all for it. What's up?"

I didn't want to be a downer, but squelched my insecurities. "Well . . . as I told you, things have been rough for Rachel." There was a short silence on the other end of the phone, and I pictured him, furrowing his brow. The lines that formed there were so cute. "Some of the girls have been giving her a hard time, and she's been eating lunch alone in the nurse's office. I wanted to get your take on some recent goings-on."

"What happened?"

"You know that game, HORSE? Well, the girls threw the ball over Rachel's head and kept it away, stupid stuff, but they videoed and sent it around. Of course all the other kids laughed at her." I was torn between wanting advice and being afraid to burden Jim or tip him off to the Lee situation.

"That's terrible." Before I could say anything else he spoke. "You should ask for a meeting with the teacher."

"Thanks. You're right."

"And don't wait too long."

I forced myself to sound perkier than I felt. "Now that you've solved all my problems, tell me about you."

"Okay, but I want you to promise to keep me posted. As far as my day, a few years ago, a kid who'd lost a parent on 9/11 was flagged for all kinds of extra support and family meetings. And now many years later, he just got accepted to his first-choice college. That's what I love about my job, being there for students, influencing their lives over time."

"That's amazing, Jim. You're amazing." I suddenly felt a little shy. "And, just in case you didn't know, you've had a positive influence on me."

"More like a long-distance influence." Jim was teasing, but I knew he was frustrated. Me too.

I was still worried Lee would do something to sabotage our relationship and tried, as I had in the past, to gauge his feelings about her. "Since you mention school, I think it's great that Lee is working to address the cyber problems at Guardian."

"Yes."

"So have you known her a long time?"

"I'd say so. More than ten years." We sat in silence for a few moments. He clearly wasn't one for gossip.

"Well," I finally said. "Miss you."

Jim and I had been getting along great. He'd given me no reason to doubt him. I took a leap of faith. "I know it's been hard for us to have weekend time. If you're still up for meeting Rachel, I'd love for us to figure something out."

After we hung up, I wrote to the teacher and requested a meeting. Just as my thoughts went back to Rachel's situation, I heard something scurrying behind the plasterboard behind the headboard. "Shut up mice!" I said, punching the wall. I heard they hated noise. Well, I hated them.

I turned off the light thinking it was ironic that the damned things sounded more robust than ever. If only I could say the same for Rachel and myself.

At least my daughter was now knee-deep in basketball. There were frequent practices and games, each one an opportunity for her to show her stuff. Rachel was athletic, a currency that really mattered at Barnum. The jury was still out about whether that would help her socially, though she had recently been invited to spend the afternoon at Katie's with the other girls in her class. When I picked her up, she told me all about it. "They invited everyone but Maya," she began.

"It makes me uncomfortable when they laugh at her or Francesca," she told me.

"So what do you do when you're in it with the other girls?" I asked.

"I try to stay clear." She looked down at her hands. "When Maya heard everyone talking about going over to Katie's, her face got really red and she went to use the bathroom."

"That situation—inviting all the girls in the class but one— you know what it feels like to be on the receiving end of that."

"It's mean." Rachel's expression was thoughtful. "But a lot of this isn't up to me. Who they invited wasn't my choice."

I turned the steering wheel and headed up the hill to our house. "Couldn't you have asked them to include Maya?"

"I just told you! It wasn't up to me. It was Katie's party. And I told you, none of them like her."

"You don't have to do everything the group does. You know that, right?"

Rachel thought for a moment. "Maya can be kind of nice," she said. "She shared her cookies with me the other day."

"Why don't you invite her to come home with you one afternoon?"

I stopped at a stop sign and glanced at Rachel. "I don't think so," she told me. "They'd ditch me. I want to be part of that group. They have all the sleepovers and parties."

I tried again. "I've said this before, but here goes. Why not make friends with kids in different groups?"

Rachel shot me an annoyed look. "It doesn't work like that."

I asked her if she wanted to go out for ice cream, but she said she wasn't hungry. It was the third time I'd heard that in as many weeks.

"No ice cream?"

Rachel shook her head.

"You weren't hungry the time we baked cookies either." She didn't meet my eye. "How 'bout you tell me what's up?"

Rachel shifted uncomfortably. "What's a makeover?"

My anxiety rose. Was she unhappy with her appearance? I forced myself to play it cool. "Sometimes people try a new style, use different makeup, or change their hair and clothing when they want to improve how they look. And some people undergo surgical procedures. Why do you ask?"

Rachel looked down at her hands. "Yesterday when Alva was picking me up from school, I ran back in because I'd left my jacket in the cubby. Mrs. DeVry was telling another mom that I could use a makeover." Her face turned a bright shade of red.

That was outrageous! "She has no idea what she's talking about. And you're perfect."

Rachel sighed. "You're supposed to say that. You're my mother."

"I say what I mean. You're beautiful—on the outside and inside."

I reached over the seats, extending my hand. As she leaned forward and took it, a tear slid down her cheek. "Collette and Lexi laughed at me in gym. They said my knees were fat." I released her hand and grabbed the steering wheel so she wouldn't feel the tension in my body.

My blood was boiling, and I felt like driving over to Lee's and telling her she needed professional help, but I curbed the impulse. "That must have really bothered you," I said. She nodded.

"May I say something?"

"I guess."

"Comments like the ones Lee and Collette made are vicious and hurtful. You need to know that, and next time someone says something below the belt, pretend you have a little suit of armor on. Or if you prefer, think of a duck's back."

Rachel's look told me I was making no sense.

"Let it go. Think 'water off a duck's back.'" I made a sliding motion with my hand.

Rachel was smiling a little now. "That's ridiculous."

We were pulling into the driveway. "I'm going to say it again: You're perfect. Not only beautiful, but equally important, you're a good person."

I got out of the car and opened the back door to hug her. "Please don't let these kids have any power over you," I said, kissing the top of her head. "I don't know why they're so mean, but when people are nasty, it has more to do with them than with you."

Rachel was looking up and to the side, thinking. "That makes sense," she said, meeting my eyes.

"Let's go inside and have some fruit and cookies."

"Okay."

Baby steps. At least I'd started the dialogue. There would be other chances to offer my prehistoric perspective on her preteen problems.

Once we were sitting down in the kitchen, I smiled as Rachel bit into a cookie and sipped her milk, but inwardly I was still seething. Lee made a habit of walking around, bragging about her charitable work and contributions to the PTA, while behind the scenes she was terrorizing my kid.

I still couldn't believe what Rachel had told me. Making fun of a fifth grader's appearance? This was war.

Get ready, Lee, I thought. You underestimated me.

Fourteen

Buckets

We were on our way to the big game, Knicks-Lakers, and even bigger occasion: Rachel's first meeting with Jim. He had a conference day, and asked if it would be okay to get tickets during a school day. I said yes to Rachel playing hooky, and moved patients around to free up the afternoon, hoping she and Jim would connect through sports talk and stadium food.

"So, Rach," I'd said a couple of nights earlier, "I have a friend I want you to meet. His name is Jim." She said very little which was her style—no reactions upfront, but there would be questions when I wasn't expecting them.

We took the train into the city and got across town on the subway. As we emerged from Penn Station and I was asking myself for the millionth time, what if they didn't get along, Rachel caught sight of the giant flatscreen above the Garden's outdoor entrance. She was shivering. "Can we run to our seats?" she asked as I scanned the crowds for Jim.

"We can't run. We have to find my friend, remember?" We headed for our agreed-upon meeting point in the huge putty-colored lobby. He was waiting by the turnstiles.

"Rachel, say hi to Jim."

"Hi." Rachel looked down at the floor, pushing her toe into the tile.

"Hi," Jim said, reaching out to shake her hand. "I don't know if you've been here before, but there's a lot of great stuff to eat: giant hot dogs, chicken fingers, ice cream."

Rachel tried to play it cool, but her face brightened at ice cream.

We stopped on the way to our seats. Jim and Rachel chose hot dogs, and I went with pizza. The meals were lukewarm, but the team sizzled, and Rachel's analysis of the players and coaches made Jim laugh. When one of the Lakers tripped after fouling a NY player, she casually suggested that he might be better at soccer. Her friend Zoe had just switched from softball to tennis, and had found the latter to be a much better fit.

"You're right. He probably should switch to another sport, judging from his stats and what I've seen so far tonight." Jim looked like he was trying to keep from laughing.

"Rachel's fun to be around," he whispered. "And she's beautiful, just like her mom."

Before I could thank him, one of the Knicks made a three-point shot. Jim and Rachel jumped up from their seats at the same time and high-fived.

The game passed quickly. We clapped and shouted and finished our popcorn, and then it was time to leave. Since Jim had driven, we all rode home together.

"I'm glad the Knicks won," Rachel said.

Jim nodded. "They have a really strong team this year."

"So where do you live?" Rachel asked, emphasizing the word "you."

"In Northfield." He glanced at her in the rearview mirror.

"Near us, then."

He nodded. "How do you like your new house?"

"It's nice. Can you help me convince my mom to get a golden doodle?"

Uh-oh. Those were cute, but a pet would be too much for me to handle. "Why don't you tell Jim what you're reading?"

Rachel played along, eager to make a good impression. "*Wonder*," she said.

"Great book. Inspiring."

Rachel looked surprised that he'd read it. "Jim's a middle school dean," I said.

"I can see it," Rachel said, smiling at him.

Mayfair was the next town off the parkway. I held my breath a little as Jim followed our directions, driving through the village and past the large homes in our part of town. He'd never driven me home in daylight before. I felt embarrassed about the long driveway, gigantic porch, and extra rooms. Would he be uncomfortable when he got a good look at the house?

"Wow. Beautiful place," he said, surveying the grounds and large white home. His tone was matter-of-fact, and that made me happy. I had let him know it had been my aunt's house. Once he'd parked, Rachel said thank you, and they did a little fist-bump before she went inside through the kitchen.

I was glad to be alone with him. "Thank you. For the tickets, for driving, for being so sweet to Rachel." I kissed him, first on the lips, then both cheeks and finally on the sides of his neck.

"You're feisty today," he said, laughing.

"I'm happy we went. Thank you again." I itched to check on Rachel, see how she was reacting to meeting Jim.

We kissed some more. "Normally I'd invite you in, but Rachel . . . . I'm not sure if it's too much for her in one day. Is it okay to wait until next time?"

"It's fine. I can wait." He smiled and promised to call later.

After he drove off I went straight upstairs to Rachel's room. "Time for a shower, sweetie."

At bedtime I gave her a kiss, and was about to turn out the light when she stopped me.

"Mom?"

"Yes, honey."

"Is Jim your boyfriend?"

"I guess that's what you'd call it. Did you like him?"

I hoped she would say yes. I hadn't even thought about what I'd do if she didn't.

"He's nice."

"Good night, Rach."

I was halfway down the hall.

"Mom?"

"Yes?"

"Come here."

I backtracked until I was standing in front of the bedroom door. "You have to go to sleep, hon."

"Are you going to marry him?"

That was a tough one. "Don't know yet."

"Will you tell me if you're getting married?"

She'd already seen one disaster at the altar.

"If Jim and I do get married, you'll be the first to know, sweetheart. Promise."

Rachel frowned. "You never told me what happened with Colin." She turned her head to the side, her thinking face. "It was weird that when you broke up, we moved here right after."

My stomach clenched. "I know. It was a lot of changes at once." I was glad she'd asked about my ex-fiancé and our move. "Want to talk about that?"

Rachel interrupted me. "Jim seems nice."

"Don't worry. It will be better this time. I'll prepare you better, and go more slowly. And don't forget, we'll always be a team. I love you. Nothing could ever change that."

I closed her door and exhaled deeply.

I'd done it: introduced Rachel and Jim. There was no turning back now.

Even though my daughter had been spending time with Maya, the school situation was far from settled. Today was the teacher meeting, and I was eager to hear what Ms. Franklin had to say. Arriving at the designated time and knocking on the classroom door, I found her at the computer working. "Hello, Dr. Bryant," she said, coming toward me.

"Thank you for making time to see me, Ms. Franklin," I said.

"Not at all. As it happens, I'm emailing parents to set up regular conferences." She motioned toward a child-size table and chairs, and we sat down. I was low to the ground, and could see the whites of Hermione's eyes on the Harry Potter rug in the reading corner next to us.

I glanced around at the map of the US and long division lesson on the walls and blackboard. "I know you have your hands full with eighteen kids and all the subjects you cover. Teachers can't possibly see everything, but I'm not sure who else to talk to about this."

She leaned forward, listening intently. "Please tell me what you mean."

"Well, even though Rachel's adjusted to the new school, in terms of academics, she's been struggling socially."

A boy with a golden retriever shirt and glasses appeared in the doorway.

"Yes?" Ms. Franklin said as he swayed nervously.

"I'm here to feed the guinea pig."

"Thank you, Lucas."

It was the boy who'd been picked on at lunch. Ms. Franklin continued to speak. "Please tell your teacher, we'll handle that today and I appreciate your diligence. You can feed him tomorrow, okay?"

Lucas nodded and rushed off.

"Sorry about that," Ms. Franklin looked at me. "You were saying?"

"Since starting at Barnum this year, Rachel's been having a hard time. I'm concerned something's going on with the girls."

The teacher gave me a sympathetic nod as I continued. "One time she was on the playground and went over to a group at the picnic table." I paused, thinking I'd have to be careful with my phrasing. No teacher wants to hear a mom speak critically about a bunch of young kids. "So, uh, these three girls who've been friends forever were there. When Rachel walked over and sat down with them, they all got up, leaving her alone. I know they're just eleven, but she was really hurt and embarrassed."

Ms. Franklin sucked in her breath. "That's terrible. We do work with them on a social developmental curriculum. We spend a few minutes each day and each child selects the word that best describes his or her mood. Plus, we speak about bullying, what constitutes an incident; about exclusion too, and what responsibility others have to help a child who is struggling—which reminds me, there's going to be an assembly to teach kids about online safety."

"I heard. But it seems like there's one more thing I should mention. Rachel's the new kid. Many of the others have been together for years, and their families socialize on weekends. I'm not sure how to help her break in. She doesn't seem to be able to find anyone to hang around with, and I want to try to help her before it becomes an even bigger problem."

"Of course. That makes sense. Let me speak to the other fifth grade teachers. They always have good ideas. Rachel does seem to enjoy spending time with Maya and one or two of the boys; you should know that. Also, I can move the kids around a little, see if that would spark a friendship."

I nodded, appreciating the thought, but noticed she hadn't

asked who had walked off and left Rachel. Perhaps she already knew. Was she signaling that those girls were off-limits, as far as any type of discipline went? Or maybe she knew that it was better to steer my child in a different direction, which reminded me that I was glad to hear Rachel continued to hang around with Maya.

"Now, let me show you some of Rachel's work." She pulled out a math test, on which was written "100% Great Job!" and started rifling through a stack of papers, looking for other work to show me. "I wanted to tell you how pleased I am. Rachel's academics are terrific."

My spirits rose. As Ms. Franklin was reaching behind her, looking for a certain paper, her cell phone lit up with a text: *"Hey, Frankie! Remember to save January 5th for the teacher appreciation luncheon—you deserve it. Lee."* I knew just who'd sent the text, and signed off with a kissing emoji.

My mood crashed, but I fixed a smile on my face. Even the teacher seemed to be under Lee's thumb. This was the land of DeVry, and Rachel and I were trapped.

My panic rose. Nothing I did made a dent, whereas Lee had the power to wreak havoc in Rachel's life. *I was alone, and I alone could help my child.*

The walls felt like they were closing in. Not only would I never forgive Lee for the nasty makeover comment, I'd just learned that her influence might even extend to the classroom. She had to be stopped.

A bell rang and scores of kids started running down the hall, screaming.

"I'd better get out of the way," I managed to utter, leaving quickly as Ms. Franklin's promised to keep an eye on the situation.

I was furious as I got into the car, vowing again to take a harder line so Lee would get the message and stop pushing us around. I'd also keep my eyes and ears open for information that would help me figure out my next step to protect Rachel.

The following weekend was Thanksgiving, our first without Aunt Pearl. Our plan was to visit Julie and Hal, but their older daughter, Carly, got a stomach virus, and we stayed home.

On Saturday, I invited Jim for a tawdry meet-up in a hotel. With Rachel having met him only once and the relationship still being relatively new, I didn't feel comfortable having him spend the night, and since I wanted to spice it up, an assignation was the only way to go.

Rachel would be okay staying alone for a couple of hours, reading or watching TV. I told her I had a meeting one town over, and she could reach me on my cell.

"Of course I can stay home without a sitter," she'd scoffed, rolling her eyes. "I've done it before—and I'm almost eleven!"

"What will you do?" I felt guilty about having fun without her.

Rachel scoffed. "I'll read the next Harry Potter book, or Face-Time Zoe. I'll figure it out, just go!"

So I did.

They put us in a quiet part of the hotel—it was far enough away from the house that I didn't have to worry about running into anyone I knew, yet close enough to get home quickly if Rachel needed me.

"I am going to give you a massage," I told Jim between kisses. We were all hot and heavy, and I was feeling adventurous. "Strawberry or yucca?" I asked, rubbing his back and shoulders with the hotel's free moisturizer.

As Jim pulled me in for a kiss, my attempts at a full body massage were cast aside in favor of his more ardent agenda. We were sweaty and all tangled up. I forgot where I was as my sense of time evaporated.

After we'd made love, Jim ordered champagne. I couldn't have much because I had to drive, but it was exciting and cozy to be sharing the hotel bed. I didn't want our time to end.

An hour later I was putting on my dress and boots and sighing about how fast the afternoon had flown by. Jim pulled his jeans on and faced me with a huge grin. "This feels kind of cheap, you walking out of the hotel, abandoning me."

I leaned over, nuzzling his neck. He always smelled so good.

Jim wrapped his arms around me again. He was such a great kisser. I wanted to stay, but it wasn't right, me here enjoying myself, and my child sitting home with nothing to do and so few social connections. I dragged myself into the hallway and promised to text him later in the day.

I stopped and pulled out my phone to see if Rachel had messaged. There were no texts, and I was about to head for the elevator, when a sound in the hallway distracted me. The corridor was long, almost the length of a football field. Way down at the end, a couple was visible. There was something about their demeanor—the man glancing behind him before grabbing the woman's hand—that made me tread slowly.

I inched forward, taking in the woman's blond hair and noting the way she threw her head back and laughed. Something was familiar about her. Then I knew: it was Lee at the end of the hallway. I froze. The man with her wasn't Jack.

I couldn't tear my eyes away, and ducked down behind a room service cart so they wouldn't see me. Lee whispered something in the man's ear and the two of them laughed. He turned and scanned the hallway again. This time I got a good look.

I was grateful I'd crouched down and grabbed hold for support. That shaved head. Those intense blue eyes! I knew instantly the person holding hands in the hotel hallway and whispering with Lee was Jess's husband, Peter.

Jess had been petty and unkind, laughing at my expense during the ladies' night, cohosting a party for all the girls but Rachel. But even if she wasn't my favorite person, she deserved better than this.

I watched them whisper and giggle, and my hatred for Lee grew. How many people did she need to harm, and how many lives would she ruin before she was stopped? I balled my hands into fists. Ouch. The edge of my cell phone was pressing into my hand.

My phone! Without thinking my actions through, I raised the cell slowly and tapped on the camera app. Jess's husband leaned into Lee, as if on cue, and I captured them smiling at one another, visible directly above them the elevator dial. Peter whispered again as she smiled up at him. This time I enlarged the image before clicking on it. I now had a photo of the two of them, with Peter bending toward her and Lee tilting her chin toward him. They hugged and I snapped that too, before the elevator doors opened and they got in and rode upstairs together. The car stopped on the eleventh floor.

Lee was obviously sleeping with Peter. I steadied myself against the cart and stood up, my heart still pounding. She went around, campaigning for sympathy and accusing everyone else of engaging in bad behavior, while she was the one who was cheating—and with her best friend's husband.

Which reminded me. I wasn't sure how I'd use the incriminating photos. For the entire ride home I couldn't shake the image of her and Peter, leaning toward each other, riding the elevator to the eleventh floor.

I pulled into my driveway and shut off the car. I needed a few minutes to clear my brain. My thoughts shifted to Rachel, how she'd been biding her time at home alone.

Later that evening, the two of us were in the living room watching TV. My cell phone rang. It was Sharon. I picked up immediately. Chatting would be a good distraction.

She entertained me with a story about a recent business lunch, and I was in the middle of telling her I'd be glad to drive Neil home on Friday, when she interrupted. "You sound like you could use a laugh. Well, get a load of this: I was at yoga, adjusting my mat before the final shavasana, when I heard two women going on and on about a parenting bulletin board, what a great resource it was."

I had no idea such a thing existed outside of school. "Who even uses those nowadays?"

"I mean an electronic message board. And there are apparently a bunch of New York area parenting sites with postings and chat rooms. Some of the stuff is hilarious. There are even women bitching about their nannies and mahjong games." That figured. "I'll send you a link," she added and we hung up, promising to make a plan soon.

As soon as Rachel was in bed, I clicked on the link in Sharon's email and found advice, info, and a community at the ready. It was easy to see how people got lost in the virtual world.

I skimmed through #MeToo discussions, sample nanny agreements, and books about sibling rivalry. There was gossip about everything, from celebrities to the best exercise classes, as well as threads to live discussions. On one called "Neighborhood," someone named "Cheerleader" was talking about her local PTA to a poster called "Bumblebee." Clicking on the pom-pom icon, reading the words, "Location: Westchester County," I felt a flutter in my chest. Cheerleader lived close by.

Reading on, I learned that Bumblebee was advocating for a democratic parent/teacher organization where everyone split the duties equally. Cheerleader was opposed: "Take our town. I've run our organization for years, working hard for the school and students seven days a week, but people still complain. Someone recently went behind my back to the principal, complaining I had shut out her *loser daughter*."

Lee's words replayed in my mind: "There's no way mah Collette would spend even fahve minutes with her loser daughter." Not only had she said exactly that, Amy had described being "shut out" from some afterschool program. And Cheerleader was in charge of a parent organization.

I searched through other chats. She'd recently advised a mom who'd lost a promotion to a colleague: "If someone threatens me or mine, I get even."

That was creepy. Was "Cheerleader" Lee? The postings sounded like her.

After bookmarking the chat room and conversation, I brushed my teeth and went straight to bed.

The next morning I woke up before the alarm. I recalled what I had seen at the hotel and read in the chat room, but managed to push Lee out of my mind.

I was still concerned about Rachel. Even though she'd become friendly with Maya and was doing well academically, our problems were far from resolved. Private school wasn't an option, homeschooling wouldn't work, given my full-time job and lack of background in education, and seeing the teacher hadn't helped.

I told myself there was a chance that once my daughter got through the rest of the school year, there'd be a larger peer group in the fall; maybe then the dynamics would improve, even with Lee and Collette still in the mix. In half a year Rachel would be in middle school, changing rooms, taking classes with different kids. That was only six more months.

Six months. That sounded like a prison sentence.

Fifteen

Dead Ends

Two things happened in the week that followed the school meeting and assignation at the hotel. Rachel solidified her friendship with Maya, and I finally stole away for a quiet escape with Jim.

It all began that Monday. I had just gotten in, and was thrilled to see that for the first time in a few months, my kid wasn't sitting home alone. "Thank you for having me over." Maya spoke softly, just like that day in the cafeteria. I was about to tell her she was welcome anytime, but Rachel's phone pinged.

"Look, I got another one," she said, showing her friend the screen. I saw over their shoulders that they were looking at Instachat. "He commented again. Just, 'hi,' like last time. He's friends with someone's camp friend," she confided to Maya.

I didn't want to interrupt. "You guys seem like you're having fun. I'm going to go downstairs. I bought some cookies if you want." They looked at one another and giggled. "Thank you, Dr. Bryant," Maya called, as I went into the hallway.

With Rachel smiling more, finally secure in a friendship with someone from her class, I worried less about the girl clique and their snotty moms, and could finally breathe a little, although there was a new source of concern. Rachel had received online comments from some unknown kid, a boy she'd met through a classmate, someone's camp friend. I recalled hearing patients describe how their teenagers met people online. Followers of the same account routinely chatted with one another. It was commonplace, and concerning. I'd have to speak to her about it.

I decided that a child should come with an owner's manual, like an IKEA wall unit, with explicit directions for start-up, use, and maintenance. This shit was hard.

At least Rachel seemed to have made a friend. Hopefully Lee, Jess, and their daughters would start to have less power over us.

Jim was laughing, probably at the excitement in my voice. We were on our usual good night phone call. "I've been thinking that you were right," I said. "We should have time alone and go away somewhere. Maybe I can try Maya's mom, see if she'll take Rachel for a couple of nights so we can we get away?"

"I'd love to." His response was immediate. "I know a mountain resort not too far upstate. Very private, comfortable, there's a spa and lots of hiking trails. It's quiet off-season, so there will be no one around," he added.

Hope there's a fireplace. "That's perfect," I said, my happiness and excitement rising. "Oh, and Jim?"

"Yes?"

"Don't expect to do too much hiking."

I told Rachel that I was going away with Jim and that she'd be staying with Maya. She barely looked up from her phone, so I said to let me know if she had any questions. Moments later she texted from the room next door—that killed me—to ask who would be bringing her to basketball. Apparently my plans had registered.

With Rachel's sort-of blessing, Jim and I left at eleven that Friday morning. The man at the registration desk gave us an early check-in, and by lunchtime, we were walking into our room. Jim dealt with the bellman as I texted Rachel, and then silenced the ringer. I went to look out the window at the rugged terrain below. It was mid-December and winter was in full force, the gray sky melting into hills and mountains in the distance. Jim came to stand behind me, guiding me backward slowly, until I was folded into the contours of his body.

"It's beautiful," I said. Then I forgot about the mountains as he kissed the back of my neck. We never bothered to order a meal; we were too busy getting reacquainted. Jim's lovemaking was steady and strong. At moments, he looked straight at me, and I felt happy and a little shy. At other times, we were moving in sync, and I wasn't aware of anything but the warmth of his body.

A couple of hours later, we sat on the loveseat by the crackling fireplace. I'd gotten my wish, actually several of my wishes, and then we talked. I felt relaxed, like I didn't have a bone in my body, and was wondering whether to share this fascinating fact, when Jim spoke first.

"I'm really glad we're here," he said.

"Me too. This is so nice. I was hoping we could have a fire. It's chilly up here. I'm so happy being with you, away from everything else."

"That's good to hear. I brought my ex here once—I hope that's not a bad thing to say—and it was a disaster. She hated everything: the drive up, remote location, and the outdoor activities. We fought the whole time, which was par for the course."

I squeezed his hand. "Rachel has shown me what it's like to have deep bond over many years." I smiled. "But now getting to know you, I know there's a whole different level of closeness that can be possible."

He grabbed my hand. "I feel exactly the same way."

We held each other and enjoyed the silence. Finally he raised a question. "You told me you lost your parents, but didn't elaborate. Is there some reason you didn't say more? You don't have to, but . . . ."

I spoke more openly this time. "It was a car accident, a drunk driver careening down a one-way street." Seeing how Jim's eyes widened, I recalled how much I hated discussing the accident. People always felt sorry for me, a sentiment I wanted to avoid with him. I'd nip it in the bud. "About my parents and Rachel growing up without a dad . . . please don't pity us."

The look on his face was tender. "Oh, Victoria. No pity, but I am sorry." He cupped my face and kissed me. "You've had to deal with being on your own for a long time. It's a lot."

"Yes, I had to grieve at a young age. People hadn't . . . stayed around." As my eyes filled with tears, Jim looked like he wanted to say something. Instead he pulled me closer.

"But I'm happy now," I said.

"Enough talking for the next, um, six weeks?" I laughed and leaned in to kiss him. His chest felt like home.

The rest of the time flew by. We didn't bother to leave the suite. We just kept putting the room service trays outside the door, not needing more excitement than each other's company, until Rachel texted on Sunday morning. She was at her team's basketball game, which had been rescheduled from the day before—writing during half time. As soon as I started reading, I knew it was time to leave our quiet idyll.

She was at her team's basketball game, writing during half-time: *"Collette just texted Lexi: 'How come you get to sit there and I'm stuck with Rachel. She's weird!' I can see her phone.'"*

I instantly felt angry—why couldn't that kid just leave Rachel alone already?—then guilty. I'd been having the time of my life while my daughter was being picked on. *"Sit with Maya!"* I wrote.

"Not allowed to change seats," she responded.

"Did you have fun at her house?" I held my breath after I'd hit "send."

"Yes. Gotta go. Biii." she wrote.

As soon as Jim went down to check out, I texted Rachel again: *"Be home soon. Please thank Maya's mom for letting you stay, taking you to the zoo and the game, and all the other stuff. Love you."*

I went over to the window and snapped a photo of the scenery. It was so beautiful. I'd have to get someone on the staff to take one of Jim and me, which reminded me of the other hotel photo: Lee and Peter. They were the last people I wanted to think about.

Jim came back into the room with the bellman, and I shoved the other thought to the side. "It's beautiful outside, though chilly," he said. "Next time we have to hike."

"Deal," I said.

I wondered whether he'd heard about Rachel's basketball game and my dustup with Lee? I'd been waiting for him to bring it up, but he failed to mention it.

On the car ride home, we spoke about our favorite travel destinations. My list was short, but Jim had traveled a lot, and told me about visiting Australia, how beautiful the shoreline was, and how nice everyone had been.

Since he was in the mood to chat, I decided to broach a topic that had been on my mind, "I've been wondering, did you ever want kids?"

Jim thought for a minute. I wasn't sure if I'd put him on the spot, or if he was choosing his words carefully. "I had a lot of things I wanted to do by the time I turned forty: make the leap from teacher to admin; get promoted on that level; see the world because my dad worked and worked, and played golf on Sundays, but he always told me he regretted never traveling anywhere exotic. That stayed with me. I took the chance to see other continents, broaden my perspective. And my ex wasn't the right person. After the divorce I dated some, but nothing ever clicked." Jim sounded comfortable, matter-of-fact.

We rode together, my hand in his, comfortable in the shared quiet.

"There's something I haven't told you," he finally said. "I met my ex-wife, Tonya, years ago, while I was living in the city. I was finishing my first master's, trying to get certified in teaching. We lived together for a couple of years and she broke it off, hoping to meet someone more high-powered, I think."

That was the Tonya that Lee had mentioned. Despite Lee's best efforts at causing tension, Jim was discussing the past on his terms. I squeezed his hand.

"I moved out and moved on, teaching, trying to figure out my life. A bunch of years later, I went back for a second master's and had to take on debt." Jim breathed. "One day, Tonya called. She said she regretted breaking up and wanted us to try again." He laughed. "I later figured out, she was turning thirty and freaking out about being single. But at the time, I followed the path of least resistance and moved back into her apartment. She paid the bills while I finished up my practicum and got licensed."

I listened, digesting it all. We were almost at my house, on a slow-moving back road. Jim cleared his throat.

"I had my doubts, but agreed to marry her." He paused, gathering steam. "She paid off my student loans too." For a second, I thought he was going to cry.

"Jim, spouses pay off one another's debts. It's not like you did anything to be ashamed of."

"I haven't gotten to the worst of it. We didn't have the best relationship. We argued constantly. I finally told her we needed to split up."

"I'm sorry; that must have been difficult," I said. "But you tried. Things didn't work out. It happens."

"Not according to Tonya. She accused me of using her for

financial gain, and threatened to take me to the cleaners. It turns out, in New York when a degree is financed by a spouse, it becomes 'property of the marriage.'" He shifted uncomfortably in the driver's seat. "The judge ruled that Tonya was entitled to 50 percent of my wages." He continued to grip the wheel tightly.

I pulled one of his hands toward me and held on with all my might. "I'm glad you told me about all that. Is this what you alluded to, the story you didn't want to get into?" He nodded and clenched his jaw. "Well, I want you to know, the money stuff, it isn't that important to me."

We were at a red light. Jim looked over and held my gaze, and then he leaned in and kissed me until the traffic light turned green and the drivers behind us started blaring their horns.

We drove quietly for a few moments. Noticing that he looked completely drained, I decided it was time to lighten the mood. "I've been meaning to ask you about the photos in your apartment. You traveled alone?"

"Sometimes. Or with friends. I once accompanied a group of students on a tour through Europe. I'll tell you about that sometime, but let's just say: never again."

We laughed.

He reached for my hand. "Vic, I'm glad I told you about my divorce." He paused and I leaned over to kiss him again. "You know," he said, "I can really see us together."

I held on tightly. "Me too."

Sixteen
Thin Ice

When I got back from the resort, Rachel asked if I could take her ice-skating during the half-day the school had scheduled toward the end of the week. When the day arrived, I switched a few patients around, and Rachel and I went to a local rink to skate and drink hot chocolate. For the rest of the afternoon, she lounged around in her sweats, reading, watching preteen Disney, and giggling, back to her old self. On days like this, I wondered if her quiet and lonely persona had been a mirage? When she wasn't in the classroom fending off the cliques, and now that she'd made a friend, she seemed like a happy and well-adjusted girl.

The next morning my daughter was back in class, and I was in the Mayfair office, finishing up with a couple I'd been seeing for the past few months. The hours flew by and I marveled at my stress-free reentry.

Then Amy strolled in, ranting about how she'd run for office in the PTA, but had been turned down. "How can they reject someone like me for a volunteer position? I have years of legal experience, great organizational skills. I swear there's something wrong with these people. All they do is follow their preteen children around and go to PTA meetings. Their worlds are so small." I'd asked her to say more about the woman or tell me what she imagined, but she'd changed the subject. Twice.

What wasn't she sharing?

I'd been wondering when all the boundary issues would come to a head. I assumed it wouldn't be long now until all my problems with Lee bled into the sessions with my patients from town.

Amy was two steps ahead: "I heard someone faced off with the PTA uber-bitch at a rec game a few weeks ago. Gave her a dirty look and insinuated she needed to get a life. My husband caught the tail end of it before Lucy's game started, but he wasn't sure who the woman was."

I was about to tell her that I lived in Mayfair and had a child at Barnum, before working my way up to the scene in the gym, but she cut me off. "I ran into a woman at the supermarket who was in tears, sobbing in the frozen food aisle about how her kid, Francesca, is being bullied and has started cutting herself. I didn't catch the whole story, but apparently Francesca got into it with Collette, and after that, Fran was done. The kids targeted her, sending texts, posting on Instachat, leaving her out. The mom, Emily, was beside herself—not that I blame her. I gave her your number. Maybe you can make a referral."

My head was pounding. The last thing I needed was another Barnum mom calling to confide about Lee. I nodded as the hour ended and texted Julie asking if she could give me another hour of peer supervision. I also filed away the story about a fifth grader who'd started cutting. That was upsetting.

Once Amy had left, I called Jim. He picked up on the first ring.

"Hey," I said.

"Hi." I loved the rich tenor of his voice. "Glad you called."

I wasn't about to mention patient problems and went with a lighter touch. "How are things with you?"

"Well with this wind and rain, no one can get around, or make it here for their interviews, and everyone is panicking. Other than that, work is a laugh-riot."

Jim sounded stressed, and I was glad I hadn't started off with a complaint. "Sounds like you need another shoulder rub. If only I were there to relieve some of the pressure."

He sighed loudly into the phone. "That would be nice . . . ."

I was worried he'd heard that Lee and I had argued at the rec game. Since he viewed her as "harmless," I wasn't sure he'd believe my side of things, though I knew what I had seen. When he failed to mention anything, I left it.

We hung up, promising to speak later in the evening. Then Rachel texted telling me she'd been hoping to move up a reading group, but it hadn't happened. She was still with Collette, who'd been ignoring her. Despite the patient conflicts, Lee situation, and Rachel's difficulties, I managed to put one foot in front of the other and go into work.

The following morning I was at the Westchester office where I started the day on Tuesdays, working until noon before heading into New York, and seeing my city patients into the evening. The red light was blinking on my answering machine. There were two messages asking me to reschedule.

Having sworn that at the next cancellation, I'd run over to Jim's school, I texted: *Can we meet midday?* If I jiggered everything in the right way, I'd have a block of free time and could stop and see him on my way into the city. He sent a "thumbs up," and said he'd see me at noon.

Two dabs of perfume and ninety minutes later, it was déjà vu as I passed through the doors of his school and walked down the main hallway to the administrative offices. I gave my name to the secretary, hoping I wouldn't run into the headmaster who'd been so condescending.

Several moments later, Jim was walking toward me, smiling. "Want to come in back?"

"Sure!" He led me toward his office and invited me to sit

down. Once the door was closed, I decided to pull his leg a little and leaned over the desk, exposing a thin red bra strap and an unflinching amount of cleavage. "Mr. Reilly, I'm here to discuss my daughter's application."

Jim reddened a little, which was adorable. "I'm sure someone, somewhere has led with that."

"You can't blame a girl for trying."

We stared at one another across the desk. "Maybe we should table this discussion," I laughed, glancing around at the diplomas and photos that lined the wall. "So this is the inner sanctum, the room where futures get made?"

Jim shook his head like I was being silly, and closed a file he'd been looking at.

"Would you like to get some coffee or something?" I asked.

"Something would be nice." Jim stood up and ushered me into the hallway. "How much time do you have?" He asked as we headed downstairs and into the parking lot.

Ten minutes later, we were in his bed, my red bra on top of a crumpled pile of silk next to the bed. Sex in the middle of the day—at my age! I felt like a character in a book or film, hair spilling over the pillow, sunlight streaming into the room, as Jim kissed my neck and shoulders.

"Lunch has now become my favorite meal," he said, pulling me on top of him. I knew just what he meant.

The time flew by. I didn't want to leave, but forced myself to sit up and resist the temptation to go in for another kiss. I lowered my left leg to the ground and was about to get out of bed, when Jim tried to pull me back on top of him. "Sorry, I have to leave. But let me make it up to you. Can you come over for dinner on Friday?"

"Definitely." We sealed it with a kiss, and then wasted no time jumping out of bed, getting dressed, and making it to the elevator in record time. Jim drove us back to his school, parking near where

I'd left my car. I blew him a kiss before making my way to the city. I let my mind wander as I drove.

Things were great between the two of us, but I knew it was only a matter of time before Lee made trouble.

Rachel was at the kitchen table when I walked in, figuring it made sense to prep her. "So, you remember my friend, Jim."

"Obviously. You just introduced us."

"Right. Well, he's coming over on Friday." I didn't know how long to wait after introducing them at the game; was a couple of weeks too much? "Is that okay?" I asked, worried she'd be threatened or overwhelmed.

Rachel gave me a "whatever" look, and told me a new planet had been discovered in the solar system, if I wanted I could read the article with her before bed.

The next couple of days passed quickly. Before I knew what hit me, it was Friday afternoon, and I was thirty minutes behind in my cooking prep and house cleaning, running in circles trying to get the place and menu in shape for Jim. Rachel was sitting on the sofa as I flew past.

"Why are you being weird?" she asked.

"I'm not."

She began staring at her phone, ignoring me. "You're not making chicken nuggets again, right?"

"I got the ones shaped like dinosaurs. I thought Jim would enjoy those."

Rachel looked appalled, and I laughed. "Kidding. I'm baking a chicken."

"That's better." She started walking up the stairs. "Getting dressed," she called over her shoulder.

Moments later the doorbell rang, and I went to peek out the

side window. Jim was standing there, his face friendly and open. He had a bottle of wine and a bouquet of flowers . . . and he was forty-five minutes early.

With circles under my eyes, pale cheeks, stringy hair and no makeup, I looked like an old mop. I glanced in the mirror by the entrance. At this rate, it would take a team of aestheticians to make me over. Jim looked freshly showered, and he was wearing a nice jacket.

I ran upstairs to my room and called for Rachel to go down and let him in. Grabbing perfume, accessories, and a hairbrush, I shoved them into a portable shower caddy. I felt like I was on the game show where you won money by being the first to fill your shopping cart. I threw on a tank top with my jeans, then dabbed my lashes with mascara. I glanced in the hallway mirror as I raced downstairs. I looked slightly improved: a mop with eyelashes at least.

They were in the living room. Rachel had changed for dinner. She wore leggings, a T-shirt, and shoes with cute appliqué.

"Candy Crush?" Jim said, pointing to her shoes.

Rachel nodded. "Do you play?"

"I get by."

They started discussing Harry Potter. Then her phone pinged and she began texting with a friend.

During dinner, Jim and Rachel talked about Dumbledore and basketball.

"Do you like teaching?" Rachel wanted to know.

"I'm more of an administrator. But working at a middle school has its moments," he told her.

"Is it anything like Hogwarts?" I couldn't tell if Rachel was trying to be a good hostess, or if she was genuinely interested in learning about Jim. "Seriously, what's your school like?"

"It looks a little like a small college campus. There are a few ivy-covered buildings. Classes are small. The students like it, I hear."

Rachel took a photo of herself and started tapping the screen to compose a message.

"Rach, no texting at the table."

"It's a 'Snap.'" She rolled her eyes. "No one texts that much anymore. Can I go upstairs now?"

"You have dishes in your future."

"Awwww."

After the dishes were done, I led her upstairs and told her she could read for thirty minutes before bed.

Then it was just Jim and me.

"Rachel is a really smart and funny kid. I like her a lot, Vic." Before I could respond, Jim led me over to the sofa and leaned toward me.

"Mom!" Rachel called. "Is my quarter zip clean? I want to wear it tomorrow."

"Be right back," I whispered. "You have to go to sleep, hon," I called up to Rachel.

When I'd come back into the room, Jim and I kissed until I tore myself away. Watching him drive off, I promised myself it wouldn't be much longer before I'd feel like he could stay over sometimes.

The next morning was Saturday. Rachel was sleeping late. It was raining hard, and the house was peaceful. I checked my machine: all quiet at the office. As the bathtub filled, I enveloped myself in soapy, hot water and wished I were splashing around with Jim. I soon heard Rachel's voice through the bedroom door: "Mom, where are you?"

"In the tub, honey."

"Zoe called. It's like the first weekend in ages that she doesn't have travel practices or scrimmages, and she's staying in the city. They invited me to sleep over. Can I go?"

The girls hadn't seen each other in a couple of months. I was thrilled she'd reached out now. A true friend was exactly what my child needed. "Of course. Just let me know what time and I'll drive you."

"I'm invited for the day, for lunch and dinner. Can I miss basketball?"

"Fine by me. Email your coach."

I heard her moving down the hallway as she FaceTimed Zoe. "Be there soon. My mom will drive me."

My heart was beating fast. Now I could visit Jim. Stepping out of the bathtub and wrapping myself in an oversize towel, I grabbed my cell and pressed his name. It was raining like crazy, and I expected his team's football game to be canceled.

My eyes fell on the FaceTime button. Did I dare? What if he was with friends and someone saw me?

Seconds later his face popped up. "Are you wet?"

I panned down to my bare shoulder, and he didn't miss a beat.

"You know, it looks like you had some trouble with the knot on your towel. Would you like me to help you tie it properly?" he said.

I repositioned the camera to capture my face. "That's the best offer I've had today."

We continued looking at each other until I finally broke his gaze. "Actually, Rachel got invited to sleep at her friend's house. And I was wondering if we could get together even though it's last minute?"

Jim looked surprised. "The field is flooded so they called the game. I was supposed to be at a dinner with people from work later, but I'll let them know I'm exercising the option to use my plus-one." He smiled at the screen. "I'm really glad you called."

"Me too."

"The dinner is for senior administrators and a few members

of the board," Jim volunteered. "Lee and Jack are hosting, and it's casual."

Dinner at Lee's home seemed like a terrible idea, but backing out now would be too obvious. I felt my anxiety rise. Lee would probably make all sorts of snide comments. Imagining tense exchanges and thinking about the nastiness that lay under her lilting tone made me feel jumpy. I couldn't discuss any of that with Jim. But at least I could ask what to wear. "She's so fashionable. Casual for her probably means a ball gown."

Jim laughed. "Let me get the invitation." He was back moments later. "Cocktail attire."

More anxiety. I couldn't wear the black sheath again. It was time to buy a new dress.

We hung up, agreeing to meet at his apartment, and my dread at seeing Lee mixed with a thrill of excitement. I was spending the night at Jim's! First, I had to get Rachel moving. "Hon, I need to run out to the County Center. Please pack your stuff. Be back in an hour and we'll leave then, okay?"

At the store, I chose an elegant black suit—on sale—and lapel pin to complete the look, then raced home in time to shove my things into an overnight bag and slip the suit on.

My nerves were all over the place, but I kept it light as Rachel and I drove into the city. "Jim's taking me to a dinner party. It happens to be at the DeVrys'." She made an annoyed face. I tried again. "Are you excited to see Zoe, now that she's finally free?" She nodded, dead-ending me. "You haven't mentioned anything; have you tried to reach out to anyone else? Are you finding nice people, not chasing a closed group?"

"You know I don't have that many choices. We mostly stay with our class. Nothing new."

"What about Maya?"

"I like her. She's really funny."

"Would you like to invite her over again sometime?"

"Probably. I'll see."

Rachel yessed me for the next few minutes, but was mostly silent until we pulled up in front of Zoe's apartment. I glanced in the review mirror. She appeared to be deep in thought, hopefully weighing what I'd said.

"Bye, Rach. Have fun."

I watched her run into the building, praying her time with her friend would go well, and hoping the Barnum cliques hadn't permanently damaged her self-esteem.

I was excited to be spending time with Jim—even if I had to share him with the DeVrys.

It took only thirty minutes to drive back to his place after dropping Rachel at Zoe's. The doorman let me go straight upstairs. Jim was in the doorway, waiting. "You look beautiful," he said, kissing me and holding me close. "Street clothes, no towel?"

I shrugged. "Hope you're not disappointed." He pulled me into the apartment and onto the sofa, and started kissing me again.

Jim buried his face in my neck: "I wish we could block out the rest of the world." I was so swept up in the urgency of his needs, the intensity of the moment that I felt like telling him he was the one.

We sat side-by-side as he ran one finger up and down my shoulder and along the length of my arm, slowly, languidly. I was free of PTA moms and problems . . . until it was time to leave.

As the navigation system announced our arrival, my stomach lurched. Hopefully Lee wouldn't provoke me.

The valet opened my door.

"Lee and Jack hire staff to park whenever they host," Jim was saying. "Despite their success, they're nice people."

That was news to me. I'd rather stick a pin in my eye than

eat salad and pheasant—or whatever was on the menu—with the DeVrys. But Jim had to work with them, and I'd have to toe the line if I wanted any sort of relationship with him.

A butler opened the sky-high metal doors. "There's a helipad," Jim whispered. As Lee came down a long hall to greet us, I glanced around at the white walls and modern art, breathing in to steel myself. The dinner would be fine. I'd make sure of it. She stared at my new suit and pin: "Victoria, welcome to our home. And Jim. Mwah."

Everyone had arrived. Lee steered us into a rhombus-shaped library filled with leather-bound volumes. Dostoyevsky, Tolstoy, Foucault. I bet she hadn't read any of them.

Jack was just as I remembered him from the evening at Jim's club: broad, probably an ex-football player. He stepped forward, handing me a glass of rosé and Jim a tumbler of amber liquid. "Thanks for coming, Victoria." His voice echoed across the room.

There were ten guests for dinner, among them Dr. Lacanne, the headmaster, who either pretended or had no recollection of meeting me, his wife, Caroline, and a couple of buttoned-down looking men, William and Henry, board members, I assumed. Their wives were named Sally and Ann. I wasn't sure who went with whom.

The talk was mostly about "numbers" and "the yield," admissions terms that were of little interest to me. Jim stayed close and even wrapped an arm around my shoulder a few times. I studiously avoided locking eyes with Lee.

When it was time to eat, we made our way to an enormous circular dining room with a cathedral ceiling and a gigantic venetian-glass chandelier that hung down two stories until crowning over the table. I was seated close to Lacanne and Lee. Caroline was at the other end of the table near Jack and Jim. Sally, Ann, and William rounded out the group.

Lacanne made a "little boys room" joke and slipped out. I got up, intending to follow.

"Victoria, please use the powder room in my office." Lee was gesturing to a stressed out looking woman in a black dress and white apron. "Josafina . . . ."

The maid led me down a long and well-lit hallway until we were in another part of the house. Lee's office was large and paneled with family photos and an oil painting of her and Jack on the wall. As I passed by the desk, a silver frame caught my eye, in it a photograph of Lee and Jim, arm-in-arm. "In recognition, Ten Years of Service to the Guardian School" had been engraved, along with the date. "I knew him first," was her message.

When I got back to the dining room, I complimented Lee. "Thanks for letting me use your private powder room and see more of your beautiful home," I said, digging into the aspic.

For the next several minutes, the guys made a number of golf jokes, and Jim smiled at me. The evening was going better than expected.

As Josefina served the Cornish game hen, William picked up a carrot with his fork, and accidentally dropped it onto his pants. "I think you need a mulligan, Bill," Jack boomed, and all the men laughed. Golf humor was even worse than the tennis stories I'd recently been subjected to.

Lee and Henry were discussing an off-Broadway play they'd seen while Jack glanced at his phone, telling everyone his fantasy football team had traded for the number one draft pick. I thought I saw Caroline roll her eyes.

And then it happened. Someone, maybe William, made a "small world" comment, and Lee pounced. "It IS," she purred, tilting her wine glass slightly toward Josefina, who rushed over to refill it. "Ah bet most of you don't know how small," she held my gaze, and I froze. "Victoria, ah've been wondering. Was that Rachel's daddy that morning at the basketball game?"

I felt Jim's eyes on me. "Just an old friend." I shifted in my chair. "So, Lee, I was looking at the portrait in your study. How long did you have to sit until the artist had finished?"

"A month, maybe less." She dismissed me with a quick wave of the hand. "Jess and I agreed your companion was a very handsome man. Your former fiancé?"

Jim winced. So Lee was willing to publicly embarrass a friend to goad me. That was low, even for her.

I smiled at Jim, but he glanced away and looked down at his plate. I'd be sure to tell him the Colin story and apologize the first second we were alone.

There was a communal shifting as Lee glanced around the table. "Mah Collette heard from Victoria's little Rachel that ah actually went to the same university as Victoria's ex." She turned toward me. "Rachel told me when we chatted that you'd called the wedding off. It was last spring, right? Ah admire you for bouncing back so quickly."

As Sally and Ann exchanged a glance, Jim fought to conceal his anger. I was desperate for a subject change when Caroline cleared her throat. "I think we should all start a school down south, move somewhere warm," she said. "Escape from the frigid temperatures we've been having." I nodded and tried to catch Jim's eye, but he was avoiding me, focusing on Jack: "That reminds me, we should have Jean send that email out to all alumni."

"Good idea," Jack's eyes were glued to his phone. "Back to business. It's almost time for the second-round pick."

I was furious at Lee, but held my head high. "So," I said, "how did you and Jack become involved with Guardian, since Collette attends a different school?"

She threw her head back and laughed. "Why Victoria, you ask the most interesting questions. Always two steps ahead, aren't you?" She took another sip of wine. "Isn't that right, Jackie?"

He looked up from his cell. "Our older daughter, Mariel, is a senior at Guardian," he said, then turned back to Jim, "they're about to post . . . ."

Caroline jumped in. "I think we should discuss the Spring

Gala. I finally spoke with the woman at the Botanical Gardens. It's looking good as far as the venue goes."

I leaned into my chair, my thoughts racing a mile a minute. Lee started pouring coffee from a polished silver service.

"We must be going. Please excuse us." Jim stood up and nodded for me to follow.

Before I could speak, he'd moved around the table, putting a hand on my back and steering me toward the hallway leading to the front door.

Lee sprinted behind. "Lovely to have you," she said as a butler handed us our coats. "I'm sure we'll be seeing a lot more of each other, Victoria."

"Everything was delicious, Lee. It's always a pleasure." Jim said, bending down for a hug.

Seventeen

Into the Dark

As the valet shut the car door and the interior lights went dark, I noticed Jim's knuckles. They were white from gripping the wheel.

We rode in silence. I knew my failure to confide about Colin had really hurt him. The tension and guilt were tearing me up inside.

We were now in his building, standing on opposite ends of the otherwise empty elevator car. "I should have told you. I was waiting for the right time. I'm really sorry."

Jim was quiet until we got into the apartment. After turning on the lights and tossing his coat onto a nearby chair, he stood in the foyer and crossed his arms.

I was about to tell him about my former fiancé's cheating, but he cut me off. "A wedding last spring? That's kind of a big omission, isn't it, Victoria?"

I nodded. "I don't know what Lee told you but—"

"The issue is what *you didn't* tell me." I hadn't seen this before, Jim's angry side.

"Lee warned me about you. I just didn't want to listen." He shifted his posture and glared. I felt as though I'd been slapped; the conversation had devolved so quickly. All I could think was that Lee was at it again, making life impossible for me, as she had for Rachel. As tears of frustration pooled in the corners of my eyes, I struggled to maintain my composure. It felt important for me to hold it together so I looked credible.

"Jim, listen. Please!" I breathed in. "Lee doesn't know anything about me. Please let me explain."

His posture was stiff. "I heard you accused Lee of laughing at Rachel, picking on her."

I wiped my tears. She'd spun things in the worst possible way. "She's going out of her way to make Rachel's life miserable, and she's dangerous. I'm just trying to protect my child."

Jim was shaking his head and closing his eyes, fighting for control. "What do you mean 'dangerous,' Victoria?"

"She's been trying to hurt Rachel. I know it."

"Hurt her how; what do you know? You're losing me."

"She's out to get us."

Jim furrowed his brow. "That's a big accusation. It sounds . . . it's not like you. Where is this even coming from?"

"I can't tell you. But I know she's out for blood."

"How do you know this?" I couldn't repeat what Maureen said. "There's a chat room," I said. My words sounded odd, even to my ears.

Jim looked skeptical. "Lee revealed a plot in a chat room?"

"It was anonymous, but I know it was her."

He was staring at me, a strange look in his eyes. "Let's sit down," he said in a careful tone that made me defensive. "Are you okay?"

We were now on the sofa an arm's distance apart. I crossed my arms and leaned back onto the cushions. "I'm a psychologist. Don't you think I'd know if I weren't?"

He rubbed his temples and shook his head. "Listen, I'm worried. This sounds . . . unusual, Victoria. You can't just accuse people of going after you based on postings in anonymous chat rooms."

"She grilled Rachel and kicked her out of a carpool, then baited me on a school trip, and along with her kid, planned events that excluded mine. Those are the things I can tell you."

Jim's face darkened. "What is it you aren't sharing?"

I thought of Maureen's story about Lee, the accusation that she'd gone after an enemy and been accused of driving a kid to suicidal thoughts and dangerous behaviors. My voice was a whisper. I was close to tears. "I'm sorry. I can't say."

Jim shook his head. Now I was angry too; he was judging me, making no attempt to see things from my point of view.

"Rachel and I haven't had the easiest time of it. A woman live-tweeted during my wedding ceremony late last spring. She posted a sex video on YouTube, starring her and my ex, and all sorts of other stuff on various social platforms just in time to steamroll the vows. My friend, Julie, pulled me aside during the Justice's remarks and showed me, and I called the whole thing off. You can ask her."

Jim's eyes were sympathetic. "I had no idea. That's a terrible story . . . on many levels." He reached for my hand. Neither one of us said anything for a few moments.

"About the wedding and cheating, that's really low. You deserve better. But what does it have to do with Lee? She's no angel. And I can see her asking Rachel questions and letting Collette exclude other girls. But why these suspicions, the idea that Lee's planning to harm you?"

I wished I could tell him what Maureen had said, but patient confidentiality was sacred. "I can't prove it yet, but it's all true. She's behind Rachel's social difficulties and I have reason to believe she'll go after me."

Jim shook his head.

"Can't you see that she intentionally caused trouble tonight by dropping a bomb, creating tension between us? Plus—and I can't reveal specifics—she takes revenge on people. I'm worried that something really bad could happen!"

Jim put up a hand, slowing me down. "I know you're the psychologist, but you sound, I don't know the exact word, 'fixated' or something. Instead of accusing Lee, why don't you look at yourself for a minute? You didn't tell me about the wedding thing, or the fact that the guy showed up recently at Rachel's game, and you keep your guard up, with me too. You haven't been fully honest."

There it was. He was taking Lee's side, overlooking how I'd told him personal things about my family and Rachel's struggles.

"So I'm just suspicious and guarded? It's all me? How come it doesn't matter that she's gone after my kid and made comments to provoke me? You still don't have enough faith in me to trust that the reasons for my fears might be valid?"

There was an unpleasant charge in the air as we regarded each other from opposite sides of the sofa.

"Putting your theory about Lee to the side for a minute, I want to have faith and take you at your word, and guess I could have asked directly about your romantic past. But imagine how I felt, hearing her ask in front of everyone about the man that attended Rachel's game, and even worse, saying that you two were engaged last spring!" He gave me a wounded look. "Do you still have feelings for him?"

"No!" He showed up uninvited to the game, and I made it clear—as I had several times in the past—that I had no interest in further contact."

Seeing the sadness in Jim's eyes, I was disgusted by Lee's modus operandi, stirring the pot to advance her own power and revenge agenda, even if it meant hurting her friends in the process. "Jim, this woman is like a powerful cyclone, destroying innocents in her path. I can't believe she'd treat you like this. And I'm sorry I hurt you by waiting too long to mention the scene at the altar." I reached for his hand. "I should have told you." He didn't budge.

I was flooded once again with the all too familiar fear that another loss was imminent. My panic rose and I kept talking, sounding angry and a bit cagier than I would have liked, "But it isn't fair to lay this all on me, you know."

"How do you mean?"

"Well you've been guarded too," I said through tears.

"I told you all that stuff about my ex, Victoria, even though it was embarrassing. But you haven't even said who Rachel's dad was. And now I find out there's this other person you were serious about. You haven't been forthcoming, and that makes me uncomfortable."

I tried again to explain. "I'm sorry you feel that way. There's no big mystery. I tried to open up to you. I don't usually talk about my parents or give details about Rachel's social problems. As for her father, it's not a secret. I used a sperm donor."

Jim flinched a little. "I didn't know." He adjusted his position on the sofa. "I want to trust you."

I felt my body stiffen. "You keep saying that. What do you mean?"

"Even if you have shared some things with me, whenever the subject of Lee comes up you sound overly suspicious, and that's concerning."

It was unfair that she came off as the sympathetic one, while I was the bad guy.

I was frustrated and drained from the stress of having to rein in feelings, even after Lee had stabbed me in the back, and felt my composure slipping and voice rising. "She's evil, okay? She whispered threats in my ear by the museum dioramas, and went door-to-door with party invitations, but told everyone she didn't have our address, and got Rachel alone so she could grill her about her biological father. Who does that?"

Jim was staring like I was a toddler who'd dropped her ice cream and began convulsing with sobs. He raised his palms and pushed them slightly toward me, in a motion that said: go slow, calm down. His eyes were sad, but distant. His look told me he pitied me for seeing the world through a warped lens.

"Victoria, you sound . . ." he chose his words carefully, "like you've lost perspective."

So, that's how it was?

He patted my hand. I hated the way he was sitting a foot away from me, offering stiff comfort, like I was an elderly aunt. My heart wrenched with sadness and fear. With no romance or intimacy in his touch, this was the beginning of the end.

"Stop patting me. I know what I know."

"Have you spoken with Julie? You've been under stress between Rachel and the move. Is there someone you could call?"

Now he wanted to pawn me off on a friend. Well, Lee was the problem, not me. My mental health was intact, even if Jim couldn't see that.

I chose my words carefully, "Don't worry. I'm fine." I stood up and he followed. "I'm going to go now," I said.

Jim was silent, willing to let me leave, and that hurt. "I didn't choose this, you know," I told him. "I've always been alone, and managed to run my practice and raise my child. Given the nature of my job, there are sometimes things I'm privy to." I could see him calculating. "My theory isn't frivolous or imagined, no matter how it appears to you."

He appeared to be thinking about how to respond. As I watched him, thinking it through and sighing, I saw again that despite the times we'd shared, the romance and friendship, there'd been a shift. Something had changed when my suspicions about Lee were mentioned—he'd chosen the DeVrys over me.

I got up and stepped into the foyer of his apartment. Standing there, sensing that we had no future, my anxiety and anger rose, until I was almost suffocating. Though it had been hard for me to get close, I'd opened up and hadn't pushed when he'd played things close to the vest. Yet, despite several apologies and clarifications, Jim still didn't believe me.

I felt like running off, but it was difficult to walk away. "I have tried opening up to you, so it would be so nice if you could just—"

"Just what? I know you have a child and you put her first, and I understand that. You're a good mother. But there are also two of us *here*." He stopped talking again and stiffened.

"And?" I said.

"And no matter how hard I try, you're still holding back and mistrustful. That's part of the problem."

There it was again. Despite all the things I'd said, he still saw my caution and fear of Lee as suspiciousness. "I guess it's good we're finding all this out now." I stepped toward the door.

"Victoria . . . ."

"What? I don't get this at all! I tried to talk to you, but you haven't acknowledged that maybe you're part of the difficulty here, siding with Lee, taking her version of events as the gospel. It's like you're under her spell or something."

Jim's expression hardened. "As I said, I told you about my ex. And right now we're talking about you—this thing with Lee, your suspicions about her targeting Rachel. She's a grown woman with a busy, fulfilling life. Why would she bother picking a fight with a fifth grader? It doesn't make sense. Not to mention the fact that she and Jack are my bosses, in essence. So, sorry to have to say this, but I think we should take a break."

I'd known that was coming, but the words still hit hard, like a punch to the gut. I fought off the tears that had started to flow.

"I really didn't expect this." I was really angry now. "I went out on a limb introducing you to Rachel. You have no idea what a big step that was, how difficult. And yet you discount it because you believe I'm making things up about Lee!!" I shook my head. "Maybe you should look in the mirror once in a while. It's not just me that's created distance, you know. Goodbye." I left the apartment and sprinted down the hall.

I walked at a brisk clip, fighting off tears, until I made it back to the car. And then the floodgates opened. "Don't think about this now," I told myself. "You tried to explain and he couldn't hear it, accusing you of being overly suspicious. You've got no time for this guy and his sanctimonious attitude—and no room for pressure. Just drive."

And drive I did.

As I steered, Jim's words echoed in my brain: "I think we should take a break . . . ."

There was a lot of traffic and the drive took longer than usual. I cried the entire time, sobbing so hard I could barely see the road. I finally pulled into a gas station and called Julie.

"All relationships have their ups and downs. I love you, Vic. But I think you should call him and ask if you could talk again, try to work things out." Julie's advice was good. I'd think about it, even if she didn't know the pressure I was under. She had it all: stability, perspective, and a glass of Chardonnay in hand.

"Even if you're right, maybe the breakup is for the best," I said. "What kind of future do we have, Jules? What if he wants children? I'm probably too old. And if that happens, a half-sibling might upend Rachel's life. There are too many unknowns. What if Rachel doesn't want him around or he freaks out and runs away from the relationship?"

Julie signed loudly. "The only one who is freaking out is you."

A half an hour later, I was home. After I'd pulled into the driveway, I texted a heart emoji to Rachel and wished her good night, before going inside, having a giant glass of wine, and falling into bed.

Looking back, I could have handled things better, been less insistent about Lee. But that night, as I hugged my pillow, prostrate with grief, all I could think of was that my fear had been

borne out: relying on other people was too risky a proposition, Jim
included. So I pulled the covers over my head and did the usual
when it came to loss. I shoved my feelings into that particular
compartment of my brain, locked the door, and threw away the
key.

Eighteen

The Arms Race

Gutted after the breakup, and unable to shake Rachel's social difficulties, I gave myself a couple of days to hang around the house, even letting Alva do drop-off. When my bathrobe began to take on aspects of my shape as though made from memory foam, I knew it was time to change my approach.

Licking my wounds, I went back and forth, considering the same dead-end options, from selling our place and moving somewhere else to homeschooling. But none of them were viable. Besides, it was possible it wasn't any better anywhere else. I'd have to make this community work.

I noticed an email in my inbox, sent by Lee in her role as PTA president, and felt an immediate surge of embarrassment. She'd broken Jim and I up after I'd made a fool of myself by accusing her of targeting Rachel. At least I knew Jim wouldn't repeat any of that; otherwise I'd never be able to show my face in public again.

The email made mention of several upcoming school events: a karaoke night, fifth grade Colonial Fair, Spring Fling, and school-wide assembly on internet dangers. I noticed that Lee was in charge of not one, but all of the events on the PTA calendar. All roads led to her.

Even though I was riddled with sadness and anxiety, being called "fixated" and overly suspicious was a mischaracterization. No matter what Jim thought, Lee had hurt my daughter and was responsible for the break Jim had requested. Now more than ever I needed to figure out my next move.

〽

Mayfair fell into a long cold spell, one day blurring into the next. I was sitting in my kitchen about to leave for work when Sharon pinged, reminding me I'd agreed to go with her to the upcoming PTA-sponsored karaoke night.

Having barely survived the past few weeks, I was in no mood for more of the school scene. *"Not singing!"* I wrote in response.

"Ha ha. You promised and I bought tickets. Pick me up at 7:00 so we can go together." She signed off and I went into the dining room to get the bag with my paperwork and planner. Rachel's group assignment was left behind on the table, an in-school science project she'd worked on with Collette and Maya. She was supposed to turn it in to their teacher. The thing was due today.

There was the "let her fail" school of parenting. If I stepped up and rescued her every time, she'd never be able to keep all her academic and extracurricular balls in the air. But after what she'd endured over the past couple of months, from Lexi and Collette ousting Francesca to being excluded from parties, I knew that all it took was one glance from a blond, bangle-wearing little diva, or a well-placed PTA mom, and you were out.

I'd bring the report to school, and we'd work on organization at some future point. For now, it was all about the social stuff.

I drove over and parked in the school lot. A door at the back, the section near the music room and gym, was propped open. Cutting through would be easier than walking all the way to the front. I peeked in—the place was a mess: cartons everywhere and chairs stacked six feet into the air. I almost banged heads with the aide who was stationed inside, standing guard, for safety reasons.

"Hi," I said to her. "Can I come through?"

"I think that would be okay. As long as you go up front and sign in at the office."

I nodded. "What's going on?"

"They're replacing the old gym floor. Don't slip. There are piles everywhere. A couple of moms are down the hall, packing up some of the sports equipment so the guys can send it to storage." Her walkie-talkie beeped. "U-haul is here. Excuse me." She went outside, pulling the door shut behind her.

I'd started to make my way down the hall, when I spotted two women several yards ahead, sitting with their backs to me, loading boxes. One was partially hidden by cartons. I recognized her as a mom who favored sunglasses and tennis whites, and seemed to be at the sidelines of every one of Rachel's games. I didn't remember her name, but recalled she always looked glamorous, even in the stands on Saturday mornings. I stepped quickly, eager to get the report to the office.

The taller woman pushed her glasses back on her head as she kneeled down to tape the carton she was packing. She was slender and sinewy. Obviously she had a lot of time and money, and made an effort to exercise often. Bodies like hers signaled resources. Now the other woman was speaking, asking to borrow the tape. I heard a drawl and caught a glimpse of blond hair, and my heart skipped: it was Lee. She was the last person I wanted to see.

I tiptoed back to the door and noticed the sign: EMER-GENCY ONLY. ALARM WILL SOUND. I'd walk by them swiftly and depart with a quick wave.

I headed back down the same hallway again, toward the area where they were working, and inched toward the women. Their conversation made me freeze on the spot.

Lee was speaking: "Those social climbers moved in and just

started bothering our family. That mother, I think she's a lawyah in the city or something. Her hair is all over the place, a big ol' mess. And she wears these boring shapeless suits, and tops them off with matching accessories—ridiculous; it's not 1990 anymore."

She was talking about my patient, Amy.

"From the time she moved in, she just wouldn't let it go, asking *mah* friend Maureen for plans, inserting herself. And her daughter, well, the apple doesn't fall far from the tree. Her kid went after Collette's best friends, Lexi and Hannah."

Social engineering was Lee's specialty. I could predict where this was going. Lee went on: "Those awful people will stop at nothing. Collette had been looking forward all week to a sleepover with Hannah, but that awful Lucy just stole it right out from under her."

"What did you do?" A voice asked.

"Well, it just so happened that the next weekend was Jack's fiftieth, and he wanted to go to our place in Florida, lounge on the boat. We thought, why not invite Hannah's parents, Maureen and Bob? It was adorable; the girls posting their every move on Instachat: bikinis, palm tree, hugging in the pool. I guess Lucy's sleepover with Hannah just got canceled."

Lee's friend laughed.

"And then that awful Lucy's mother invited Hannah to go with her wallflower of a kid to Radio City to see the Rockettes and go ice-skating.

"Was Collette upset?" the disembodied voice wanted to know.

"Absolutely crushed. So I told her she could have a wonderful sleepover party. We spent all day the following Saturday getting decorations and picking a theme. That lawyah was calling and emailing everyone for playdates. She looked so desperate. So finally I sent her an email. I said, 'Look here: Hannah and Lexi are mah daughter's friends.'"

"Good for you."

I stood silently, digesting it all, when Lee started in on me. "Oh and you know who turned out to be the biggest phony of all? The psychologist. I tried to be nice, seeing as she has no husband and she's kind of mousey and all."

Mousey? I wasn't a Ford model, but *mousey* I was not.

She went on, "I actually felt sorry for her, having to work full-time to support her daughter, alone in that big old house, until she started draping herself on our friend Jim like a cheap suit."

Bitch!

"From the minute they moved in, she was just awful. She tried to discipline my child in the hallway, telling her not to bother some girl. And get this—ah tried to be nice at dinner and warn her about the social scene in town, and she lectured me about all people having value. It was hard to take. She thought she was too good for mah friends, she and her PhD."

I was strangely relieved to hear that Lee had it in for me, and I hadn't misread the situation.

She was still speaking. "And as far as that house, well, she took me around. The place was a disaster: leaks and patches, everything in a state of disrepair. Ah wouldn't let a feral cat live there. I don't know who she thinks she's fooling, with her 'elegant mansion on a hill,' but she's a nobody, living like that. Not my kind of person. Let's just leave it at that."

I heard Lee shifting in her chair, sharpening her fangs: "Oh, and I warned all the other women about her house—so unsafe— *told them not to let their little darlin's go over there.* They should avoid these people at all costs."

My chest muscles seized.

"What about the kid?" her friend asked.

"Oh. Collette took pity on her, and tried to do a makeover, but there was no helping that child. Like ah said, the two of them were just awful. *Ah had to get rid of them.*"

I couldn't hear the other woman's response because my heart

was pounding so loudly in my ears. Just as I'd thought, she'd black-balled us, like we were pledges in her college sorority.

It was time to get even. My only question was how.

I couldn't remember the last time I felt this much anger. I wanted out of there . . . and bad. Suddenly the back door opened again. The aide had returned. I raced out and around front to the office, handing the secretary the report.

Lee's version of events confirmed exactly what I'd suspected about Rachel's abrupt shift in fortune. That horrible woman had used the fifth grade girls as pawns, galvanizing their moms to join in her secret revenge scheme. Even if she hated me, I couldn't believe she'd bully my child—and other moms would follow so blindly.

Now I knew for sure what kind of people I'd been up against. This was how Sisyphus must have felt, pushing that boulder up hill, only to have it roll farther back down each and every time.

I vowed to make Lee suffer like Rachel and I had. And then I thought of the photos. I was definitely using them. I'd have to figure out when.

I called Julie, placing the cell phone on speaker, deciding not to mention my revenge scheme. "Hey. It's me, in the car. Can you talk? I won't bore you with the latest developments here in Stepford."

"What happened now?"

"I'll cut to the chase. Lee, the ringleader, thought I insulted her daughter when I told the kid to 'be nice' to another girl. Plus, she didn't like a comment I made about 'finding something inter-esting in everyone.' She thought it was psychobabble, and because of her dislike for me, went around, campaigning, urging others not to spend time with us. That's why Rachel was shut out."

There was silence on the other end of the line. "Get out of here. Are you sure?"

"Yes. It's been a long time coming, and now I'm really done

with letting them push me around and watching them hurt Rachel." Julie cheered me on as I changed gears. "Now I have a question for you about Jim."

Julie waited as I chose my words. "I seem to embody some pop culture phenomenon, the type of thing Dr. Oz would have a show about: professional women who fear abandonment." Under my joke was a well of sadness. I felt the tears start to fall. "Seriously, what's wrong with me?"

She didn't miss a beat. "Your parents' death caused a deep wound. You're still reeling and terrified of getting close, and the possibility of another loss terrifies you, so you pushed him away."

As I was thinking, she spoke again. "Have you heard from him?"

"Not since we broke up."

"You could call him, apologize."

"Maybe. He might not want to hear from me." I decided to bring the conversation around to Julie. "What's going on there?"

She described the latest melee between her daughters, and we laughed for a few seconds before hanging up. I knew Julie's take on the Jim situation was correct. I had been too caught up in suspicions about Lee, and now it was probably too late to fix it. I could call him, but didn't have the energy. I needed all my resources to deal with Lee.

Nineteen

One For the Team

The mom chat room was busy with lots of talk about the upcoming holidays, getting kids through the winter, and dealing with cabin fever. I read different threads, but nothing caught my eye, and no Cheerleader, aka Lee. Maybe I could get something going, entice her.

It was even easier than it looked. Minutes later I'd made an anonymous account and started a thread: "Party Lists: how many is too many?" That was right up Lee's alley. I'd been chatting with a woman from the Midwest about her fourth grader's ice-skating party. A few people chimed in, voting for a large gathering where no one was excluded, especially in elementary school, and I decided to sign off.

If not today, next time. Being blackballed had reinvigorated me, and I was now all in, and swinging. I hated Lee. If there was a way to take her out while modeling decency and kindness for Rachel in other areas of my life, I was going to find it. I had the photos in my arsenal and would continue to gather intel until I figured out exactly what to do to get even with Lee for bullying Rachel and coming between me and Jim.

Which reminded me, I'd been putting off talking to Rachel about that. It was time. First, I'd have to sort out my feelings. And there were so many.

I hadn't fully grieved when my parents had died. After the car accident, Aunt Pearl and I had checked out a library book about orphans. I'd devoured it, and watched "Annie" a thousand times, becoming terrified about how alone I really was. At the time, I'd said goodbye and focused on moving forward. But burying feelings made it hard for me to get close to others and brought a whole new set of problems.

Compartmentalizing clearly hadn't worked when I was a teen, and it did not provide all the answers with the man I'd loved—that I now knew for sure. For the first time in my adult life, I'd make it a priority to process my grief.

I made myself remember everything about Jim from his blue eyes, strong jaw, and the way his arms engulfed me when we had sex, to all the laughter. There were tears sliding down my cheeks as I sobbed. I'd lost him for good.

Other losses ached in unison: our last apartment, the dining alcove where I'd nursed my daughter, memories of her with her BFFs, Zoe and Savannah, playing softball and hanging out at the science club. And Aunt Pearl. I missed her every day. She'd clapped and cheered at my college graduation, presenting me with an envelope from the bursar's office, a receipt signifying my tuition had been paid. She'd adored Rachel, insisting our girl would be the first woman elected president.

The hurt was there when I thought of my parents too. It was just a duller, broader version. I'd never gotten to find out about their childhoods, hear how they fell in love, or ask for advice.

People always seemed to go to their mothers in times of need. I'd learned to lean on my friends. Birthdays were particularly hard; I forced myself to ignore the sad and empty feelings. But no more. I allowed my mind to process the losses even further. My parents would never hear Rachel giggle, or know I'd gotten a PhD. The tears fell until my head hurt and I couldn't think anymore.

Rachel finally texted. She was almost home from the library. Maya's mom was dropping them off.

I went downstairs and opened the door. "Hey, honey. How are you?"

"Good." She put her backpack down in the hallway and turned around to look at me.

"Lots of homework?" I asked.

"Some. We also hung out."

"I still want to have Maya and her mom over. Is that okay?"

"Maybe. I'll see." She raced up to her room. At least she seemed happier.

Later in the day, I was in the living room plodding through my billing, anything to distract myself. I wasn't used to the heaviness that had settled in my chest, the shadows playing in the corners of my mind. Rachel came into the room. "Mom?" She waited until she had my full attention. "Everyone plays soccer, fall and spring. I'm done with softball and I'm switching this coming season."

After being in my head for so many hours, it wasn't easy shifting gears from my parade of losses to my child's real-world concerns. Rachel was folding her arms and stuck her chin out. "Can you please find out what the other girls are doing to get ready for the soccer season?"

I sighed. "It's probably better if you ask them, Rach."

She shook her head. "They might not tell me."

Then why would you want to be with people like that? Preteens were mystifying. Though I did understand that she didn't want to be the only one who hadn't adequately trained. "I'll do my best to find out, but you should try to ask around."

"No! I want you to do it for me."

As she dug her heels in, I found myself thinking again of Jim, how I'd taken a stand and blown it, and still hadn't told Rachel. She'd asked if he was coming over again and I'd said something innocuous like "not sure," and changed the subject.

I made a mental note to reach out about preseason soccer and be sure to discuss the Jim breakup with Rachel.

The following afternoon I was at pick-up and overheard a couple of fifth grade moms discussing a carpool. "Hey," one said, looking cornered, as she brushed past. "You were on that email, right? See you at soccer."

When Rachel appeared, we started walking to the car and I told her there were probably clinics we didn't know about. She texted Maya, and they decided to check with Collette.

We were now belted in and driving. "So, hon." she didn't look up from her phone. "Well, I'll just say it. Although there were a lot of nice things about Jim and he's a decent guy, it didn't work out between us." I exhaled and quickly brushed a tear from my eye.

She looked off to the side, thinking about how to respond. "I'm sorry because I know you liked him and he seemed nice. What happened? Was he like Colin?"

I shook my head, worried my worst fears were realized, and that she'd gotten used to having him around and would now be scarred. "He *was* nice. But we had a disagreement and couldn't settle it," I told her.

I wiped my eyes as my daughter responded, "Remember how you told me to be friends with Maya, even when I wasn't sure? Well, maybe you should take your own advice and work it out. People deserve a second chance."

I felt a surge of pride. Rachel was compassionate and valued people—not like some of the kids I'd seen around. "I'll think about it," I said as we drove up the hill to the house. At this point, I doubted whether Jim would even take my calls.

A couple of days later, she showed me an entry on her phone's notepad app. She and Maya had approached Lee during pick-up and asked about soccer. Lee had spelled the practice turf's name and dictated the time and day slowly, waiting until each girl had typed in and saved all the info. She'd made them read it back just to be sure. The note said everyone was practicing on Tuesday evenings at seven o'clock.

"Mom, are you listening?" I hadn't been. Hearing Lee's name brought me right back to the dinner party, the night she'd caused my fatal argument with Jim. "Sorry, honey, what were you saying?" Rachel gave me an annoyed look. "Please pay attention. Lee gave us the info. Can I go tonight?"

"Sure."

Had I not been so preoccupied I might have thought twice; after all, it was Lee we were dealing with.

We arrived at the turf a few minutes early. Rachel scanned her phone. "Maya just texted. Her mom left late; they're almost here." As we waited, Rachel strapped on her shin guards and sipped water. Suddenly the facility door opened and I started to get a funny feeling. Several moments later there they were: all the girls in the class exiting the facility. Running two-by-two toward the parking lot, they were all in matching shorts and cleats.

Lee had intentionally told Rachel and Maya the wrong time, ensuring they'd miss the practice.

I told Rachel to wait in the car and then got out and walked in the direction the girls had gone, until I found Lee's giant black SUV. She was in the passenger's seat, reading something on her phone. I motioned for her to open her window.

"This was really low, Lee, even for you."

"Ah have no idea what you're talking about." She was smirking.

My stomach clenched as I tried to stay calm. "Rachel and Maya. Spelling out the name of the turf, dictating slowly and checking twice; only you gave them the wrong time. They missed the practice and probably pissed off the coach. You made sure of that."

My palms were sweating and my heart was hammering in my chest. I could barely contain my anger.

"Mah stars. You give me way too much credit, Victoria. And

since you and Rachel are here, ah don't understand whah you're so worked up. All's well that end's well, isn't that right?" She was smirking again.

I imagined slapping her and leaving finger marks on her perfectly rouged cheeks. "Stay the hell away from my daughter, Lee," I said, a little more loudly than I would have liked, before turning on my heel and walking back to the car.

⋔

"What happened after that?" Julie asked. We were having coffee near my office at a city Starbucks a few weeks after it had all fallen apart with Jim. She and her family were in the city for Christmas, visiting relatives in New Jersey.

"I took Rachel and Maya out for a smoothie."

I rubbed my temples while pausing for breath. The holidays were lonely this year, depressing without Aunt Pearl and Jim. I decided to tell Julie how I'd made things festive by handing Rachel a box the size of a kayak and watching as she unwrapped it to reveal a smaller box, repeating this exercise several more times, until coming upon a small jewelry case. She smiled when I described the scene: Rachel jumping up and down after discovering the pair of gold heart earrings, centered in a tiny velvet nest. "Pierced?! Thank you," she'd screamed. "You know, Jules, it was a bright spot in an otherwise joyless month, make that year."

Julie was making soothing sounds. "You guys have been through a lot. It will get better. I know it. These women are a bunch of assholes, Vic. Rachel will come through this and it will all be fine." She waited for me to go on. "What did Rachel say about missing the practice?"

I barely had the energy to recap. "Later when we were alone in the car, Rachel was upset. She asked if Lee had made a mistake about the schedule. I said 'perhaps,' and bit my tongue."

"Why didn't you tell her it was deliberate? Let her see what lowlifes you've been dealing with—better yet, make a plan to get even," Julie wanted to know.

"Rachel asked if we could organize a soccer class and not include Collette and a few of the others. I told them that we shouldn't stoop that low. We're really better than that. But between you and me, I'd love to get revenge."

"I would have told Carly the same thing. But the nastiness you describe makes me burn."

"Things were good in the city." I sighed. "I pushed the move to Mayfair, and since that day I haven't done anything right."

"Don't sell yourself short, Vic. What happened between you and Jim isn't your fault. And as far as the soccer thing, I can't blame you for being furious. They've made your daughter miserable and lied about the practice location. I wonder how these women sleep at night." She paused for a breath.

"I wish you lived here." I said, speaking rapidly, cramming it all in before our short visit was up.

"Next time, I promise I'll stay longer." We hugged and said goodbye.

Later on at dinner, I told Rachel that it was time I put Lee in her place, and tell everyone in town who didn't know what a bully she was.

"Please don't say anything! They already don't like me and you'll make things worse." Rachel's eyes were panicked. "Promise me you won't do anything. I can handle it."

It was a dilemma, choosing whether to let the world know how aggressive and nasty Lee had been, or respect Rachel's wishes for me to put Lee's treatment of us to the side. I told Rachel I'd never intentionally do anything that would harm her, but reiterated that I had to figure out something to make sure Lee stopped picking on her.

While we were speaking, Rachel asked if I'd called Jim. I told her that I cared about him, but we weren't suited for a long-term relationship. She nodded, and in her characteristic preteen way, displayed no further interest in my love life.

That made two of us. Given how dispirited I felt, I couldn't imagine entering into a romantic relationship ever again.

Twenty

The Social Networks

It had been a few weeks since the scene at the turf, and even though there had been no further incidents with Lee, I told myself it was merely the calm in the eye of the hurricane. A major storm loomed.

I was in my Upper East Side office where my first patient had canceled; his OCD rituals were too debilitating and he couldn't get out of the house. I left a message, encouraging him to think about a medication consult, and then distracted myself by scrolling through Facebook.

I peeked at Julie's page. She'd posted a picture of herself and Carly shopping for bathing suits. They were going on a Bahamas cruise, nice.

Against my better judgment, I went to Jim's page. I had been expecting to look at an old photo like the one he showed me from a college reunion two years ago: seven men in flannel shirts and jeans, all covered in five o'clock shadows.

I should have stopped looking, but I couldn't. My jealousy was a riptide, reeling me in deeper and deeper. Seeing Jim's handsome face just made me miss him even more, and I sat, paralyzed as the page loaded with photos. The first revealed Jim, arm-in-arm with an auburn-haired woman who was so beautiful, I couldn't breathe.

Not only was he seeing someone new, she was a tall, gorgeous red-head, different from me in every possible way. The pictures broke my heart. He and the woman, together in every shot, smiling and laughing. In one photo, she was whispering something in his ear. I glanced at Jim and the redhead laughing in Yankees hats; eating ice cream; ice-skating. What was next: sandcastles on the beach? I couldn't stand it.

It was out there for everyone to see: a love affair between my ex-boyfriend and this mysterious woman. If he'd moved on that quickly, he'd never really loved me at all. I thought back to the dinner party, how Lee had broken us up. Jim and his new girl-friend were probably double dating with the DeVrys at this very moment.

I started to cry, but stopped myself. If I gave in to this, I wouldn't get through the day. I dialed Julie, but her cell just rang. I thought of going for a run, but I didn't have my workout stuff. So I sat feeling sidelined, the wilted wallflower at a high school dance.

Change the channel, I told myself. Do not think about Jim and his new girlfriend. Or Lee. It was her fault we'd broken up in the first place. "I hate you, Lee," I told the empty room.

It was juvenile and reminded me of how Rachel had been angered by the villain in a princess movie—she was two at the time—and shouted at the TV, "I hate you, evil queen!" She'd stomped her foot and balled her fists. I'd bitten the inside of my cheek to keep from laughing.

Thinking about Rachel's childhood grudge cheered me up a lit-tle. To get myself through the rest of the day, I made a mental plan:

Step 1: Eliminate all social media, at least for today (who was I kidding? It would be years before I'd be able to get the picture of Jim and the tall beautiful woman out of my mind).

Step 2: Think about something else. Visualize a pleasant image, like a puppy. We had an Irish Setter growing up. He was so sweet, with his big brown eyes and soft sweet tongue, and silky red hair. Red hair! Ugh. Next.

Step 3: Distract yourself. Read a magazine.

I went to the waiting room and grabbed a copy of a news magazine. The lead story was about adolescents and bullying. Not exactly the thing to calm me down.

I clicked on Rachel's classroom's home page, wondering if there were any updates about what they were working on in school. A photo of three small blond girls laughing and smiling came up. I recognized Lexi and Collette, who were photographed on a field trip. They looked so happy and carefree. I wished it were my kid giggling with friends.

The phone rang, startling me. It was later than I'd thought. Amy had missed her hour and was leaving a rambling message. She'd gone over to Barnum because her daughter had received hurtful texts from some kid at school, and after meeting the principal, had "gotten caught up in something." Hopefully she wasn't trawling the internet again, or—worse yet—posting.

My next clients, the couple with the infertility issues buzzed. After ushering them in, I tried my best to listen as the woman described pregnancy symptoms, but I felt like I was sleepwalking, lost in a stiff-limbed trek through my own worst nightmare. The session ended. I put the tea kettle on and willed myself to keep going.

This is your fault, Evil Queen. My blood boiled. I couldn't wait to get even with Lee. There were still five minutes before Maureen's appointment. Maybe there would be an interesting development in one of the chat rooms; something I could use to get revenge.

When the buzzer sounded, I reluctantly closed the laptop. I still had the photos but hadn't yet come up with a way to put them to good use.

I managed to focus on the last hour of the evening before

closing up the office and driving home where Rachel and I had dinner together. She showed me a website on her phone. It was for the store in the closest mall where all the kids got their accessories.

"Subtle, Rach."

"Come on. Please. Can I get these ear cuffs? I'll only put tiny studs next to them. It's not like I'm going to wear five hoops at a time."

"I'll think about it. So still eating lunch with Maya these days?" I asked.

"Usually." I was relieved to hear she'd been maintaining that friendship. "At the risk of becoming repetitive, Rach, want to invite her over again? Or all go to a movie?"

"Maybe."

The next morning I unlocked my city office. Amy was waiting, squeezing an appointment in before work. She'd finally spotted me around school and had wasted no time in announcing that she'd seen me at the other end of the campus fields over the weekend, and had heard from one of the moms that I was the parent of a fifth grader, and lived in town.

This was the boundary stuff I'd been dreading. Amy was still speaking; hopefully she hadn't noticed my nervousness. "Why did you listen to me say all kinds of things about Barnum, and never let on that you lived in town?" As she shifted and grabbed a tissue from the box on the table, I groaned inwardly and adopted a neutral look. I wasn't up for this.

"Obviously you know the people I talk about! Do you talk about me?" She stuck out her chin. I knew she was vulnerable underneath the defiant stance. Who wouldn't be? I had to answer. I thought it would destroy her trust if I let her associate without answering her questions or confirming her perceptions. "You are correct. I do live in Mayfair. But I hadn't had a child at Barnum until recently."

She stared, waiting for more.

"And I would and could never say anything about what we discuss in session. Not to anyone. It's confidential."

Amy nodded.

"I'm sure you will have more questions. For now, why don't we treat this in a way that will allow us to use them in a therapeutic context," I said. "For example, you have been through a hard time recently. And it seems like running into me has brought up a lot of feelings."

"It's fine. I want to talk about a couple of other things, like what happened before Ellie's game."

She was off, describing a coach's mistreatment of her younger child. I was just glad we'd gotten past her anger.

After work I was driving north, eager to see Rachel. When I walked in, she was in the living room, sprawled out on the sofa, playing on her phone. Before I could speak she told me how Lexi and Collette had set her up, texting that a boy named Dylan had broken up with his girlfriend, asking her to pass it on. After she'd relayed the message, they'd told Dylan that Rachel was "obsessed" with him, and everyone had laughed at her.

I was amazed that any learning went on at school. The kids were all so busy with senseless playground drama. At least Rachel didn't seem as upset as I would have expected.

"So what did you do?" I asked.

"I went over to Maya and we tried to ignore them, playing Candy Crush on our phones."

"Good for you," I said, putting my arm around Rachel and walking her up the stairs so she could get ready for bed. She smiled a little. Even if Collette and company had gotten under her skin, I was thrilled to hear that she and Maya had banded together.

Rachel finally acquiesced, and we invited Maya and her mother, Ellen, for dinner. She turned out to be the woman with the solarized glasses I'd met the first day. We laughed at the memory of the weirdness in the classroom, and said we hoped things would improve next year when both elementary schools combined.

"So who is this camp friend they've been writing to on Instachat?" Ellen asked. We were sitting in the living room drinking mint tea after the girls had gone upstairs.

"Not sure. The whole thing makes me uncomfortable. I've talked with Rachel about social media. It's concerning that these kids put everything out there and are in touch with strangers."

Ellen shifted her posture and seemed to be thinking about whether to speak. "Is something wrong?" I asked her.

"So you don't know then?"

This didn't sound good.

She breathed in before speaking. "The one who has been writing to our girls, someone's camp friend, asked Maya, and Rachel, to send him—" she stopped and covered her eyes.

I sat forward in my chair. "Please go on."

"He wanted naked photos."

It felt like my air supply was cut off. Rachel and Maya weren't even eleven years old. I prayed my daughter hadn't done something stupid.

Ellen read my thoughts. "They didn't send anything. And they both blocked the account. This was a few days ago."

My pulse was moving in double time. The photo incident could have ended in disaster. I told Ellen that I needed to talk to Rachel. She said she understood and took Maya home. After they'd gone, I asked Rachel to help me fold up the tablecloth and napkins.

"Maya's nice," she said as we moved toward one other, collapsing the fabric into a perfect half, and then a smaller folded square. "But the other girls make fun of her." She appeared to consider something before speaking. "They're all teeny-tiny, and really pretty, and rich, and they think they're better. It used to bother me, but now I try to ignore them."

This was an opening. I'd follow up on the sexting in a minute. "Rach?"

"Um hmmm." She was texting and ignoring me.

"Rachel?" I waited.

"What! I'm done talking about this."

"Please listen. You're perfect, beautiful and smart. I mentioned this before and meant it. If the girls act this way, excluding you or any other person, it says more about them than it does about you."

I inhaled and looked her squarely in the eye. "There's something else. I just spoke to Ellen."

Rachel hung her head. "I should have told you. But I handled it."

I waited until she was ready to say more.

"The camp friend was nice in the beginning. And it felt good to message with a boy." She looked sad. Poor kid. After all she'd been through, of course the attention was flattering. "So, he said, 'I want to see more of you. Send photos.' And when I refused, he kept trying to convince me, like, 'don't be a baby. Just take your top off.'"

I felt like jumping out of my skin, but forced myself to remain composed.

"When I said no, he got mad and called me a 'tease.' He did the same thing with Maya. We decided we would block him. And that was the end."

I went over to where Rachel was sitting and hugged her tightly. "That was the right thing to do. Sending photos like that, sexting, is never okay. Don't let anyone try to force you. And please come to me if anyone bothers you again, in person or online." I made sure our eyes met. "Promise?" She nodded and we hugged again.

I was relieved that Rachel and Maya had stood up for them-

selves, but the incident had spooked me. I wondered again who
the camp friend was, and emailed Ellen, asking if we could talk.
Maybe we needed to go together to the police? She was going
out of town and promised to get back to me. I felt better having
reached out, and managed to get through the next couple of days.

On Friday, while Rachel and I were eating dinner, she told me
a new girl had started school. She and Maya had invited the girl
to eat lunch with them.

"That's great, Rach." Maybe our talks about the cliques had
made a dent. But I still felt a chill in my blood thinking about her
close call on Instachat.

"It sounds like you and Maya have each other, and maybe this
new girl too. But I've been meaning to go over something. Any
word from the camp friend?"

"I told you. We blocked him."

"Do you have any idea who it was?" She shook her head, and
I decided to take her pulse one last time about the girls in her
class. "Since you'll be at school together in the coming years, it's
important to have a handle on the group stuff. Have you thought
any more about why Collette needs to run the show?"

Rachel sighed. "I have no idea, but you're about to tell me."

"Wealthy and attractive people can be just as insecure as everyone else. Everyone has something they worry about, and she's no
different. But it sounds like these girls don't matter as much now.
You've found other kids to hang around with." I stopped talking
because Rachel's eyes were starting to glaze over.

She was glancing at her phone. Apparently even a minute was
now too long for a talk. Time to wrap up. Rachel yessed me and
stood up to bring her plate to the sink. At least she seemed to be
putting the social stuff in perspective.

The next morning, I drove into my city office, feeling better
than I had in awhile. My daughter was navigating well, both in
school and online. And I was too, having relied on the wisdom of

my personal moral compass to teach her while modeling kindness. Even though I still wanted to settle the score with Lee, my heart felt lighter than it had in awhile.

The good feelings were short-lived. This became clear after work when I climbed the stairs and opened the door to my daughter's room. She was hunched over and didn't move.

"Is everything all right? Did something happen today?"

Rachel's eyes were swollen and her face was tear-streaked. She opened her laptop to Instachat, a page I'd never seen. There was a photo of Dopey, one of the Seven Dwarfs. His hat was pulled down and he had a confused look on his face. Underneath was a bio:

"Rachel Bryant"

"Loser.com"

I forced myself to look further. Rachel scrolled down. The first and only post was a stock image, a large flapping bird, the Domesticated Turkey. It had the following preprinted caption across the top: "World's Stupidest Animal." Posted right underneath was the phrase: "That's me." The account had sixty followers and the post, seventy-eight likes.

Rachel spoke through sobs. "This was made by the camp friend. I'm pretty sure. It has a lot of the same followers and he used the same font and lettering as the account I blocked. I got a notification from his new account and clicked on it and found this page. The first time I looked, it had only eighteen followers and twenty likes. More and more people have been viewing it and laughing at me. Collette and Lexi and some of their friends wrote stuff like: 'I want a slice of that' and 'OMG' to make fun of me." She sniffled and wiped her eyes with the back of one hand.

What was going on? First a request for nude photos, and now this? I felt the hair on my arms rise, and leaned in, unsure about what I was even looking at. All I knew was that it was a nasty display, intentionally targeting my daughter.

I clicked on the profile picture of the account that had notified Rachel about the cruel turkey photo. It was a cartoon of a basketball and hoop. "BucketBeast," it said. "Living the Life."

"He wrote a couple of times before. The first time the account said BucketBeast, and there wasn't a picture with it. He just wrote 'hi.' But now suddenly the account has a photo and is posting mean messages, sending private DMs and commenting here and on other posts I made."

I scrolled down. On the turkey post, he had commented, "You're ugly. Go hide in your house!"

Rachel peered at me through red eyes. Why would he write something like this?"

I went over and kneeled down next to her. "We're certainly going to get to the bottom of this. I don't care what it takes, sweetheart. Let me think a little bit." Rachel nodded and I went on. "Would you like to do something nice, like go out for ice cream with Alva while I make some calls?"

"Alva couldn't come today. You were busy and forgot that she texted. Neil's mom gave me a ride home. I'll just stay here and do my homework."

I'd forgotten that Alva had called in sick again. Hopefully she'd be back before too long. Rachel and I needed her.

I distracted myself by calling Julie, who was outraged by the online cruelty. "That's horrible. Poor Rachel."

I pictured her puzzling over our situation in the silence that followed. She finally said. "So what do you think you should do?"

"I wish I knew. It's so cruel. And I don't even get what this stupid account is. I was about to go online and try to figure it out, but I thought I'd call you. Maybe Carly would know?"

"When in doubt, ask a teen. They know everything. Carly!" A few moments passed, then I heard her daughter's voice asking what was up. "Can you tell me about Instachat?" Julie asked.

I prayed she wouldn't out us. We all got together for a road trip every couple of years, and I didn't want Rachel to be embarrassed when she next saw Carly.

"Later. I have to FaceTime Ally."

Julie spoke again. "I know someone who needs information about cyber stuff *now*. So here's what we need to know: What does it mean if you look at Instachat and there's a page with an unflattering or mean photo and bio, and the whole point of it is to make fun of a person?"

I thought I heard Carly make a snorting sound. "I don't get the question."

"So let's say you found a page with your name on it on Instachat. Only it was really mean and you didn't put it up."

"Oh. Someone makes an account, pretending to be someone else, and puts really mean things on it?"

I was nodding along.

"Yes, exactly."

"Is it, like, self-deprecating?"

"No, it's more humiliating and mean-spirited than self-deprecating."

"Well, it kind of sounds like a fake account, a second Instachat feed. Just so you know, there's also something called a Finsta, which is different; we all have them. They're for fun. So you have your regular Instachat, where you show more public things, and your Finsta, which is more private."

Carly was losing me.

"So you have another account?" Julie sounded annoyed. I pictured her, hand on one hip, challenging her daughter about social media secrets.

"It's not a big deal. I have like five hundred followers on my Instachat: kids from camp, teams, whatever, not just close friends. But on my Finsta, I have a lot less. And the posts are a joke, but kind of making fun of myself, private jokes. Like you only show your real friends if you are pissed off at a teacher or you tripped in the hallway at school. You don't want everyone to know that stuff. Getting back to the question, I think what you are talking about is a fake account. People sometimes make those to poke fun at someone. Can I be done, now? I have to go."

I heard Julie remind Carly to finish her homework, and waited as they had a muffled exchange. Once her daughter had moved on, Julie came back on. "Wow. Fake Instachat and accounts."

"I know. I had no idea. Thank you so much. I appreciate your finding out about that. And thanks for keeping Rachel's problems a secret. Now I have to deal with this online bullying. I really can't take much more."

"I know. It sounds really bad, Vic. From what you described and what Carly explained, someone made a fake account and, posing as Rachel, put humiliating things and threatening comments on it?"

I massaged my temples. "Apparently. I've got to get off the phone now so I can try to do something. Should I wait—every-one's saying it's some troubled kid—or go to the police? I want to nip it in the bud."

"Going to the police is probably a good idea. Please call me when you get home—or before."

We hung up and I went downstairs. Rachel was in the kitchen, mixing eggs and flour in a giant bowl.

"How are you doing, Rach?"

She shrugged. "Show me your phone. I want to see if there's been anything new."

As I feared, BucketBeast had been busy. He'd branched out, commenting on a few of Rachel's recent posts: "I hate you," one of them said. "You're a whale!!! What's your BMI, like 1000?" a second one read. "GO KILL YOURSELF!" the third one screamed. I had to steady myself against the desk. This was awful. The account now had 460 followers.

"Why is this happening to me?" Rachel was pacing. "Everyone in the school probably knows. They'll all make fun of me."

"I'll be acting on this immediately." She gave me an exhausted shrug. "What's a BMI?"

"Just some disturbed kid's attempt to disparage you. It's an abbreviation doctors use." She buried her face in her hands. I was furious now.

Rachel looked up and wiped the tears from her eyes. "I know it has to do with body size. I googled it." She was crying harder now, and I knelt down next to her. "Remember at my last appointment, my height and weight, I was in the fifty-something percentile? I'm in the middle, not the biggest, not the smallest."

I nodded. "Sweetheart. You are absolutely beautiful and healthy and just the right shape and size. I'm going out so I can deal with this now. Do you want me to drop you at Maya's or Neil's on my way?"

She shook her head. "I'll be fine here."

"Just hang in for a little while until I get back, okay? Love you," I said as I grabbed my coat.

▥

Mayfair shared a police department with several other neighboring villages. The precinct was housed two towns over in a small white house adjacent to a gas station off the main drag.

I walked onto the porch of the police station and said my name into an intercom next to the front door. Someone buzzed me into a large room. A gray-haired receptionist sat behind a desk several feet in front of me. I stepped in and smiled in her direction, closing the door behind me. She peered over her glasses. "Hello," I said, unsure of the protocol.

"My name is Victoria Bryant. I'd like to speak to one of the officers."

She cocked her head, waiting for more.

"About a potential criminal matter."

"Okay. Sit down over there and someone will come and get you."

As I took a seat in a boxy steel chair and waited as the receptionist went into a back room. I thought about what I'd say during the meeting.

A uniformed officer opened the door and extended one hand. "Officer Giles," he said, ushering me into the main part of the precinct. He looked to be about my age, and probably had a decade or more of experience. That was promising. Although I wasn't too keen on getting involved with the criminal justice system and preferred to keep our problems private, I'd file a report.

The officer brought me into a large room that had several desks across the interior and a table.

"So please tell me your name and address, then let me know how I can help you," Giles said as we sat down.

"Dr. Victoria Bryant. Two Long Pines Drive, Mayfair. I'm here about my eleven-year-old daughter, Rachel. She's a fifth grader at Barnum."

Giles made notes as I told him the whole story, from girl troubles to the bullying comments on Instachat to the fake account and BucketBeast. As soon as I mentioned BucketBeast, he stopped writing and put a hand up. "I didn't realize it was connected to that. Let me get you over to Detective Weiner."

We stood up and walked over two desks to the woman who'd been filing. "Laurie, this woman is here on the 'BB' matter," Giles said before looking back at me. "This is Detective Weiner. She'll take it from here. Good luck."

The detective took all the information as she brought the BucketBeast account up on her screen. I felt sick looking at the now-familiar turkey photo profile pic and growing number of accompanying jabs. "318 likes and 494 followers," she said, eyeing me across the table.

So hundreds of people had seen this humiliating photo and

horrible display. How would Rachel ever show her face in public again? And the comment, "Go kill yourself." I thought about how Rachel had tried to help herself, blocking the kid who was doing this, talking to friends. But all he had to do was make another account and go after her again. Kids were so vulnerable these days, with all the time they spent online. The pain caught in my throat and came out as a small anguished gulping sound. The detective handed me a box of tissues. As I cried, she sat silently, hands folded on her lap.

She was tall and dressed in all black with almost no makeup and long straight blond hair, which she'd drawn into a tight, high ponytail. "We're looking into this, Dr. Bryant. I can't discuss an ongoing investigation, but over the past twenty-four hours, we've received several similar complaints. The school is also concerned and cooperating in our investigation."

"I guess that's something. My child wasn't singled out." Weiner nodded and brought her fingertips to her lips before inhaling deeply.

I wondered whether Collette had been on the receiving end of a fake account from BucketBeast. Then Lee would know how it felt to see her child bullied while being unable to help.

"I appreciate that this is rough for your daughter and you. But this incident isn't a lot to go on. And normally I'd tell you that we don't open a criminal investigation for something like middle school shenanigans . . . however hurtful they may be."

I shifted uncomfortably. "Any idea who is behind this?"

"Like I said before, I can't comment, but in this case, there are several people who've made similar complaints, and for reasons I'm not going to get into right now, the department is pairing with another police organization and investigating further. So please be available."

"Okay. But is there some help you can provide until the investigation precedes any further? My daughter's turning eleven, and this cyber stuff is brutal.'"

Weiner nodded. "We're doing everything we can. Just sit tight." She ushered me to the exit. I texted Rachel, *"leaving now."*

"Finished baking," came the response. *"Doing homework."*

I was relieved she'd back-burnered the fake account, at least for now.

I'd put my coat on and started to walk out the door when Detective Weiner reappeared. "Dr. Bryant? I forgot: Here's my card, in case you think of anything else or need to speak to me again."

Once I'd left the station, I slid into the driver's seat of my car, feeling a little more hopeful. I'd taken concrete action by going to the police, and Rachel wasn't the only one targeted. I hoped things continued to move in a positive direction.

When I arrived at home, Rachel asked me a lot of questions. "Was there a police dog at the station house?" she wanted to know.

"Nope, just a coffee maker. What are you going to say the next time you're at school, and someone asks you about the fake account?"

"I'll tell the truth. I ignored it."

"Rach, telling the truth is always good. But since we don't know who BucketBeast is yet, and we don't want to provoke him or cause him to make another fake account or bother you in some other way, I think you should say very little, okay? Until we get it all sorted out?"

"I forgot to tell you, BucketBeast made fake pages about Maya and Francesca. Those accounts also had a lot of followers."

I nodded, waiting to hear more.

"Neil got one the other day, but he didn't tell anyone. I'm glad I wasn't the only one."

Apparently BucketBeast was an equal opportunity hater.

"So if someone asks me about the turkey account, I won't respond," Rachel continued. "I'm going to make a new account, and if they bring up the other one, I'll just tell people to follow the new one I'm making."

"Great idea."

"I'm going on Urban Dictionary." As she went upstairs to her room, I overheard her, trying out puns, seeking a name for her fake account: "The Rachel," "Pulling a Rachel," "Code Rachel," "Rachel heart—wait that's it." I heard her closing her door.

An hour later, I called her to come downstairs for dinner. "Let me see the fake account, please," I said. She handed me her phone. There was a profile photo of Rachel, winking at the camera. The bio said: "Rachel < 3"

"What does that mean?" I was confused by the symbols after her name.

"A Rachel with a sideways heart means 'awesome Rachel. A great friend, the person everyone wants to be around.'"

I smiled, despite the fact that her handle and explanation made me sad. Rachel was obviously trying to display an image of what she wanted to be, the girl at the center of a core group of friends.

I thought about my daughter and her peers, living their lives online, their social lives commoditized for all to see. It was so complicated, growing up in front of an audience, in a world with no boundaries, no privacy, no accountability, and where bullying was the norm.

Twenty-One
Cyber Nothings

Next morning, all was calm as Rachel and I drove to school. She'd heard from Neil and Maya that other kids had been targeted by BucketBeast. He was school-wide stalker. Come again? Barnum had a stalker?

Rachel told me all about it. "Neil tried out for a soccer travel team and saved a goal by a seventh grader, who then got really mad at him. Later, Neil saw the kid in the bathroom. He was on his phone, posting on Instachat, and told Neil to "fuck off." Rachel paused, studying me through the rearview mirror, gauging my reaction to the language. I nodded and she went on. "So after the tryout, BucketBeast targeted Neil and another kid with fake accounts. That's why everyone thinks the seventh grader that got mad at Neil is the stalker."

"That's a big coincidence, isn't it?" I glanced back. She was deep in thought. "Why would some seventh grader go after you?"

Rachel was nodding. "Good question. No one can prove it, but he was really mean to Neil and was on his phone posting. And BucketBeast sent the notifications right after that. He probably made accounts for Maya and me because he knows we're friends with Neil."

I'd dropped Rachel off at school, relieved that she and her friends were all sticking together. For my part, I was glad she was comfortable going to class, though I was still eager to hear what the police had learned.

An hour later, I was in the city office listening to Amy tell me about a huge blowout she'd had over the weekend with Lee, Maureen, and several PTA moms. She'd gotten in their faces, accusing them of purposely closing the registration in the afterschool class she'd told me about. She said she was sure they'd excluded her daughter out of meanness. I couldn't believe she'd gone off on the group like that.

Since the argument, Amy hadn't been sleeping or eating and had been having trouble concentrating. There was no doubt that she was under tremendous stress. After I pointed this out, she finally agreed to discuss medication with a colleague of mine.

After the session, I recalled the conversation in which Amy had announced she'd been trawling a bunch of kids' social media pages. I pictured the horrific turkey account. *What if?*

I pushed that thought to the side. Not only was it was ridiculous, I now had a more pressing concern: Amy, Maureen, and the resulting clinical conflict. My head felt like it was about to explode. I made a note on each woman's chart that I was in the process of referring her to a different therapist, and decided to discuss the change with Amy when she was stronger. But something else nagged at me.

Amy's comments had brought it all back. She and her daughter had been through hell, and Rachel and I hadn't had it much better, but Lee, who'd caused trouble for all of us, was getting off scot-free. That wasn't right. Why was that woman above it all, immune from suffering or payback? She'd made Rachel's life miserable, and been the catalyst in my breakup with Jim.

The BucketBeast incident had served as a disturbing distraction, but now I thought back to what Maureen had said several weeks ago. Lee was planning something behind the scenes, intending to come after me. My resentment burned. I had to do something to stop her. And even though Rachel had begged me not to, I still wanted to get even with the woman for all the cruelty she'd visited upon us. With my daughter handling the social stuff and the police getting involved in the cyberstalking, I could once again focus my attention on the PTA chair.

I went back to the same chat room I'd visited before, being sure to sign in under a newly minted alias: "Observer," and looked back at the thread I'd started weeks earlier at the postings of the woman I'd concluded was her. Someone had written: "inclusion is always the way to go," while Cheerleader, the woman who'd recently used the phrase "loser daughter," had responded: "Not every situation is alike. For example, we'd gotten along fine, minding our business, until *these social climbers started messing with our daughter.*"

My heart stopped. That was exactly what Lee had said to her friend that morning I'd overheard her in the back hallway at school.

If it looks like a duck and walks like one . . . . Cheerleader had added: "sometimes less is more when it comes to birthday parties. There have been tons of threads on this." She provided a few links to other discussions, and I clicked on them.

One conversation was about group vacations, how to limit the number of families who wanted to join. Next. Another had to do with holidays and annoying family members. Not a surprise.

"Social Climbers" was certainly a common phrase. But given what I'd heard about her behavior in the New Jersey school, plus the "loser daughter" comments and Westchester location, connecting the account to Lee wasn't out of the realm of possibility. I was almost there. I could feel it. My fingers itched as I typed and searched.

What was I not seeing?

Think, Vic. Maureen had said in session that Lee got revenge.

That was a good jumping off point. Thinking like the enemy would make her posts easier to find. I trawled the chat room, scrolling through current discussions and archived ones. I clicked on a link, a thread someone had started a couple of days ago, a debate about a woman down south who'd fought back when certain parents had campaigned to have her kid kicked off the cheer squad. That mom wanted blood.

Someone named "Shih Tzu Lover" disagreed. "Steer clear," she'd counseled. "In my northeastern town, one mom took another to court over a spot in the local brownie troop. It was not worth the aggravation." People were adding responses, weighing in as I read.

The pom-pom icon popped up with a message: "I disagree!" Cheerleader was on; my pulse began to race. "I'm plotting something that will have a tremendous impact on the community. I can do so much with so little—it's almost too easy. I'm going to put a certain holier-than-thou mom in her place. My methods are right at my fingertips."

My heart felt like it was beating out of my chest, and I thought I'd faint. On the one hand, connecting an anonymous poster to someone I knew, even if she used similar phrases and discussed certain topics, was crazy, but I'd received a credible warning about Lee from Maureen. Truth was, she *had* made threats and gone after someone in the past.

And though I had no concrete proof that Cheerleader really was Lee, she did live in Westchester and use similar language. She had just bragged about putting a "holier than though mom" in her place. I'd overheard Lee say something like that about me. Saving the page on my laptop before copying and pasting it into a document, I took a screen shot on my phone, being sure to record the exact date, time, and link I'd read.

I typed furiously, searching for more clues. But the battery was drained and the laptop powered down. In the dark screen, I saw myself reflected, eyes wild, angry looking, frantically pressing buttons. Like Amy, I'd been all over the internet, trying to find out ways to get even.

I called Sharon, who made me laugh and feel more like myself again. We were about to hang up when I mentioned the upcoming Colonial Fair. She'd howled about my decision to sign up as a volunteer.

"Everyone knows that's the worst possible gig. Lee and her nearest and dearest get all the good jobs, and the mere mortals are stuck with manual labor like moving picnic tables and hauling out the trash. You won't get to spend a minute with Rachel. Next time, please ask me before you sign up for anything."

I recalled an email from Lee, directing me to purchase bottles of water and serve them at 67 degrees. Hearing the directions about the temperature only made Sharon laugh harder.

I felt calmer and was even able to smile a little at the absurdity of it all. I had Sharon to guide me through the Barnum maze, just as Rachel had Maya and Neil. That was progress. Despite Lee and her machinations, our new house and school were finally starting to feel more like home.

Sharon had been so nice, I felt like confiding in her. "Why do they all follow Lee?"

"You're the psychologist. You tell me."

I told her my working theory. "When people are insecure, desperate even, it's generally due to something old, a childhood wound."

Sharon snorted. "Well, they have all known each other for years. I learned that the hard way. Back in pre-K, Neil had a few playdates with Lexi. And I'm remembering something now, although I'd done my best to block it out, I once went to Jess's to pick him up. She offered me a cup of tea and bragged about being best friends with Audrey, the pediatrician, and Lee, their ringleader, pulling out shots from their college sorority years and bridesmaid photos. New nose, by the way." Sharon paused for breath.

"Who?"

"Audrey. Jess kept referring to the others as her 'dear, dear friends,' and I was wondering how to extricate myself when she crossed the room to the baby's bouncy seat. As she was readjusting it, I saw an old yearbook mixed in with all the albums. Would you believe, the high school photos of Jess and Audrey were like something out of that old '*Revenge of the Nerds*' movie."

She barreled on. "I know, I sound bitchy. It was not smooth sailing for those two growing up. Jess has worked her ass off—literally—since the yearbook days. Plus, she got contacts and lightened her hair. And Audrey has the best face that money can buy. Now they and their pals do whatever it takes to preserve their place in the Lee clique. Popularity is the most important thing to them. It's pathetic."

Sharon softened her voice. "I've wanted to tell you because they've been so horrible to you guys, but whenever I raise the subject, you put up a wall."

Jim had said something similar. I was obviously telegraphing a "stay away" vibe. Well, no more. "I'm glad you're going into all this, Sharon. I didn't mean to act like I was holding back, or keeping you at arm's length. It's not easy to talk about, but these women have been awful to us. And it makes sense that if they felt ugly and unpopular, they'd need to feel their children weren't flawed in any way. But they must have a sense of the harm they do—"

She barely let me get the question out. "Look at Francesca's mom, Emily. Since Lee froze them out, Francesca has no friends, is constantly being picked on, and Emily is off all the PTA committees. I heard she's even worried about losing her club membership. Jack is on that board too, of course."

Sharon paused. "Why don't you stick up for yourself, Vic? I

know you did that one time, but these people have been walking all over you."

"Sometimes I want to tell Lee that I think she's a total asshole. I did call her out for laughing at basketball, and at the turf, I told her to stay away from Rachel. But I can't go around arguing with people, making a spectacle. There's my practice to consider." Sharon agreed and we decided to talk later that day. After hanging up, I went downstairs to look for Rachel.

It had been a week since BucketBeast had struck, and more than six months since the first day of school. Spring had almost arrived. I smelled the buds that were blooming on the bushes at the side of the house, and listened as cicadas buzzed, splitting the silence in two.

I was at the office, looking forward to a weekend off when Amy came in with fresh stories of bullying. The school called as the session was ending. I closed the door behind her and answered the phone.

"Dr. Bryant? This is Principal Burke. There's been an incident. We need you to come in. Rachel wasn't harmed, but we are concerned."

What had happened? My heart thumped inside my chest. "I can't get there for another forty-five minutes. I'll leave now. But can you tell me more?"

"We found something in her backpack; actually the gym teacher noticed it as your daughter was changing into her sneakers. It fell out. He cleared his throat. "It's a Juul." He was referring to the small device for smoking all kinds of substances; the kind that didn't give off smoke or odors.

There was no way. I was angry now. I'd know if Rachel were

using substances. The whole thing was ridiculous. "Put her on please."

"Mom?" She sounded upset, though it was difficult to hear. We'd both spoken at the same time. "What's going on?"

"One of the teachers saw this silver thing fall out of my backpack. She picked it up and told me to come with her and we went to the principal's office. It isn't mine." She sounded scared.

"What is it?"

"A flash drive. You know, the thing that looks like a pen. For the computer, extra memory.

"Stay where you are, and explain to the principal what you just told me. Then put him on."

"Yes?" He was saying as I spoke, "I'll be there as soon as I can. Rachel doesn't have a Juul. She thinks the device is a memory stick for the computer. I'd like you to have her teacher there when we meet today so we can all discuss this." We hung up.

It was all I could do to stop myself from vomiting. Rachel was being accused of carrying illicit paraphernalia. I locked up without even turning off the lights and called my scheduled patients as I walked to the car, apologizing for the inconvenience. I had an emergency and would make time to see them over the next couple of days.

I could barely concentrate on the road, I was so worried about Rachel. While I didn't think she was using tobacco or worse, I was concerned about a smoking device making its way into her backpack. That was "the how," and it was confusing. There was also "the who," and I had my suspicions.

Forty-five minutes later, the principal and I were sitting down in his office along with Rachel and her teacher, Ms. Franklin. Principal Burke was tall and balding, lanky, with a pallid complexion. There was a wood desk with a few papers and a gold nameplate, along with a matching chair. A coatrack and wall calendar were the only things in the room.

The air was tense. When Ms. Franklin put a hand on my shoulder, I smiled, grateful for her kindness. Rachel was on the other side of the teacher, red-eyed and quiet. She'd been crying. I blew her a kiss.

The principal got up and closed the door before sitting back down.

"Some things are very unpleasant." I waited.

"This is what the gym teacher found." He held up a three-inch long object; it was silver and shaped like a stick, but thicker. I looked over at Rachel, who was starting to cry again, and at the teacher, who put a hand on her shoulder and gave her a tissue.

"Did you ask Rachel about this?"

"I did. And she has said that it's not hers." I was furious that an educator would be so left-footed, putting my fifth grader through this, like she was a criminal on the witness stand. "Anything else?"

"I'm not sure what you mean."

"This is what I mean." I was working hard to control my anger at the way he was accusing my daughter. "Rachel, is this yours?" She shook her head violently. "What is it? Can you tell us?"

"I told you before; it's something for the computer. A flash drive, extra memory."

I glared at the principal. "My daughter doesn't even know what it is. She's ten-and-a-half years old. Do you realize how over the top this is, accusing her?"

Ms. Franklin chimed in: "Robert, I agree. Rachel has no idea what this is, and says it isn't hers. I believe her." My chest expelled a rush of air. The teacher's words were a huge relief. "And she's had a rough time since moving in last summer. So who knows what even happened here."

I'd been thinking the same thing.

The principal was speaking again. "I'm sorry, but I have to ask these questions. Juuls are not allowed at school. We normally suspend a child for bringing one in."

Rachel let out a piteous cry. "Am I being suspended?"

I was so angry I'd been grinding my teeth. Was this guy serious? The kid thought it was a flash drive. We all waited for him to speak. "Have you ever heard of a Juul?" he asked.

Rachel shook her head. "I've heard of jewels, like in a crown or something." I felt my anger rise. She was telling the truth, cooperating, and he was treating this like a major narcotics investigation.

"How about vaping? Do you know what that is?"

Rachel shook her head again.

"Is that satisfactory, Mr. Burke?" I really wanted the meeting to be over so I could comfort my child.

"Yes. I'm sorry, but things like this happen from time to time. We'll have to look into them when they do. Electronic cigarettes are against school rules. Thank you for coming in."

Fortunately, it was well after three. The halls were deserted. I took Rachel by the hand and led her down the hall and to the car.

"Are you okay, honey?"

She shrugged. "Why wouldn't he believe me? I don't smoke! No one does!"

My heart broke again. She was so innocent and really didn't deserve this harassment.

As we drove home, I thought about this latest infuriating development and how it fit in with all the other pieces. It had to be Lee; she had motive and access. I was dying to use the dirt I had on her and get even. Maybe obtaining records from the school in New Jersey, proving she'd been asked to withdraw her older daughter for bullying another girl, was the way to go. Then I wouldn't be violating Maureen's confidentiality. I still had the copy of the chat room discussion where "Cheerleader" had bragged about "getting even when threatened." And then there was what Amy had said about Francesca's mother describing how that child had been cutting, after Lee got the girls all lathered up and they kicked her out of Collette's clique, although I wouldn't reveal what had been told to me in session.

Lee was making life impossible for Rachel. At points, she'd been isolated and restricted food intake. Would she get depressed like the kid in New Jersey? My head was spinning the entire way home. There had to be a way to put it all together without violating confidentiality and make sure Lee got what she deserved.

After we'd gotten into the house, I heated up some leftovers. Rachel was quiet, eating a couple of bites of chicken before heading into the shower. Poor kid. The stress was getting to her. First, there had been the BucketBeast incident—what if it were Amy?— and now, days later the Juul affair.

I'd thought the targeting and cruelty was bad when it was the girls excluding her as their moms looked the other way; likewise when Lee provoked me, and served as the catalyst in my breakup with Jim. But this?! Lee hiding the Juul in Rachel's backpack felt much worse.

The following morning, I woke Rachel up early so I could see if she was okay and we could spend a few minutes together before school. Her eyes were sleepy and she had pillow creases on her cheeks, at least she'd slept. That made one of us.

After we ate breakfast together, I walked around the table to kiss her head. "Are you okay?"

"Fine. Ms. Franklin was really nice to stick up for me. You too."

"Honey, it was ridiculous. People use substances, as we've discussed, but the principal was barking up the wrong tree with you. We all knew it. Probably even him." Rachel looked like she was thinking. "At least no one saw. The gym teacher brought me to the office, but didn't make a thing about it."

It was time for school. "You'll be okay, right?"

"Yes. Maya and I feed the turtle on Thursdays. I want to go."

I parked on the street behind the school, so Rachel and I could take the short cut. She let me hold her hand. Spring had almost arrived. I smelled the buds that were blooming on the bushes at the side of the house, and listened as cicadas buzzed. As we walked around to the front, I noticed Lee, standing in front of the school, checking her messages, hanging out in what looked like skintight white leggings, furry boots, and a white puffy jacket with fox-trimmed hood. Was it my imagination or did she seem surprised to see Rachel?

I pulled Rachel along, willing her to walk faster. As we made our way up the path and brushed by Lee, I was furious. She only looked away. My kid was called into the principal, and this woman got to stand around, planning workshops and school events, and act like the queen of it all? I asked myself again: How was it that we all rolled around in the muck while she was above reproach?

I kissed my daughter on top of her head and watched her walk into the building. I was disgusted by Lee's selfishness and unabashed bullying, and after the Juul incident, was blinded by hatred.

It was time to use the photos. I'd show them to Lee in private, and let her know I was onto her. Then maybe she'd leave Rachel alone once and for all.

Another idea popped into my head. Since the principal had treated Rachel like a drug kingpin, he owed me one. I wrote to him, mentioning that I was a psychologist. I asked whether I might present on internet safety at Lee's upcoming Cyber Crimes Workshop. I'd figure out a way to mention her bullying during my talk. Since the administration, local police, PTA moms, and rest of the town's parents and students would be there, it would be a great chance to let the community know about Lee. People deserved to know the kind of person she really was.

The principal responded immediately that he'd be glad to have me speak at the workshop, and I felt excited for the first time in a while.

Fasten your seat belt, Lee. You've messed with the wrong psychologist.

Twenty-Two

Beasts of Burden

A few days after I'd contacted the principal, Rachel was at her desk, earbuds inserted. "Rach?"

"I'm busy now." Her face was tense.

"What's going on?" I asked.

"It's nothing. I'm handling it." That didn't sound good. I sat down on her bed.

"Rach?"

"Okay, we had a rehearsal for the Spring Fling next month, and everyone was learning this dance. Maya and I were practicing with Neil and a couple of the boys. When the teacher wasn't looking, Lexi and her 'BFF,' Katie, came over and tripped me. Some of the kids laughed when I fell on the ground."

Did these people have nothing better to do? My pulse was picking up, but I forced myself to speak calmly. "What happened then?"

"I ignored her. She went back to Collette and Hannah, and they started whispering." Rachel shook her head. "I was embarrassed, but Neil and his friend said Katie was really lame, and then Maya imitated how she snuck over. Whatever."

I got up and walked over to where Rachel was sitting. "Anything else?" Rachel hesitated.

"Well, Mrs. DeVry was there during the rehearsal. She was holding her phone up, taking photos because she wanted to do a montage for the end of the year."

I nodded. What now?

"So . . . Lexi and Collette were standing near Katie and this girl from the other class, Hannah, and Ms. F, my teacher, asked a few of us to gather for a photo, and she put me near Katie, Collette and Lexi." Rachel paused for breath, "and then she ran off because this boy Lucas was pushed down to the ground."

No adult supervision. This sounded bad.

"I was standing in between Collette and Lexi, near Katie, when Mrs. DeVry came over and held up her phone to take a picture. In front of everyone she said, 'Rachel, please step out of the photo. You don't belong in it.' Everyone was whispering and staring when I moved aside. It was so embarrassing." Rachel started crying, but shook me off when I went to comfort her.

"I'm glad your friends stuck up for you on the playground. As for Mrs. DeVry, honey, just ignore her. You have your own friends now. If she's that petty, well . . . ." I wondered what to say, how to wrap things up.

Rachel laughed. "How about just saying, 'Who needs her?' I have my group and I don't care what she or her kid says or does. I'm over it."

I felt like applauding. Instead, I kissed her, and extracted a promise that she'd go to bed within twenty minutes.

I went back into the chat room. In a Neighborhood conversation, Cheerleader had been active a couple of days ago, posting "#MissionAccomplished," and bragging about "putting people in their place." She was probably talking about the Juul. I bookmarked the exchange.

The next day I was at the office, happy to be engaged in meaningful work, but exhausted after the most recent travails. It had been a long day and I was ready to go home.

But first I had to see a couple that was worried aboout their twelve-year-old son who was performing below expectations. Phil, the dad, ranted about Xboxes, while Jen, the mom, described hiring tutors.

"Hard as it is, you have to let him wrestle with this problem, resist the urge to fix it. Sometimes a kid just has to fail," I said, aware of the irony.

My thoughts went to Rachel, and how she'd struggled socially all year. Lee had seen to that. My pulse began to race, but I forced myself to focus. Jen was speaking. "You promised to discuss the below-the-belt stuff today," she said as Phil rolled his eyes. "I'm sick of being criticized for everything I do." They sat silently, staring in opposite directions.

I was angry with myself for getting distracted and with Lee for invading my thoughts, but pushed my personal difficulties to the side. "Sometimes couples get into knots. Let's hit pause on the anger, live through this together, and consider how you two tend to resolve things." I turned to Jen. "You prefer to broach your grievances and clear the air." She nodded as I looked at Phil. "You hear Jen's feelings as criticisms, and pull back. And I think this causes even more hurt feelings, making her want to talk more directly, and you, in turn, retreat even further. Together, you perpetuate a never-ending cycle of conflict and emotional pain." The hour ended with Phil smiling at his wife and grabbing her hand on the way out.

During the ride home I thought about Jen and Phil, and how they were deeply bonded to one another. Their interactions were sometimes tense, but always loving, authentic, and meaningful. And then it hit me: I'd been pulled into the sandbox with Lee, but I didn't have to remain there or continue to lower myself to her level. People and relationships were what mattered, not winning at power plays or getting even.

I began to feel ashamed for focusing so keenly on gathering

intel and seeking revenge. I liked the work I did, and felt at home being a caregiver. I didn't want to stir up additional discord in my community.

My doubts about using the speaking gig at the PTA workshop and getting even nagged for the entire ride home and throughout the evening.

Seeing the couple also made me think about Jim. Even if he had someone new, he deserved an apology. I'd have to figure out a way to make that happen sooner rather than later.

The following Saturday, we were at Rachel's first soccer game. I watched the opening. She had starting at midfield and didn't want me to miss a minute, but it was cold, so I ran to the car to get the blanket we kept in the trunk for such occasions. Rooting around under the rear hatchback, I heard voices.

"This isn't our second grade Brownie troupe. You're a grown woman. Act like it."

"I'm the one renting the condo in The Caymans, and I get to say who I invite."

I couldn't resist peeking out. It was Jess, car key in hand, standing with Audrey. Both were wearing matching exercise clothes and formfitting jackets. Since their daughters were also on the team, I assumed they'd left the bleachers around the same time I had, and wondered why they were squaring off in the school parking lot. "It may be your condo rental, but Lee can't stand Phoebe. You're asking for trouble," Audrey said.

"But Phoebe invited us to *her* destination birthday. You put the photos all over Facebook."

They were now heading in my direction. I slid out and leaned on the back of my car.

"Phoebe will just have to get over it. Lee will make your life— and Lexi's—hell . . . ."

They stopped talking the second they spotted me. I thought I saw Jess blush.

Audrey seemed annoyed at being caught off-guard. "You know what they say about eavesdroppers, Victoria."

I shook my head. "Let's not do this, Audrey."

I closed the hatchback and left them open-mouthed, then strode back to the field, hugging the blanket to my chest. As I stepped away, I thought again that I wanted to use my presentation at the Cyber Crimes Workshop for good, teach people about internet safety, and explain the psychological toll bullying has on kids and adults.

As clear as I was about not wanting to be divisive, there was still the matter of the Juul. Assuming Lee had planted it in Rachel's backpack—and, again, who else would have had access or motive?—I intended to let her know privately that I was onto her and ready to get even. As long as it wasn't against the law or in violation of my profession ethics, I'd do what I could to stop her from doing further damage.

Sharon texted. Tonight was the PTA karaoke night. With all the other goings-on, I'd almost forgotten about it. Few things sounded less appealing than singing show tunes with Lee and her pals. I told Sharon an old war injury was acting up, rendering me unable to hold a mic or hit a high C, but she ignored me. "Well then, I'll have to use my 'get out of jail free' card," I said.

"Nope," she said. "You promised, and we've already paid for the tickets. Pick me up at seven thirty."

"No way I'm dressing up though." Being forced to attend a school-sponsored event brought out the oppositional teen in me.

At least Rachel was taken care of. She'd been invited to dinner at Neil's. I closed up the office and did a quick check in the restroom mirror. I was good to go in a black dress, silk scarf, and heels. I never usually accessorized, but it made a difference.

Before I knew it, Sharon was sliding into my passenger seat. Her metallic silk tank top and gold mesh earrings were fun. "You look so pretty," I said, trying to get into a party frame of mind.

"Thanks. You too. I've actually been looking forward to this. Mike got home early and is watching the kids. I'm sure the place will be a disaster when I get back."

Fifteen minutes later, we drove up and parked in front of a white brick building with a sign that said, "Dorry's Bar."

"Let's get a drink," Sharon said, pulling me toward the bar. We joined a gaggle of women dressed in tight jeans, heels, and tank tops. Almost everyone had a killer blowout; I smoothed my flyaway hair, looked around the room, and waved at Joelle from cafeteria duty before turning my attention back to my Sharon.

The line for alcohol was three deep. After being served, we stepped into the middle of the room, making way for new arrivals.

"I feel like I'm back in college," Sharon said.

"Can you believe we all used to do this on a regular basis? Go out and party with friends?" I asked.

She nodded. "It was another life."

"We could dress Neil and Rachel up and force them to go out drinking and dancing with us?"

"As long as the club has an Xbox, Neil's in." We laughed and then overheard one of the women suggesting karaoke. All it took was some pink stuff in a highball glass (a lot of pink stuff actually), and we were ready to meander over to watch everyone sing.

"I'll find you. Need to use the restroom," I mouthed. Sharon nodded, and I made my way there.

As I was reaching for the door, a tall woman with long blond hair emerged and nearly banged into me. It was Phoebe, Lee and Jess's on-the-outs friend, who'd blown me off that morning at the basketball game. "Hello, how are you?" I said, trying to use my most pleasant small-talk voice.

She looked me up and down. "Are you coming from work?"

I made a joke about a mom's night being just the cure for a long day at the office and moved into the safety of the stall, hoping she'd be gone when I'd finished. I lingered a moment or two longer than necessary, but as I emerged from the restroom, still came face-to-face with Phoebe, who looked like she was about to say something, until she saw Lee moving across the room. She rushed to catch up, calling a hurried goodbye over her shoulder.

Wow. I stifled a laugh, as I made my way back to where Sharon was standing by the side of the bar. Phoebe just has to climb.

Lee, Jess, and Audrey were by a window, whispering as usual. Giving into my hatred for Lee would ruin my entire evening, so I decided to be cheery, act like she and her friends meant nothing to me, and smile. Lee waved back, and then Jess and Audrey got in on it too, grinning and nodding.

I sighed at the absurdity of it and told myself that now that Rachel had a firmer footing with some other kids, all of those women had become irrelevant.

Scanning the room, the smiling faces, I recalled how Sharon had watched Rachel a few times when I couldn't, how Maureen had warned me about her friend's history, and how some people had been welcoming, nice, and helpful.

There was good in Mayfair.

I was deciding whether or not to get another drink when I spotted someone familiar on a barstool, did a double take and froze. It was Jim. What was he doing there?

"The guy I used to date is over there," I said to Sharon. "You see him, the tall guy?" I nodded toward a smaller bar on the other side of the room, and Sharon nearly dropped her glass. "Stop staring," I hissed as she craned her neck.

"Jim, right? He's hot." Sharon giggled and elbowed me.

"I've had one too many. I'm afraid I'll say something I'll regret. I'm calling an Uber and getting out of here."

I snuck into the front entrance hall. When the car arrived, I sank into the back seat, but not before I managed to dump the contents of my purse all over the floor. I groped for my phone in the darkness, and texted Julie, *"Can you talk?"* I added a heart for effect.

"Surprised you wrote," came the response.

Call it a slip of the finger. I had texted Jim, inadvertently entering *"Ji"* instead of *"Ju"* in my contacts.

My pulse raced at the sight of his name on my phone. Even though he'd moved on so quickly—the memory of the other woman in the photos still stung—he still deserved an apology. I knew it was wrong to omit the Colin story and accuse him of siding with Lee. I wanted to own my part in the breakup.

Emboldened by the Cosmos, I wrote back. *"Would it be possible for us to speak sometime? I'd like to apologize."*

He answered immediately. *"Will come over. Please let me in."*

I was too exhausted to argue.

Jim looked almost haggard when he arrived. Blame the pink stuff, for better or worse. My guard was down, and I felt a familiar excitement as I opened the door.

I took a close look as he walked into the house. His eyes were hollow and his skin was pale. I had no idea what he'd say and was glad Rachel was asleep and wouldn't be subjected to a messy show.

We went into the living room, where he sat on the sofa and I took the chair to his left. I inhaled deeply and spoke from the heart. "Thank you for coming by. I wanted to apologize. I should have told you about my engagement and breakup at the altar before you heard it from someone else. That must have hurt, having it sprung on you, and in public." I felt a tear slide down my cheek and quickly brushed it away. "And I'm sorry for accusing you of siding with Lee. That was ridiculous. I didn't mean to involve you in that whole mess."

Jim was studying me closely. What was he thinking? I exhaled again. "You probably have to get on the road. It's late. Thanks for hearing me out."

Jim looked miserable. "Victoria . . . I accept your apology. I've been out of my mind. Things were great, and then we argued after the thing at Lee's. I also said some things about not trusting you. I know that being a single mom is hard, and you were protecting Rachel. I'm sorry too. I never meant . . . . I've missed you so much."

The look in his eyes was sad, raw. But even if he was hurting, so was I. He'd asked for the break with no attempt to work it out or give me a second chance, and that was painful. And there were other problems—for starters, his new red-haired girlfriend. Our mutual apology hadn't stopped the ache that had taken over my chest, the sadness that filled me.

He shifted awkwardly on the sofa.

"Jim, please don't act like you care, and say things you don't mean . . . ." My voice cracked and tears were sliding down my face.

He reached out and pulled me onto the sofa. Our shoulders were touching and he held my hand. For a second, I wanted to melt into him. Then, I thought again of the redhead.

"Why are you hanging out at Dorry's anyway?" I asked.

Jim sighed. "It's a long story."

"Come on. I know about her." A shiny tear slid down my cheek.

"Who? There's no one else."

"Please don't do this. I know you're seeing someone. I saw the photos on Facebook."

"What photos? I have no idea what you're talking about."

I grabbed my phone, and clicked on the site. I typed until the images of him and the smiling woman appeared. Jim leaned in and stared. I watched as he scrolled down and did a double take at the sight of the photos: he and the redhead in Yankees caps; the two of them seated in a hot tub; and one of them arm-in-arm in front of a skating rink.

Jim started to speak, but couldn't seem to find the words. "Listen, Vic. I know this sounds crazy, but I'm not seeing this woman."

The stakes felt so high I could barely breathe. Jim was actually telling me he hadn't met someone else? I was sobbing now.

Jim shook his head. "I don't get it. The photos are two years old. These are pictures of me and Tonya." He looked really upset, and then tugged on his earlobe. It killed me when he did that; it was so adorable. I felt my resolve waning.

If that's the case, why did these pop up now? And why wouldn't your friends tell you they were up?" I said.

"Good questions, but you have to believe me. This is the absolute first I've heard about it. See!?" He was pointing to the friend column. There were only three listed. "I never use Facebook. I'm not into it. I never monitor my profile or use the site. And my 'Facebook friends' use it less than I do. It's just not something any of us guys are interested in." Jim stopped talking and looked into the distance for a minute. "I can't believe this . . . ."

I waited. All of a sudden Jim got a strange expression on his face and let out a groan, then stared straight into my eyes. "You weren't wrong; what you said that evening in my apartment." He rubbed his temples as I tried to follow his line of thought. "Lee took the pictures a couple of years ago. I'd forgotten about it. Tonya and I had gone away for the weekend with her and Jack. We broke up like five minutes after we got home that Sunday night, so I never saw any of these photos, but I recognize the inn in the background."

He scrolled through the site. "Look," he said, handing the phone to me.

The site was open to Lee's profile. She had recently posted the photos, tagging Jim so they appeared on his page. My fury rose. I'd fallen victim to that woman and her machinations yet again.

Jim's look was part shocked, part angry. He stared into the distance. "I don't get it. She has everything. Jack's a great guy. They have two beautiful daughters and a gorgeous house, and they seem so happy. I can't believe she'd do something like this."

He reached for my hand. "Now, sitting here with you, I guess I'm having a light bulb moment. The only explanation for these photos is that she wanted to mess with us."

My anger immediately mixed with relief. Even if Lee had deliberately put up damning pictures on her Facebook page to cause confusion and drive a wedge between Jim and me—the lengths to which she would go no longer surprised me—her post meant that Jim wasn't involved with the redhead! If I hadn't been emotionally drained and physically exhausted, I would have jumped up and down.

Jim spoke softly. "Vic, I swear I had no idea these were up, and I haven't even seen Tonya in a couple of years. His eyes were raw. I've been out of my mind, kicking myself because I was too hard on you that night. But I was embarrassed and hurt. I've wished a thousand times I could take back what I said about not trusting you and asking for a break. I really regret that. Even if you held back at times, you never lied or gave me reason to doubt you. So I'm sorry. I've even hung out at the Starbucks near your office up here, hoping to run into you."

I took a good look at him. There were dark half moons under each of his eyes. He looked like hell, poor guy. I felt my resolve melting. I'd missed him so much.

"Actually I know I acted kind of crazy, making you choose between me and the DeVrys. I'm sorry I pointed the finger that night at your apartment, and got angry at you for setting things straight."

We were staring into each other's eyes when my phone started vibrating, startling me. I reached toward the floor for my purse, and grabbed my cell. There was a text, alerting me to a voice mail at work. Recognizing the number as Colin's, I groaned inwardly. It was time to put an end to his calls forever.

I showed Jim the screen. "This is my ex-fiancé. I blocked him on my cell. But he calls work every so often, even though I've made clear it's over between us. So if you don't mind." Jim shrugged his shoulders as I dialed. Colin picked up immediately. "Look, I'm calling as a courtesy—and this is the last time, so please listen: We are not getting back together." I smiled at Jim. "I've met someone."

There was silence on the other end of the call until Colin finally spoke. "Really? Who is it?"

"No one you know. Please do not call me again."

As we hung up, I breathed a sigh of relief. Colin had finally gotten the message, and I'd delivered it in front of Jim.

He was reaching for my hand. "I'm glad you called him while I was in the room." Jim said as we locked eyes. With the trust stuff behind us, we were free and clear to start fresh.

He went back to scouring the phone screen and, I assumed, thinking about Lee. I felt like announcing, "one down, one to go," but bit my lip. After a few moments, he shook his head. "Seeing this display, well, you were right. Lee's a huge troublemaker who obviously had it out for you. And she definitely baited you at her house that night. I see it all clearly now. I'm sorry, Vic. I should've known better."

I was flooded with relief. Lee hadn't won after all.

Jim pulled me toward him and I didn't resist. We sat together, intertwined, and I let myself enjoy the feel of his arms, the warmth of his body. "I missed you, Vic."

I was glad to be in Jim's arms, grateful Lee hadn't managed to keep us apart.

"It amazes me," I said. "She's made a full-time job of torturing my daughter and ... which reminds me, since you and I have been getting everything out in the open, you said once that you grew up in town, but wouldn't elaborate at all."

Jim looked beyond me, like he was thinking about something painful. "Who wants to return to the town where they grew up: small town, insular and gossipy, some snobbiness and climbing? There were some nice people, but overall, it was an oppressive environment. I had no desire to revisit the place." Jim paused and gave me a meaningful look. "But you lived there."

He continued to gaze at me steadily. My heart swelled up and pulsed like one of those old cartoons where it beats outside of the chest and goes back inside. He'd just implied he was willing to spend time in the area he wasn't fond of, just to be with me.

Viewing everything through Jim's eyes, the hurt and struggles finally unmasked, seeing his gaze, which was so intense and pleading, it was obvious he really cared. My heart did a flip. I'd see things through. I owed it to myself. Jim's look of affection made every awful thing that happened in the past seven months, even my schoolyard nemesis, almost worth it.

Twenty-Three

Him

The entire time Jim and I were talking, a small part of me had difficulty suspending disbelief. After so many empty weeks and all the pain, could it be true that he still wanted me? The more we talked, the more my hopes soared. I stared at his face—those eyes and that jaw!—and had trouble looking away from his lips, which were familiar, yet off limits. Would we ever kiss again?

Jim pulled me close. "Can we keep seeing each other?" I let my eyes do the talking as he leaned in, his mouth approaching mine.

Our reunion kiss lasted for two hours.

We sat, my head on his shoulder, me feeling like I'd never let go.

"Please believe me. I want to make things right between us. And I understand you have to do what you think is right when it comes to Rachel. I felt terrible that your fears about introducing us were borne out when I asked for a break. Was she upset?"

"She thought you were 'nice,' but kept most of her reactions to herself. That's the family way."

He laughed. "I'm really relieved you're willing to give me another chance."

I faced him, placing a hand on each shoulder and tilting my head. "Yes, but first you have to alter your Facebook settings and make it a closed account. While you're at it, you might want to change your password too."

"What do you suggest?" he asked, "How 'bout a random series of letters and numbers?"

I shook my head. "How 'bout 'Lee666?'"

"I've really missed you," Jim said, pulling me close. "And your sense of humor."

I told him about BucketBeast and the upcoming workshop on cyberbullying. Since there had been a similar incident at Guardian, he offered to share articles and resources, volunteering to speak to Rachel if I thought it would help, and made me promise to call if any further threats arose.

We kissed good night at the front door, and he asked to see me again the next day. After he'd gone, I turned off all the lights and tiptoed upstairs and into Rachel's room, laying down with her and burrowing in. Her breathing was so soothing. I soon dozed off.

A couple of hours later, Rachel shook me. "Why are you in my bed?"

I said I'd dozed off mid-hug, and she pulled the blanket over me and told me she didn't mind if I stayed. Then, we fell into an exhausted sleep. It was the happiest I'd been in months.

▥

We were having breakfast when the text came through. *"There's a casual thing at my club tonight. Can you make it?"*

I responded with a photo from the internet: a tow-headed toddler with thick sports glasses clapping and hooting after he'd opened a large gift box and a yellow puppy emerged and started licking his face.

"Am I the puppy or the kid with the bowl haircut?"

"Either/or! I was going for the exuberant vibe."

He texted a red dot that grew into a line and began to sketch a heart. The image continued beating after the drawing was completed.

"Save?" the phone asked. You bet. I hit "enter."

I raced home after work and put on a black pantsuit with no shirt, just a low cut camisole. My only accessory was a spritz of perfume. Once we were seated at the table and I removed my coat, Jim's eyes got wide. "You look gorgeous. How . . . .?"

"I didn't wear this combo to work."

He nodded. "Different slacks?"

"Exactly."

As he played with my fingers, I spotted Lee and Jack across the room. They'd stood up and were coming toward us. My shoulders stiffened. Jim rose to shake Jack's hand and kiss Lee hello. She was getting ready to pounce.

"Victoria. Isn't this cozy?"

I stole a glance at her husband. Did he notice his wife was acting like a jealous girlfriend? Apparently not; he was staring at my "camisole." I felt a blush creep slowly over my cheeks as Jack reluctantly raised his eyes to meet mine. "Nice to see you," he said, bending down to kiss my cheek.

Note to self: no cleavage at the country club. "Looking forward to your workshop, Lee," I managed.

"Ah heard you wrangled a speaking engagement." Her tone was so sharp, Jim blinked. "Exactly what qualifies you as an expert in the area of cyberbullying?"

Jack put an arm around his wife and pulled her in the direction of their table. "Baii," she called over her shoulder.

I kept it light for the rest of the dinner.

We were driving down the road that led from the club entrance to the street. "Can you stay over?" I asked. "Rachel is at a friend's."

"How could I possibly refuse?"

I decided not to bring Lee up, but he did.

"So, I noticed that Lee definitely baits you," he said, glancing over at me after stopping at a red light. I sighed and shrugged as he added, "Jack thinks she's high-spirited."

"Do you think she's interested in you?" The words slipped out, but the question had been weighing on me.

"What? No!" Jim shook his head. "Even after seeing the photos she posted, I still think she and Jack are happy."

I used the gentle-sounding voice I reserved for delivering bad news to patients. "I'm sure they are. But she seemed peeved to see me with you tonight, and she calls and texts you a lot." I felt like shaking him and screaming, "The bitch tried to break us up!" Jim held my hand, but remained deep in thought for the rest of the ride.

When we got to my house, we sat down on the living room sofa. He had that preoccupied look that had made me worry so many times before. Uh-oh. What if he thought I was accusing him of flirting when I asked if he thought Lee was interested?

"I'm sorry. I shouldn't have mentioned anything. Lee's fine. I'm not invested in figuring her out, or engaging with her in any way. I know the DeVrys are your friends."

Jim's back was still to me as he stood by the fireplace.

"Have I upset you?"

He turned around. "No," he said, with another tug of the earlobe. "I'm not sure if I should say this."

I went over to the fireplace and threw my arms around his waist. "Let's not worry about her. I'm just thrilled to be in the same room with you two days in a row."

I tried to pull Jim back to the sofa, get him to sit back down, but he continued pacing in front of the fireplace. His pants were hanging off; during our hiatus he hadn't been eating right.

"This past month or so has been hell," he said. "I'm not letting

anything get in the way this time. I'm just going to say it." He took
a deep breath. "What my friends think is not important at all,
Victoria. I'm in love with you."

〽️

Jim loved me!

I imagined us running off to a seedy chapel in Vegas, grabbing
our happily-ever-after. Then I slowed it down. Rachel would hate
Vegas, and if we did get married, I wanted everyone I loved to be
there.

We sat on the sofa, my head on Jim's shoulder. He'd used the
shaving cream and soap I loved.

"Are you smelling me?"

"Maybe." We laughed.

"I don't want to go," he said. "It's so good to be with you."

He kissed me and I felt the familiar tingle.

"I missed you too," I traced his cheek with my finger.

He moved his hands down the sides of my body, caressing me
at the waist, and then pulled me on top of him. "We fit together
perfectly," he said.

I suddenly felt shy, and hid my face.

"What is it?" Jim cupped my chin and raised my face to look
up at his.

"A lot of emotions. I don't know." *Yes, I do. I'm crazy about you,
but I'm not saying a word, not yet.*

I felt safe for the first time in so long, being in Jim's arms.

Jim looked closely at me. My stomach lurched. What else
could possibly come to light? I prepared for some horrible revela-
tion. "You'd have no way of knowing this," he told me. "But there
was an incident at Guardian. The DeVrys' older daughter, Mariel,
was struggling. A psychologist evaluated her and wrote a report
recommending she be counseled out. Lee and Jack fought it like

crazy, and worked out a deal where their daughter would supplement with tutors, consultants, whatever was needed." He seemed to weigh his next words. "You know how hard it is for parents who stress achievement. They can't handle watching their kids get bad grades or switch schools."

The fact that Jim was actually able to empathize even after the DeVrys had made a stink told me he was even nicer than I'd thought—if that were possible. "You are very kind to your students and the school families." I made a heart shape with my hands and held it over my chest.

He leaned over and nuzzled my cheek. "It was a mess. We were patient with them. After the deal was reached, Lee strutted around telling everyone what a quack the psychologist was. Since then, she's talked to anyone who'll listen about how she hates psychologists." Jim paused and gave me a sympathetic look. "You never even stood a chance."

So Lee had been primed to hate and mistrust me. That made sense. I was grateful to Jim for filling in the blanks.

"She definitely twisted my attempt to help a bullied kid in the hallway. She experienced it as an insult to her daughter."

Jim nodded. "There's more. She did get into some kind of trouble years ago at another school. I asked another friend of mine. I get that there's tension between the two of you, and you've had to protect your child. In retrospect, I don't think you were overly suspicious."

I was thrilled he no longer thought I was "fixated." "As you know, it's been very difficult since we moved here. This town, Mayfair, can be a rough place, and it trickles down to the school. I see why you didn't love growing up here." I stroked his cheek.

"It was a tiny village," he agreed. "Everyone was in each other's business. If you drank a beer in the parking lot behind the A&P, seven mothers called your house before you'd finished the can,"

Jim rolled his eyes. "It was insular, oppressive. I was glad to get away."

"It's still that way," I said. "Only now the mothers have branched out to running every aspect of their children's lives. They get involved in the classroom stuff, coach some of the teams, do the fundraising for the school, organize all the parties, drive every carpool, and choose their children's friends."

"There's some of that at Guardian too. Is it really that bad here?" Jim asked.

"It's worse. These women make drug lords look like kindergarten teachers. I don't really mind it for myself. It's Rachel I'm worried about. And I recently learned that most of the moms have actually steered their daughters away from her."

"What? Come on." Jim's expression was incredulous.

"It's been terrible. A few people thought I was something I'm not because of my aunt's house." I swept my arm toward the cavernous living room.

He nodded. "We used to drive by growing up." He grinned for the first time in a while. "I might have thrown eggs on the porch one Halloween."

"That was you?"

We laughed.

"Please finish what you were saying."

I had nothing to lose. He'd just said he loved me, and I wanted to tell him everything. "Well," I sucked in my breath, gathering courage. "Lee came over here and saw that the pipes were leaky and the wiring was ancient. She didn't like that I asked her daughter and a couple of others to leave another kid alone. So she told everyone not to let their daughters come over to play, and since then, Rachel has been excluded. I overheard Lee laughing about it in one of the back hallways at school." I couldn't believe that Rachel's struggles still stung, but they did.

A few tears started to fall. I looked down, ashamed, and brushed them away quickly

"I knew you were friends with them. And when you said you wanted to trust me, but I was too 'fixated,' and pulled away, I thought the line in the sand had been crossed and you'd sided with them; after how long you knew them, I could never compete."

Jim was thoughtful. "I had no idea that any of that happened. It's terrible." He hugged me tightly. "You thought I'd chose my friends over you?"

I looked down, but he slowly raised my chin until our eyes met. "I choose you, hands down."

We kissed again until Jim pulled away, his face an inch from mine. "I'm sorry I didn't trust you. So when you and Rachel moved to town and she started at Barnum, Lee came after you?"

"Pretty much. It's been very hard on Rachel, which was no picnic for me. I was helpless. Lee had all the power. I know I sounded crazy after the dinner party, but she doesn't like me, that I know. And the worst of it all is that someone planted a Juul on Rachel, and I'm almost certain it was Lee. I'm glad you heard there was an incident at that other school because I don't want you to think I'm 'fixating.'"

Jim's eyes were wide. "A Juul? Poor Rachel. What happened?"

"The principal let her go. She had no idea what the thing was."

Jim nodded. "I know I said you were being 'suspicious,' but given Lee's past, that incident, it does cast things in a different light. The Juul thing is really troubling."

I shrugged my shoulders. "That's pretty much it. As far as Rachel, that's a whole other story. I've been coaching her on how to deal with bullies."

"Only in this case, the bullies are the mothers." Jim said.

It was after three o'clock in the morning. We had talked for so long, I'd almost lost my voice. I was floating, feeling closer to him than anyone on the planet—except maybe my daughter—but it was way past my personal witching hour. I had to send him on his way.

He rose to leave, and I walked him to the door. Once we were in the foyer, he turned the knob with one hand and fastened his remaining fingers around mine. He kissed me again, a long, slow caress. When we finally managed to pull away, his mouth twitched a little at the corners. I knew that look. Something playful was coming.

"I'd love to see you again, but your plumbing is old, so I can't hang around with you anymore."

I loved Jim's sense of humor. Standing on my tiptoes and raising my face until I was kissing his lips, noticing how familiar they felt, I whispered a response, "I'm glad you have priorities." Then I closed the door.

Jim turned around as I peeked through the little window in the side of the hallway, and I blew him a kiss.

Moments later I was hopping into bed, hoping the recent reunion with Jim was a sign that Rachel and my fortunes had shifted. I drifted off, thinking of nothing but him as the memory of his kisses lulled me to sleep.

Twenty-Four

Working It

Running on only a couple of hours' sleep would normally bother me, but today I was bolstered, secure in Jim's love. I felt energized. It was Friday, my Westchester day, and I was working locally, then heading to school in the evening for the cyberbullying workshop.

At drop off, I spotted the poster out in front. My name was on it with the other presenters. I'd been waffling, but knew in my heart I'd go through with my plan to exact revenge on Lee. Rachel didn't want me to antagonize her, but I felt as though I had to act. In the talk, I'd allude to how awful she had been, hosting parties that excluded, shaping carpools, and forming closed sports practices. If nothing else, I'd cast a shadow over her reputation—that was all she cared about anyway. I'd also explain the psychological effects of bullying, cyber and otherwise, then close with the statement that this new breed of "bully moms" was indicative of a depressing cultural trend.

Calling attention to the cliques and social aggression would send Lee the message that I wasn't a pushover and bullying wouldn't be tolerated. And while I'd vacillated about being divisive, I still burned with rage any time I thought of Lee and the Juul, how she'd targeted my poor kid. I was ready to execute phase two of my plan.

I headed home, waving to Rachel, who was in the living room watching TV, before stealing away to the small home office. I grabbed my phone and hit the "print command," smiling as the pages slid out.

They were scans of the photos I'd taken at the hotel. I'd enlarged them before printing. The images clearly showed Lee and Jess's husband smiling at one another, leaning toward each other, embracing and entering the hotel elevator.

Lee certainly had it coming. Placing the pictures into a manila envelope and stashing them in my tote bag, I knew what I had to do: corner her alone at the back of the auditorium and tell her to stop messing with Rachel or else. The photos would wipe the smirk off her face, that I knew. For months I'd been polite and tried to set firm limits, but nothing had stopped her bullying. Now I was in the position to show her I meant business; it was the only way she'd leave Rachel alone.

It was almost time to go. I gave Rachel an early dinner, and we chatted between bites. "Neil and I are entering the science fair together. We're building a volcano. Last night when I was at his house, we managed to get some lava to flow out of the bowl we were using. His cat jumped on the counter and licked the stuff. His dad thought that was hysterical, but I don't think Sharon would have found it funny."

"Glad you had fun. Was the cat okay?" She laughed. "The experiment came in a box that said 'organic.'"

"If this were a cartoon, that cat would be glowing in the dark," I said hoping for a giggle, but Rachel didn't like my joke. "Neil's very nice," I said, trying again as we put our dishes in the sink, grabbed our jackets, and headed for the car.

"Are you nervous to present?" she asked after we'd backed out of the driveway. "Not really," I said, glancing over at her. "Well, maybe a little." She smiled as I added an afterthought. "The other night I went to an outing with a lot of women from town, including Neil's mom . . . and guess who else was there? Jim."

Rachel stared and waited. "So anyway, I took your advice about giving him a second chance—"

"That's good. He was nice. And you were always moping around after the two of you broke up."

There was nothing like preteen pearls to spice up a conversation. "I didn't mean to make you worry, sweetheart."

"I know."

We'd arrived at school and secured a spot in the lot, which was nearly full. Tonight's presentations would be well attended. "So what are you going to talk about?" Rachel asked as we were walking up the path.

No need to make her nervous by revealing details of my plan. "Just explain some of the dangers inherent in cyberbullying. I'll quickly outline the different social sites and provide examples of how they've been misused. And I'll outline social media safety— don't worry, I'll be brief."

"Doubt it," Rachel smiled.

We made our way through the lobby and down the long hallway to the auditorium. I looked around at the familiar faces that were heading down the hall alongside me, and waved at Mrs. Franklin and a couple of moms I recognized from pick-up. In the distance, I spotted Ellen. She was walking briskly and finishing up a call, with Maya at her heels.

The auditorium was large, shaped like a giant clamshell. There was a stage in front with a thick velvet curtain hanging down the back, and three sections of seating, two aisles and middle. Rachel and I took seats on an aisle toward the middle of the room.

Lee was milling around down by the stage. The principal was standing with her group, hugging his right elbow with his left arm, smiling and nodding at whatever Lee and the man to her left, the police chief I assumed, were saying. A large poster, advertising the workshop was displayed on a giant tripod at the front of the room.

I suddenly felt like I needed to use the bathroom. "Mind if I make a pit stop?" Rachel shrugged. "Be right back." I hung onto my bag and its precious cargo, and headed toward the exit.

Jim was in the doorway with a tall, leggy young woman. He kissed me on the cheek. "This is Mariel." I recalled that was the name of DeVry's older daughter who was a senior at Guardian. "Mariel, Victoria."

We smiled and shook hands. Before either one of us could say anything else, Lee wedged herself in between Jim and her daughter. "Do you two need seats?"

Mariel stiffened as Lee moved to place a hand on her shoulder. "We'll figure it out," she said, backing away slightly.

"Come find me later. Baiii." Lee flitted over to the far corner of the room, where she proceeded to make a show of kissing every attendee in the vicinity.

I smiled at Mariel. "Your mother put this whole evening together. I'm sure it was a lot of work."

She shook her head. "Not my mother."

Had I had mixed up the name of Collette's older sister? Mariel was rolling her eyes. "I think we have an audience," she said, raising her chin slightly to indicate Lee. She crossed her arms over her chest as Lee's eyes darted from Jim to Mariel, and back to me. "I wish she'd stop staring."

Jim must have sensed my confusion. "Mariel's mother, Jack's first wife, is named Eva. I don't think you've met her." He pivoted quickly. "You two have something in common. Victoria's a psychologist. Mariel told me she's interested in studying psychology, isn't that right?"

She nodded. "Where do you practice?"

"My office is on the Upper East Side."

"That's where my mom works. She's a clothing buyer at Bergdorf."

As I was taking that in, I looked closely at Mariel, who was almost as tall as Jim, and all legs. Her eyes were seafoam green, flecked with blue and gold, and her hair was smartly cut, skimming the tops of her shoulders. She was a beautiful girl. I could only assume her mother was equally gorgeous and statuesque. If my calculations were correct, Jack's first wife had professional accomplishments, a lovely daughter, and was blessed with knock-out looks—a combination that probably drove Lee crazy. She breezed by us again, and I thought of the photos and how she had no idea what was coming.

Lee was now talking to two women I didn't recognize. She glanced in our direction several times while pulling at her mini-skirt and smoothing down her hair.

"Lee keeps looking over here," Mariel said to Jim. "Did you know she used to make digs about my mom always being at work?" Interesting, but I'd have to wrap this up; there wasn't much time before the speeches, and I still needed to go over my notes and figure out when to confront Lee. "I was young, maybe twelve or thirteen, but I finally said, 'Lee, you don't need to be jealous of my mother for having a high-powered job. You're really good at tennis.' Lee turned beet red, and after that she stopped making nasty comments."

Jim and I exchanged a glance. So under the polished veneer, Lee felt threatened by me and other women who worked outside the home in professions she perceived to be high-powered. Bullies often targeted others to deal with their own insecurities. I glanced at my watch.

"I'm sorry, but I have to run," I finally said. "I'm one of the speakers tonight. It was nice meeting you, Mariel." I blew Jim a kiss and headed for the lobby restroom.

To my surprise, Lee was now in the hallway, her back to me, speaking to a dark-haired woman I didn't recognize: "Well, Dana, since you're new in town and I promised Jocelyn I'd look out for you, these are the fifth grade girls you want your daughter to be friends with. There's Lexi, she's adorable, and Hannah, they're at our club . . . ."

Ranking kids? That was shameless. I pushed past, my jaw tightening, as I thought back to the Juul. Even though Mariel had given me context for Lee's shallow and nasty attitudes and behaviors, I couldn't have cared less about her insecurities. Feeling threatened by my professional accomplishments didn't give her a pass for the things she'd done.

I'd proceed according to plan, use my talk to hint at the bullying and cast doubt on her reputation, and later on, find a way to get her alone and show her the photos. That was the only way to make sure she left Rachel alone once and for all.

I peeked out of the restroom. The coast was clear. I headed back into the auditorium to take my seat. The program was about to begin.

I shuffled through papers rehearsing in my head, the hypotheticals and allusions I'd drawn to Lee's cruelty and bullying: "Imagine a small, close-knit town with excellent schools and an active parent body where some had something to hide," it began. I'd tried to write it like a mystery novel.

"Mom!" Rachel had been pulling on my elbow. "Look over there. Up at the front of the room, Lexi's mom and her friends, whispering and looking people up and down. They're like teenagers."

Rachel was tugging my arm. "There's Jim." I waved and blew another kiss toward the rear of the room where he was seated.

We settled in to watch the presentations. I decided to wait until the end of the evening to find Lee and show her the photos. She'd just grabbed her laptop and started walking up the small wooden staircase at the base of the stage. In a couple of minutes, she'd be standing behind the podium. I reached for my notes so I'd be ready when she called my name.

"Well, hello everyone," Lee said into the mic.

She opened the laptop and plugged in a cord on the side. Her desktop screen appeared as a giant projection above the podium. She'd posted a miniature of the poster, listing the speakers on the top left and beneath it a PowerPoint with the first guest's name and credentials. The icons of her favorite apps were displayed along the right. I saw Hermès and Harry Winston, and then stopped looking.

"What a lovely turnout," Lee was saying as people were filing in. "Ah'd like to thank each and every one of yew for coming out this evening to support the PTA and taking part in our workshop on cyberbullying."

The room was buzzing as parents shoved their way down crammed aisles and rows. Lee clapped her hands. "Let's get started." She began introducing the panelists, starting with the police chief, then the detective. She provided highlights of their years on the force before setting her mouth in a hard smile. "And also on the program, one of our own, Victoria Bryant . . . . Are you here, Victoria?"

You just saw me, two seconds ago. I gritted my teeth and waved from my row in the middle of the room.

"Victoria will speak from a psychological perspective. I'm sure everyone will be most interested in that part of the evening." Her tone made a psychological perspective sound as interesting as the manual explaining how to program a VCR. "And now without further ado." She motioned for the police chief to take the stage, and people began clapping as he stepped up to the podium.

The chief outlined the law as I reviewed my notes. I glanced at my bag and spotted the envelope, and my heart skipped a beat. The evidence was at my fingertips. And I was eager to use it.

I took the envelope out and peeked inside, and had noticed my pulse starting to quicken, when Rachel started shaking me on the shoulder. All the proof I needed to show everyone in town exactly how awful Lee was! Right here in my hands! Rachel's insistence reminded me I'd tuned her out.

She was speaking to me again. "Mom." Her tone was serious. I pulled myself away from the photos and glanced up. She appeared to be deep in thought. "Why does Mrs. DeVry get to stand up there and act all important? She's done all kinds of awful things like telling me the wrong practice day, and asking me to step out of the photo." My stack of papers was momentarily forgotten. Where was Rachel going with this?

I'd been convinced that after months of mind games and cruelty, it would feel good to take Lee down, hopefully even the score. What was with the questions? I fingered the envelope again.

For every impulse that encouraged me to go ahead, there remained seeds of doubt. Part of me worried about going low. Public smackdowns were petty and risky, and not my normal modus operandi. But there was more to it. What if I didn't act? Then Lee would go after someone else.

I began to sweat as I glanced over at Jim. Life was pretty good now. If I stood up and started to hint at everything that had gone on, would he accuse me of being fixated? I breathed in and relaxed. After seeing Lee in action with the Facebook posting, he'd understand. I'd stick with the plan.

Rachel was now tugging at my sleeve. I'd been too preoccupied to answer her question. "Mrs. DeVry put this whole evening together," I whispered. "But I agree that the way she treated you was very wrong."

My daughter nodded. "You know, she and some of the other PTA mothers just come to school so they can push people around. One day, Mrs. DeVry screamed at Maya's mother at the front door because she'd bought the wrong flavor of ice cream for some teacher lunch."

That figured. "I didn't know, honey." Rachel's whisper was conspiratorial: "I think people like Mrs. DeVry and her friends act really crazy and mean. *I'm so glad you don't.*"

I didn't know what to appreciate first: the fact that Rachel had paid me a compliment—the rarest of occurrences nowadays—or that she saw through Lee, straight to her nasty core.

I'd almost succumbed to the temptation to go at it with her again, and in front of everyone. What was going on with me, and what would Jim have thought?

Rachel was still staring at the PTA moms. After watching Jess and Audrey whisper to one another, Rachel added: "I'm glad you're not like them."

I was so shocked. I dropped the envelope back into my bag and froze.

I'd been planning to be very much like them in about five minutes, but Rachel's comments had snapped me out of it. All my doubts about exposing Lee's cruelty and using the platform to cast light on her in-group/out-group behaviors came flooding back. It occurred to me that I'd been justifying bullying *her* in the guise of providing information to the community.

Lee stood up as the police chief was concluding. *Oh shit.* What was I going to do? The parts about Lee's meanness made up at least half of my prepared remarks. I couldn't use them now. I'd rather have Rachel's admiration than a moment of hollow satisfaction.

I'd edit out the hypotheticals about town and go with the part of my talk that described the effects of cyberbullying on school performance and overall mental health. I had collected statistics and summarized recent research, although I hadn't practiced reading that part aloud. My panic rose. Hopefully, I'd have enough material.

And I'd keep the photographic evidence to myself. No need to engage with Lee on such a low level, in such a petty way. Rachel and I were on the other side of it now. My daughter was happy and had found friends; what Lee said and did no longer mattered.

Lee was back at center stage. "Our next speaker is Victoria. Or should I say Dr. Victoria." She bared her teeth. There was a smattering of applause. "But first a quick thank you to the police chief."

Rachel started whispering. "Hey Mom, I bet BucketBeast is here! Whoever made up the account and sent all those messages might have shown up to see everyone talk about the stalking!"

"Maybe."

I was barely paying attention to her; my thoughts were going a mile a minute. For weeks, I'd fantasized about hinting publicly that Lee had planted the Juul—I'd outed her in my mind a million times, and tonight had been a close call.

I stood up and smoothed my pants down, still wondering exactly what the heck I'd say up there, as Rachel continued to whisper. "I blocked BucketBeast, but I can unblock and message him; Maya dared me." I put a finger to my lips. "Shh. No phones in here." I started to walk down the aisle.

I was standing a few steps away from the podium when the room went wild. There were oohs and aahs and gasps.

Not another sex video! I stepped forward and grabbed hold of the wooden stand, wondering if Lee had done something to ridicule me. But she was frantic, wild-eyed, moving her arms back and forth, and wailing. She was staring up, and my eyes followed hers to the screen above our heads.

Her desktop was still projected onto the screen. A pink square icon was blinking in her toolbar. It was her Instachat account with a notification: "@BucketBeast, you have one new message!"

The notification was from Rachel. My heart stopped. *I knew it now for sure: Lee was BucketBeast!*

The audience had gone mad. The scene looked like one of

those old newsreels reporting on the 1929 stock market crash and ensuing bank panic, with everyone gesticulating and moving their mouths all at once. I was having trouble processing and believing it all, but one thing was certain: I was furious at Lee for threatening and scaring my child with her anonymous posts. I hoped the DA got involved and hit her with every charge in the book.

Why would she do it? For control? To maintain her popularity? I thought about her kicking Rachel out of the carpool, and her and Jess inviting everyone, but my daughter to a party. While Lee's behavior was ridiculous and over-the-top, it was part of a larger societal problem. She and her friends were completely over-involved with their daughters.

I didn't want to be too smug. All mothers stepped into their children's shoes, and I always felt Rachel's pain. But some of us were also able to maintain some distance and step out again. And while blurred boundaries were an occupational hazard for all moms, the ones whose primary identity centered on parenting were the most vulnerable. Moms like Lee, Jess, and their friends struggled; they were lost in a pattern of relentless, over-involved mothering.

I glanced down to the front of the room. Lee's head was tilted slightly, her jaw set and arms crossed in a defiant manner. She didn't seem cognizant of the trouble she was in.

The chief of police and detective from the cyber crimes unit were nodding and walking down the aisles, converging on the stage. The chief asked Lee if she wanted to call an attorney.

She raised her chin, giving him an angry and defiant look. Lee was so arrogant she was almost delusional. I guessed her PTA and social power had gone to her head.

Rachel was sitting with her hands knitted together in her lap. Her brow was wrinkled. "Did I do something bad? Will Collette's mom go to prison?"

"Don't worry, honey. It's not your fault. These detectives told me they've been looking into this. Instachat can trace the people who make accounts."

That was all true. I couldn't believe she had been so careless, messaging kids from her computer and making accounts to target others. I put an arm around Rachel. "I don't think she will go to jail for posting on your Insta or for receiving your message just now. You didn't do anything—promise. Actually, you're kind of a hero!" Rachel smiled and sat back to watch the rest of the drama unfold.

The room quieted as people sat forward in their chairs and listened. The detective was speaking. "You know you have the right to counsel, Mrs. DeVry. I can't advise you about that, but we are going to take you in for questioning." After reading Lee her rights, he added: "commenting online on the posts of minors, threatening them, is a crime, Mrs. DeVry. If tried and convicted, you could face jail time." There was a collective exhale of shock and disbelief.

The detective glanced at the principal, who looked slightly green, as though he might pass out. The principal stepped into action as the officers led Lee down the aisle and out the door. He went up on stage and over to the podium and spoke into the mic. "Uh, we are going to end for the evening. Please drive safely. Thank you and good night."

Jim texted that he'd meet us by the double doors. Rachel went off to compare notes on BucketBeast with Maya. After the crowd had filed out, I made a beeline for Jim.

"I've been meaning to tell you something. I love you," I said, burying myself in the strong arms he's just finished wrapping around me.

Twenty-Five

Front Row Action

After exiting the building, I saw Lee out front, flanked by two
burly officers, walking toward a waiting police car. She didn't meet
my eye and I no longer cared. She put on a pair of dark glasses,
and lowered her head. Someone called her name, and Lee pulled
her glasses down the bridge of her nose and glanced over. Our eyes
locked, and on impulse, I lifted my fingertips to my lips and blew
her a kiss.

She was not amused.

I knew there would be reverberations from today's events. For
starters, there was Amy. I'd have to deal with her when we next
met. She was bound to have an intense reaction to what happened
at the workshop, as was Maureen. In each case, I'd discuss my
patient's feelings about the presentations, before I referred her to
another therapist. As for Peter getting away with cheating on his
wife? My going public would only hurt their kids. I knew how it
felt to be on the end of a cheating scandal, and I'd think about
whether to tell Jess, or instead, confront Peter and insist he tell the
truth to his wife.

A couple of Saturdays later, I'd glanced down at Jim. He'd
stayed over and was lying next to me on the sofa, wrapped in a
blanket watching TV. We'd been talking about moving in together
and hinting about an engagement. I asked what would it be like,

going from a bachelor pad to rooming with two females. Maybe he'd feel suffocated having our clutter and schedules imposed on him. I was sure he'd miss having time alone.

"I've had forty years of that," he said, pulling me close. "I want to be with you and Rachel."

I hugged him tightly, thinking how thrilled I was to have him here, but also wanting to be sensitive to Rachel's feelings. I'd spoken to her before he came over. I'd put a toe in, hinting that Jim and I really cared about one another and he'd probably be staying over sometimes. She wrinkled her nose in disgust, lifted a hand, and uttered only one syllable: "Ew!"

I was figuring out how to prepare her that he'd be sleeping in my room when she said, Stop!" and covered her ears, groaning, "TMI."

Now Jim was nudging me: "I think it's time you got out of your comfort zone, Vic."

I um-hmm'd. A show about undercover bosses was on, and I was riveted.

Jim rolled his eyes. "This program is unwatchable. Hey, Rach, come in."

Rachel was nowhere to be found.

We looked around, calling out until we found her, in the kitchen, FaceTiming Maya. They were playing chess in a group chat with a couple of kids from the next town. Rachel had played in a tournament and started texting and chatting with kids in that club. I could hear her counseling a curly haired girl who was complaining about how she'd been left out of a big party. Rachel advised, "'Quality is better than quantity. Who cares what the popular kids do, as long as you have real friends who like you for you?'"

Jim glanced in my direction. My advice had sunk in. My daughter was making new friends, and sounding much happier. Just yesterday she had announced her intention to quit soccer and go back to her old mainstay, softball.

Rachel's growth filled me with pride. She was finding herself, just as I knew she would. I inhaled deeply, and she looked over at Jim and me.

"Later. Bye," she clicked off her phone. On the floor next to her, there was a large box. "This is for you, Mom." She handed the package to me. I could see that she'd wrapped it herself.

"What's this, honey?"

"Open it. You'll see." I pulled off the shiny paper and stared, unsure of what to make of the item in front of me. It was domed and hard, a thick black strap hung from the side.

"It's for zip-lining, Mom! I've got one too. Jim drove me to the store yesterday. He wants to take us this weekend."

Jim took one look at my face, and started to laugh. He turned to Rachel. "Remember, I said this is provisional. Obviously, we need to ask your mom's permission."

"Come on, please? It'll be fun!"

I nodded, clearly outvoted. Though I knew it would probably be fine. The closest facility had safeguards in place, and a lot of people had children's parties there. I preferred terra firma, but Rachel and Jim looked so excited that I realized I had to let go, on many different levels.

Two hours later, we were at the climbing area adjacent to the old apple orchard at the outskirts of town. The technician, a guy in cargo pants and Ray-Bans, wearing a name plate that said "Dave B.," spelled it all out to me: "Hold on clearly and firmly. Tighten the buckle, and keep your helmet on at all times. Whatever you do, don't let go."

Dave B. released his hold on the rope, and I flew forward. I could hear Jim and Rachel cheering as I slid across the line, over the old barn. Gliding as never before, I held onto the ropes as my feet swayed and my lungs filled with fresh air. I was making up for lost time, my spirit soaring.

Acknowledgments

I am very grateful to the people at Skyhorse Publishing: Tony Lyons, thank you for letting me tell this story; Rebecca Shoenthal, my talented editor, advocate, and cheerleader: working with you has been a dream come true; Kathleen Schmidt, I am in awe of your knowledge of the book business and your always entertaining Twitter feed; Daniel Brount, your cover design captured perfectly the essence of this story; and Kirsten Dalley, you don't miss a thing; and to Candace Nicholson, Jill Schoenhaut, and the rest of the team. Thank you all.

To my agent, Karen Gantz, who worked tirelessly to bring this book into the world: you have my undying appreciation. I heart you!

I especially want to acknowledge Leslie Wells, gifted and generous editor from whose vision and assistance this story benefited immensely, and Jane Rosenman who provided thoughtful input and support.

I would also like to thank Will Weisser for his invaluable guidance on all aspects of the publishing process, and Eric Rayman for his wise counsel, and give special thanks to my writing buddies, Aimee Trissel and Sam Panzier, as well as our fearless instructor, Arlaina Tibensky.

To Jimin Han and Pat Dunn, my teachers at The Writers Institute of Sarah Lawrence College, as well as Julia Sonenshein and Susan Weissbach, thank you for weighing in; to Daisy Florin, Gloria Hatrick, and Nancy Adams Taylor, thank you for reading an early draft of the story.

I am also grateful to my colleagues, Rebecca Mannis, PhD, Nancy Stuzin, and Rita Clark, MD, for sharing their expertise.

I would like to express my deepest appreciation to the many friends who have helped this book find its way to the finish line: Dana Greissman, I appreciate your eagle eye and uncanny ability to spot factual inconsistencies. Carrie Rabuse, Jared Thaler, and Amy Westerby, your help with the visuals was truly meaningful. To Mardee Handler, Joy Thaler, Sharon Ho, Wendi Strier, Valerie Golden, Erika Lederman, Anita Bae, and Duane Desiderio, I know you guys are rooting for me, and it means more than I can say. Likewise, Brenda and Joe Berger, thank you for encouraging me to see this through.

And finally, I owe a debt of gratitude to my family: including, Michael, for his tireless support, sage advice, and willingness to brainstorm and share his spectacular vocabulary (while suffering through five o'clock in the morning coffee and banana deliveries); Arianne, my English and Latin scholar, grammarian, and constant source of pride and inspiration; Peyton, my IT department and go-to source for all matters social media: you are always a bright spot in my day.

I am enormously grateful to my parents for their continued encouragement. Take a victory lap, Mom. This never would have happened without you!

Book Club Questions

1. Social aggression, cliques, and exclusion among adolescents and adults is nothing new, but this story deals with a crossover between these two age groups: moms bullying adolescents. Did this take on the age-old phenomenon of bullying surprise you? Why or why not?

2. Do you know anyone who actively campaigns to ensure that certain kids and parents are marginalized, excluded, or left out? Why do you think they behave this way?

3. Psychologists maintain that parental overinvolvement harms adolescents by interfering with their ability to develop the capacity to make choices and decisions about their own lives. Do you agree or disagree?

4. Should children and teens be allowed to exclude, even if it means some are left out of social events? In these situations, should parents step in to help prevent exclusion or should adolescents be allowed to fail? What are the potential upsides and downsides of "fixing everything" versus letting teens or pre-teens navigate for themselves?

5. Parents of teenagers and beyond: now that you are on the other
    side of school yard bullying and social engineering, comment
    on what you have noticed about the effects of social aggression
    in the phases that followed early adolescence. For example, do
    children of overly involved parents face more difficulties when
    they go away to college or start their first jobs? Or does the
    level of parental involvement during adolescent development
    not have a significant impact on the psychological and social
    functioning of young adults?